LONG JOURNEY TO DEEP CAÑON

LONG JOURNEY TO DEEP CAÑON

T. T. Flynn

GUNSMOKE

This hardback edition 2011
by AudioGO Ltd
by arrangement with
Golden West Literary Agency

Copyright © 1997 Thomas B. Flynn, M.D.
All rights reserved.

ISBN 978 1 445 85631 5

British Library Cataloguing in Publication Data available.

Printed and bound in Great Britain by
CPI Antony Rowe, Chippenham and Eastbourne

Table of Contents

THE OUTLAW BREED

"The Outlaw Breed" was written for the première issue of *Dime Western*, dated December, 1932, when it was launched by Popular Publications. T. T. Flynn was already well known as a result of numerous detective, crime, railroad, and adventure stories he had written for other magazines. *Dime Western* proved an immediate success. Compared with the leading Western pulp magazine on the stands at the time — Street & Smith's *Western Story Magazine* — *Dime Western* was a monthly, not a weekly. It only cost ten cents, whereas *Western Story Magazine* cost fifteen cents, and Fiction House's equally popular *Lariat Story Magazine*, also a monthly, was priced at twenty cents. While both *Western Story Magazine* and *Lariat Story Magazine* had been wont regularly to feature serials in installments in their pages, *Dime Western* boasted "all stories complete" within each issue. Rogers Terrill, the editor, in an unsigned dedication in that first issue promised readers that *Dime Western* pledged itself to "the tradition of courage and resourcefulness and loyalty which made possible the winning of Western empire over obstacles and dangers the like of which have never quite been duplicated before or since!" In addition to Flynn, Terrill had commissioned stories by Walt Coburn and Eugene Cunningham, the "star" authors in *Lariat Story Magazine*, and Cliff Farrell who enjoyed a similar status among readers of Clayton House's *Ace-High Magazine*. Yet, it was Flynn's story for that first issue — titled by him "The Outlaw Breed" and retitled

"The Last of the Black Tantralls" by Terrill — more than any of the others that introduced the new tone that would define *Dime Western* and would have such a significant impact on how the Western story would be written over the next three decades. The protagonist is seen to be a man forced into isolation by social and economic forces rampant within the community, often being made to appear an outlaw, but who is able by the end to win new stature through superior courage and moral fortitude. Such a protagonist undoubtedly was an inspiration to readers who, flogged by the Great Depression, felt lonely and isolated and vulnerable. However, the theme of the nearness to us of death in all that we do and are, that Flynn carried over into his Western stories, was more a personal hallmark of his own fictional odyssey, the consequence of the painful memory of his beloved wife, Molly, who had expired in his arms in Santa Fé where they had moved for the sake of her health, a victim of incurable tuberculosis.

I

"THE NEW SHERIFF"

"So we got a new sheriff?" There was a sneer in old Jared Jines's voice — ugly dislike in his laugh that followed.

Brad Tantrall turned slowly from the bar and was conscious of the group of friends around him, turning also, conscious of the hush that fell over the big room. For not a man in here but knew first hand or by hearsay the story behind that sneer. Not a man but sensed the possibilities of drama and tragedy that had suddenly broken loose among them. Brad Tantrall knew better than they, but a slight wave of color that deepened the tan on his cheeks was the only outward indication he gave of it. Brad stood two inches shy of six feet, and age had not yet put lines in his youthful face. Little sun wrinkles at the corners of his eyes, a slight quirk at the sides of his lips gave hint that he smiled much, but that was all. His face was sober as he leaned both elbows back on the bar and looked at Jared Jines.

The old man topped him by four inches and, even now in age, was broader. There was a suggestion about Jared Jines of a hoary old oak, bruised by life, but still stubbornly holding erect. His whitening beard, flowing in a majestic sweep across his chest, gave him a patriarchal air. But his voice, manner, and gnarled, knotted fists wiped away the illusion. He swayed slightly as he stood there. Brad saw that Jared had been drinking, perhaps to drown the sour taste of his defeat, for he had bitterly contested the election that had put Brad in office.

"A new sheriff!" Jared rumbled through his beard. "An' what a sheriff!" He rocked on his heels and glared around the room. "Didja hear what I said?" he roared. "I spoke plain! A hell of a sheriff!" And one gnarled hand dropped to the horn butt of the gun at his hip as he spoke. No one answered him. There was a noticeable shifting away from the spot by several men who were not close friends of Brad's.

Men stood around who would have willingly taken up the quarrel, Brad knew, but they did not. This was a matter no man but himself could handle, and on the outcome of it much depended. There were men who had said publicly he was too young to be sheriff. And others had maintained privately that the sheriff's star should never be worn by one of the Black Tantralls. Old Jared had said worse before the election.

Brad leaned easily against the bar and said nothing. There was pity in his glance, if one looked closely, and regret that drink and hate had driven old Jared to this. He had been a mighty man in his day, fair, just, wise. It had taken great grief, lost hopes, gnawing loneliness to bring him to this.

Jared spat on the floor, glaring at Brad. "Well!" he shouted. "Didja hear what I said?"

"Were you speaking to me?" Brad asked slowly.

"You know damn' well I was."

"Is there anything I can do for you?" Brad was conscious of the drag of his gun at his hip, feeling his eyes drawing down to watch old Jared's gun. There was no telling. It might come to shooting. This thing had been in the air for years, and it looked like a showdown tonight.

Brad was not afraid, but a small voice inside was whispering that it must not end in a blaze of gunfire. He would probably win, and have all men agree it was self-defense, but it would be an empty victory.

A half bellow, half snort came from the old man. "Do fer

me! Anything a Black Tantrall can do fer me? Why, you chicken-livered young whelp, I oughta pistol whip you fer that impudence. The very sight of one of your blood puts a bad taste in my mouth."

"I'm sorry," Brad said quietly, and meant it.

He saw Buck Rogers at the end of the room smile and say something behind his hand to Wallace Morgan, owner of the Ladder U outfit. He knew what that smile meant. Already there were men watching who wondered if he was afraid of old Jared.

Afraid! Brad felt a tightening in his throat as his eyes swept over their faces. There was no way he could make them understand that he was afraid of himself, of what he might be goaded into doing.

Jared thrust his face close. "Sorry, are you?" he rasped loudly. "Is that all you got to say when I tell the world you're a yellow-bellied bluff, like all your damn' outlaw breed."

Brad's face whitened. He heard a swift angry suck of breath at his side from between Glory Pat Malone's black-bearded lips, sensing, rather then feeling, Pat's move to give him room. Pat, Slim Parks, Canby Jack — all those friends of his at the bar expected him to act on that insult. The men standing silently and watchfully throughout the room were waiting to see what kind of a man they had elected sheriff.

For one tense moment Brad balanced in indecision. He was at the parting of the ways. One path — by far the easiest — was plain before him. Take up the quarrel. But it was the other he chose.

"That's all I've got to say." He spoke mildly, turning his face to the bar and his back to Jared Jines.

Glory Pat Malone nudged his elbow, whispering hoarsely: "Fer God's sake, don't take it like that, Brad. Don't let him get by with it."

"Have a drink," Brad said conversationally and to the bar-

11

tender: "Set 'em up for the boys, Fred."

Pat stifled something under his breath, averted his eyes when Brad looked at him, and mumbled to the bartender, "Rye, I reckon." Behind him old Jared's bellow was rich with triumph and satisfaction.

"I told you all he was yellow! His whole damn' outlaw breed is yellow, crooked an' two-faced. He'll slap your back, laugh with you, an' treat you to likker fer your votes. But he'll back down and stab you in the back when it suits his purpose. His breed ain't men, an' they can't face men. Ef you want proof . . . *look*."

Jared's great weathered hand slapped to Brad's shoulder with a force that was audible throughout the room. With an angry wrench he spun Brad around. And Jared's other palm struck Brad's cheek with a crack that could be heard from one end of the bar to the other. Jared released him and stepped quickly back, holding his gun hand crooked at his side, ready for instant action.

"Now draw and make me out a liar!" he taunted loudly. "I've waited seven years to get a Black Tantrall. Draw, you cocky sheriff, an' give me what I've been waitin' fer."

A spinning red haze shut out everything to Brad but the bristling white beard and the blazing eyes before him. Jared had damned him with that slap. If he didn't accept the challenge, he might as well turn in his star and leave the county. A man could kill and brawl, could fight and plunder, even rustle cattle, and still claim a measure of respect. But when the brand of cowardice was laid on him, there was no redemption. Anything could be excused but that.

The rage passed and left only a sick feeling in the pit of his stomach and his face deathly pale. This was a mocking climax to the triumph of his election. Was it true, Brad wondered, that the sins of one were passed along to others of the same blood?

12

"Draw!" old Jared taunted again.

"You're drunk," Brad whispered.

"I slapped your face! I called you outta your name! Ain't there nothing I can do that'll make you stand up like a man an' take it?"

Brad held both of his hands up, so there could be no mistake. "You can stand there all night and all day, but I'll not draw a gun against you, Jared Jines," he warned unsteadily.

"Bah!" snorted the old man. He turned to the room and said contemptuously: "There's your sheriff! You elected him, an' now you can have him. But the Lord help this county till next election. You got yellow law . . . crooked law . . . and every mother's son that voted fer him'll regret the day you turned the office over to one of his breed. Now take what you asked fer!"

Old Jared turned and walked to the door, his broad shoulders erect and his patriarchal beard thrust out belligerently before him. Only the slightest deviation of his steps betrayed the heavy load of liquor he was carrying.

The split doors swung back behind him, vibrated to and fro for a moment, then were still. So was the room. Silence — thick, heavy, eloquent.

Buck Rogers, solid, stocky, bull-necked, laughed hoarsely. "I guess that settles that," he said to Wallace Morgan, loudly enough for everyone to hear. "Boys, drink up with me . . . at this end of the bar."

Glory Pat Malone was almost weeping as he demanded: "Why did you let him get by with it, Brad? It ain't too late. Go out an' make him eat his words."

"No," said Brad tonelessly. He was still looking at those swinging doors through which Jared Jines had disappeared. But his eyes were seeing beyond them, far away.

"You've got to," Pat pleaded.

13

"No," said Brad in the same toneless voice. "He was drunk."

"It don't matter. He's said the same things sober. He was sober enough to know what he was doing."

"He's an old man, bitter with sorrow. I feel sorry for him, Pat."

"You'll never live this down."

"Then," said Brad, "God help me. I'm still glad I did it."

He walked away from the bar, toward the swinging doors. As he went, silence went with him. Once the doors closed behind him, a sneering laugh came from the end of the bar where Buck Rogers was standing.

II

"NIGHT RIDERS"

It was midnight when Fritz nickered softly and dropped to a walk on the high shoulder of White Mountain. The reins hung slackly in Brad Tantrall's hand, and the horse, unguided, picked his way through the low piñons and junipers that studded the mountain side.

Brad had been riding for hours with no particular destination. Anything to get away from the lighted bar, the contemptuous glances, the scornful silence that had followed him out. The sheriff's star was still pinned to his shirt front, but with each hour that passed the conviction grew that his usefulness as sheriff had been destroyed. Only a long list of fights, of gun battles, of dogged resistance to contempt would bring back the prestige the wearer of that badge must have.

Brad shivered. It was cold up here on the high slopes. Two or three thousand feet higher snow still lay on the ground. Far below, the silver headlight of a train was crawling through the low pass.

Brad had wanted to make a name for himself as sheriff. All the Tantralls had been exceptional in one way or another. Old Whip Tantrall had been a cattle king back in the days when a 'puncher rode with one eye on the restless longhorns and the other cocked for raiding Apaches. Whip's brother had stayed East and made a fortune in lumber. Brad's father and three brothers, starting from scratch when old Whip gambled away his fortune as magnificently as he made it, had been known

15

far and wide as the Black Tantralls, famous outlaws and cattle rustlers. They had all died with their boots on, in a last glorious blaze of gunfire.

With such a background it would have been hard to forecast the future of Brad and his brother, Luke, but in a way they had held true to form. Luke, eight years older, had whipped a man twice his size, beaten him so badly with bare fists that he had died. It did not matter that the quarrel had been a just one, that death was perhaps not too much payment for the sins of Jared Jines's black sheep son, Carl. For it was Carl Jines that Luke had killed, bringing an end to a short, unsavory life, taking from Jared Jines the spoiled son he adored, leaving the old man alone and bitter. Their mother's heart had broken the day the jury had found Luke guilty and Judge Bronson had sentenced him to the penitentiary for eleven years.

Brad had been thinking of Luke as the miles dropped behind. Tonight he had paid for Luke's folly. Jared Jines had hated everyone who bore the name of Tantrall with increasing bitterness as the years had passed. He had remained a widower, living alone and aloof in his big ranch house, mixing little with the hired men of his Bar X Ranch.

It was seven years since Luke had gone to prison. Brad had visited him once, and Luke had made it clear that he desired no visitors. Memory of Luke's unshaven, surly face had stayed with Brad ever since. He had never gone back. His letters were not answered. Luke would be getting out one of these days, allowing for time off. What then?

Fritz ambled along, his shod hoofs now and then clicking against a rock. Brad idly watched the bright shaft of the train's headlight down there in the pass. Glowing windows farther back proclaimed it to be Number Seventeen, the limited that roared through Vaca Prieta at one o'clock in the morning. The labored spat of the distant exhaust pulsed rhythmically on the night air, barely audible.

Suddenly it stopped. The crawling advance of the light ceased. Brad wondered why. There was no scheduled stop down there in the pass. He could see the track clear to Vaca Prieta. No train was in sight there, blocking the way.

Crack . . . crack-crack-crack . . . crack!

Brad reined Fritz in abruptly as the first report came to his ears. It was so faint he might have thought himself mistaken if it had not been followed by others. It was too far away to make out anything that was happening, but Brad did not need to know, as he neck-reined Fritz around and sent him plunging recklessly down the mountain side. The train had been still when he heard the reports. They could not have been signal torpedoes on the rails. Only one thing could have made those reports down there where the train stood still. Gunfire.

As Brad rode, he drew his revolver and thumbed the empty cartridge on past the firing pin. Gunfire and a halted train meant trouble. Forgotten now was Jared Jines and all that had happened back there in Vaca Prieta. Brad Tantrall, sheriff, rode recklessly down the mountain side.

He had two full miles to go. As Fritz slid and lunged past trees and rocks, lights flashed along the length of the stalled train. One more shot barked out, louder, clearer. It was followed a few moments later by the booming blast of an explosion. That would be the safe in the express car being blown.

Fritz made the last gentler slope at the bottom of the pass in a drumming rush. The train lay motionless not a hundred yards ahead, visible through a screen of low piñons. Brad could hear the air pump of the engine, exhausting through the stack.

The door of the express car was open. Lights were on in the coaches. From the saddle he saw the white coat and staring face of a Pullman porter at an open vestibule door. Then Fritz snorted and swerved aside. A horse whinnied before them. Half

17

a dozen animals stamped uneasily in the faint moonlight.

Brad acted instantly, swinging Fritz's head. He had stumbled on the most vulnerable part of the hold-up. Left afoot, the bandits would be helpless. A posse could soon round them up.

A man holding the horse swore and called: "Who's that?"

Fritz leaped mightily as Brad roweled his flank. They struck the group of horses hard, splitting them, sending them plunging, snorting away from the man who held their reins. He swore and fought them. Lost one and held onto the rest as Brad wheeled Fritz around on his hind legs and spurred back. A gun spat flame from where the man stood. Brad felt the jerk of the bullet as it cut through the side of his coat. Then his own gun was blasting back over Fritz's head, throwing lead at that spot where little livid tongues of light were licking out at him.

It was all over in an instant. Fritz stumbled, pitching forward as a bullet caught him between the eyes. Brad catapulted over his head, able only to slip his feet out of the heavy stirrups. He struck on hands and knees, rolling like a helpless sack of meal for ten full feet.

The plunging horses were right above him when he staggered dizzily up. He had lost his revolver in the tumble. He had no weapon but his fists now. He balled them as he came up.

The man in the plunging vortex of frightened horseflesh was cursing loudly as he tried to steady them. Brad dodged past flying hoofs and plunged in after this man. When he reached him, he grabbed his gun wrist before the fellow realized he was there.

They both fought silently, Brad to keep the gun muzzle pointing away and wrest the weapon from the man, the other holding the frightened horses with one hand and hanging onto

18

his revolver desperately with the other.

The whole thing lasted only a few short seconds. A flying hoof numbed Brad's right leg. He got both hands on the revolver and twisted violently. The other swore as his fingers were wrenched and lost their strength. In that same instant the muzzle of another gun shoved hard in Brad's back.

"Reach high!"

That bawled order brooked no delay. Reach — or die. No time to think, to argue. Brad acted as quickly now as he had when he charged the horses. False heroics and a bullet through the back wouldn't help the situation any. He dropped the gun and shoved up his hands.

He was seized by his shoulder and hauled backward away from the horses. The gun continued to dig into his back.

"Who the hell are you?" a rough voice demanded angrily.

"Right back at you," Brad panted. "Who are you?"

Another man ran up. "What is it?" he called excitedly.

The horses had quieted somewhat. Their guard bawled: "That crazy fool tried to ride me down an' scatter the bronc's. I don't know who he is. I shot his hoss from under him, then he jumped me, an' tried to take my gun away. Let him have it!"

A flashlight blazed out, washing up and down Brad's figure. The man behind the flash swore.

"He's wearing a sheriff's badge! There must be a posse around here!"

But the man behind Brad denied it quickly: "Ain't no chance. If there was a posse around, the whole lot of 'em would've jumped us at once."

"You ain't sayin' this fellow run in all alone?"

"That's what I'm sayin'. Can't figger it. But he sure sashayed in an' tried to make a one-man job of it."

"The crazy fool! Plug 'im an' let's get busy. They're bringin'

19

the stuff outta the safe now."

"Guess we'd better. Can't leave no sheriff runnin' around loose behind here."

Brad blinked and turned his head away, tensing for a wild leap to the side. He knew there wasn't a chance of making it successfully. That gun, thrusting hard against his back, could not miss. But at least it was better than standing here and being shot down like a trapped coyote. Just before he took the plunge that would bring lead blasting into his back, a thick, husky voice barked from the darkness.

"Don't shoot that *hombre!*"

Brad poised motionless in sheer surprise. It was the last thing he expected to hear. These men were desperate and in a hurry. They couldn't waste time with him, or afford to take chances and leave him behind. The man who held the gun on his back thought the same thing.

"We got us a sheriff!" he protested. "Look at thet star under his coat. He come hell-tailin' along an' tried to scatter the hosses. We got to get rid of him."

A pause followed while two more men came up, dropping heavy sacks on the ground. The voice from the darkness said harshly: "Sheriff, is he? What's his name?"

"Tantrall," said Brad coolly.

"Huh, Tantrall. That name's familiar. Remember the Tantrall brothers? The ones they called the Black Tantralls?"

Grunts of assent greeted that recollection. "But they all got shot down years ago," snapped one of the men.

The harsh voice said musingly: "This is Lode County where the Black Tantralls hailed from. Mister, was they any relation?"

"Father and uncles," said Brad briefly.

"An' you're a sheriff?"

"Yes."

"Ridin' alone out here?"

"You've got more room to answer that than I have," Brad said. "You don't see anyone else piling in to help me, do you?"

"How long you been sheriff?" the harsh voice demanded.

Brad had been trying to make out the source of it, but the flash stayed in his eyes, and he could see nothing. There was something familiar about that voice. He answered readily enough, since to talk was to gain time. "Just elected."

"This your first trouble, eh?"

"And a nice piece to cut my teeth on," said Brad grimly.

"What you doing out here around the mountain?"

"Riding."

"Jest riding?"

"Just riding."

"Married?"

"No," said Brad, wondering what purpose lay behind all this questioning. The feeling was growing that he knew the speaker.

The others felt the same way about it evidently. The man who held the gun on Brad said impatiently: "We can't stand here, workin' our muzzles all night. An' we got to do something with this fellow."

"Where's his gun?"

"I dropped it," said Brad.

A heavy hand was already patting over his body. "Nothing on him," was the verdict.

"His hoss is dead?"

"Yep."

"Turn him loose."

That order evoked a storm of protest from all of them. But the harsh voice cut in angrily. "Turn him loose, I say! He can't do anything without a gun an' hoss. And the train'll get in and have a posse started just as quick without him."

The man behind Brad started to argue hotly. "Now looky

here, Slash, we all got something to say about this. An' I say we better shut him up afore he makes trouble for us."

"If that kid ain't walkin' free an' easy in ten seconds, real trouble'll hit you *pronto*," the harsh voice said ominously.

"Aw, hell, let 'im go. This ain't no time to start pourin' dirt amongst ourselves," one of the men burst out disgustedly. "First thing we know, we'll do us more harm than a dozen posses."

A final punch with the gun, a hard shove, a gruff — "Git, an' keep goin'!" — followed that.

As Brad skirted the horses hastily and hurried down toward the train, his pulses were pounding from a thought that had flashed over him. But there was no time to dwell on it now. He heard the men swearing and talking as they mounted. Before he reached the train, the drum of departing hoofs led off through the piñons, heading back through the pass away from Vaca Prieta.

The train had started. The coaches were rolling with increasing speed. Brad ran for the door where the porter was still standing. It slammed almost in his face.

He waited until the last coach rolled swiftly by, leaped for the hand rail, and swung to the steps heavily. The conductor, flagman, and half a dozen passengers were standing in the aisle inside, peering through the open door. They shuffled back with alarm when Brad appeared suddenly before them. Plainly they suspected some trick about his appearance and looked for more trouble.

Brad had lost his sombrero along with his gun. His hands were bruised, his trousers and coat covered with dirt and piñon needles. He limped a little from the leg that had been kicked. He was still breathing hard.

" 'Evening, folks," Brad greeted them. He grinned as he dusted off coat and trousers with his open palm.

The men and women in that little group, some of them half dressed, stared at him uneasily. City folks, still nervous over the hold-up. But the conductor, a thin, wizened, elderly man, wearing steel spectacles, pointed a finger at Brad's badge, which showed as his coat opened.

"Who are you?" he questioned uncertainly.

"Sheriff Tantrall of Lode County," Brad answered.

Then they crowded toward him, all trying to talk at once.

"We were just held up!" the conductor told him excitedly. "The express messenger was shot and his safe blown open!"

"I figured something like that happened," Brad agreed. "Anyone else hurt?"

No one had been. The rest of the shots had been fired in warning. None of the passenger coaches had been entered. In fact, men had strode up and down outside, calling warnings for everyone to remain quiet, and they would not be bothered.

"What was in the safe?" Brad asked the conductor.

The old man adjusted his steel spectacles with fingers that were still trembling. "Bar g-gold," he stuttered. "S-sixty thousand dollars' worth of it, shipped from the mines back at Tanger. The messenger was telling me about it at Tanger station."

As Brad listened, his eyes found the one person in the party who looked cool, calm, as if this sort of thing was not unusual. She was fully dressed, the only one who was so besides the conductor and flagman. Her intent scrutiny had drawn his gaze. She had stood there, just back of the conductor, from the moment he entered, watching his movements fixedly. A strange smile had touched her lips for an instant, and then vanished. There was no fear, no nervousness about her. In her sensible brown traveling suit she was the best-looking woman there.

Her eyes held his until Brad looked away. Something was

happening to him. He felt embarrassed, uneasy before her scrutiny. It irritated him.

"I reckon I better have a look at the express car while we're pulling into Vaca Prieta," he said brusquely. "There ain't no hospital for your messenger there, but, if he's bad hit, there's a doctor of sorts. I'll get a posse started after those *hombres* right away."

III

"LAST OF THE TANTRALLS"

They walked through coach after coach of excited, wide awake passengers who were still discussing the hold-up avidly. The express car door was unlocked. Half a dozen men were standing around the messenger's cot. Brad spotted the news butch and baggageman among them. The messenger's coat and shirt were off. A bloody towel was wound around his shoulder. Another one that had been used was lying on the floor. The young man lay there, pale and weak, his wound evidently bleeding badly.

The baggageman was manipulating the towel. He looked up with a worried expression on his face. "Find a doctor on the train?" he asked the conductor.

"No. But this man says there's one in Vaca Prieta. He's sheriff."

"If you don't mind, I'll do what I can," a cool voice said behind them. "I have studied nursing."

It was the same girl who had regarded Brad so intently in the last coach. She had followed them forward.

"Go right to it, ma'am," the baggageman said hastily, moving over to make room for her. "He's shot right bad in the shoulder, an' I can't seem to stop the bleeding."

She was kneeling by the cot before he had finished speaking. "More towels," she requested briskly. "And some cold water. A disinfectant, too, if there's a first aid kit on the train."

Brad noticed the safe in the farther end of the car, lying on its side. The door had been blown off the hinges. Parts of the

25

contents were still lying in a heap on the floor before it, where someone had hastily tossed them.

"What happened?" Brad asked the young man. The train was rocking and swaying as it pushed through the night, and he wanted all the information possible before it reached Vaca Prieta.

As the girl worked swiftly and efficiently on his shoulder, the stolid-faced young man talked. "I didn't think anything was wrong when we stopped. I'd been riding with the door part way open. But as soon as we stopped, I walked over to close it. Got it almost shut when a rifle barrel shoved through the crack an' someone, standing outside, yelled to open up. I grabbed my gun and tried to shoot through the door. Just as I did that, a six-gun poked through higher up an' cut loose. Got me in the shoulder and kind of spun me around. It was a Forty-Four, I think. Numbed my whole arm, so I dropped my gun. And before I could do anything more, they had the door open and the drop on me. Wasn't nothin' to do but take it or eat lead. I got a wife and two kids."

"You did the wisest thing," Brad agreed. "They would surely have shot you down, if you hadn't backed water quick. Did you see any of their faces?"

"No. The three I saw were all masked. They jumped in the car and went to work on the safe. I guess they were experts. It didn't seem more than a few minutes before they lit a fuse and dragged me down out of the car with them. Then, after the explosion, they made me get back in again with them. They shoved the bar gold in sacks and dragged them out. Didn't touch anything else. Looked to me like they must have known it was there.",

"Carry many gold shipments?" Brad asked.

"Quite a few. There's a lot of mines along the road."

"Probably took a chance on it," Brad decided.

26

The girl looked up from her work. Her dark eyes challenged him. "You know a lot about what they did, and what kind of men they are, don't you?" she asked. There was a vague suspicion in her voice.

She was pretty, little enough to come about to his shoulder. Her lightly tanned features were regular and even. She had a small, determined chin and a firm mouth. Soft waves of brown hair showed under the edge of her small hat.

Brad grinned at her. "It's easy to guess things like that, ma'am."

"Easy to guess just where they would be, I suppose?"

Brad frowned. "I don't understand, ma'am."

"I think you do. How do you know exactly what sort of desperadoes they were, as you just told this man a few minutes ago?"

Brad chuckled. "I oughta know that. I tangled with 'em. Almost got a back full of lead myself."

"That is what I have been wondering about," she said. "How did it happen that you were in that isolated spot in the middle of the night, just when the hold-up happened?"

An awkward silence fell. There was no mistaking the girl's implication. She had indirectly charged him with being one of the gang. Brad felt his ears reddening. If she had been a man, he could have handled the matter better. But one didn't call a woman a liar.

"I was riding up on the mountain," Brad explained to them all. "I saw the train stop down below, and then heard shooting. Right off, I knew something was wrong. So I rode down to see about it. I ran into their horses and tried to scatter 'em. Got my own pony shot from under me. Lost my gun as I went down. They doubled up on me and stuck a gun in my back. That sort of put me out of things, seeing as I was alone."

"And they let you walk away?" she challenged.

"There was some talk about shooting me, but they changed their minds. Figured I couldn't do any more harm alive than dead right then. So they rode one way, and I just caught the train as she pulled out."

"And did you see any of their faces?" she questioned. She might have been the sheriff and he the one under suspicion. Brad couldn't account for her interest in the matter. Just a city girl who liked to poke into everything, he decided, like she had come here in the baggage car and taken charge of the wounded man.

"It was dark," he explained patiently. "One of them held a light in my eyes all the time."

The conductor broke in nervously: "I don't see where all this is getting us. The hold-up was in this man's county, and it's up to him to track down the gold and get it back. We'll be in Vaca Prieta in a short while, and he can take charge."

She had been working as she talked. Now she finished tying a clean towel over the wounded shoulder and got to her feet. Her eyes were flashing as she faced Brad. "What did you say your name was?" she asked him pointedly.

"Tantrall," said Brad.

"Wasn't it from this county that the famous Black Tantrall gang of train robbers came?"

Brad's face was crimson again. Sudden anger swept him. It didn't look as though he could ever get away from the heritage of his blood. "It was this county," he agreed. "They were my father and uncles. But they're dead, and I'm sheriff now. And the Black Tantralls are gone."

"All but you and your brother," she said coolly.

"Yes," Brad agreed.

"Where is your brother?"

Brad's self-control snapped, as perhaps she had intended it

28

should. "This isn't any of your business, ma'am!" he said furiously. "I don't aim to drag out the family history for strangers to paw over. But since we're on it, how come you know so much and have so much interest?"

Her smile was scornful as she turned away from him with a little shrug. "As a passenger who was at the hold-up, it interested me," she declared — and walked out of the express car.

Brad stared after her slender figure with his lip caught savagely between his teeth. The pain snapped his thoughts back. He turned to the men, who looked embarrassed.

"That's all," he said curtly to the conductor. "You can unload this wounded man at Vaca Prieta if you want to. Get all the evidence you can from the passengers for your report. Some of it might come in handy at the trial."

The conductor cleared his throat and said uncertainly: "Do you think you'll be able to catch up with them?"

Brad's teeth clicked together with the violence of his feeling. "We'll get 'em if we have to trail 'em from here to hell and gone!"

There was still a good size group of men in the Bankhorn Bar when Brad stepped in through the doors. The conversation hushed abruptly. Some of the men turned their faces away, ignoring him pointedly.

Glory Pat Malone stepped from the bar, his face grim under his short black beard. "Jest in time to cut in on a round, Brad," he said loudly enough for everyone to hear. And Glory Pat shoved his worn gray sombrero back on his head and looked around the room challengingly. His purpose was plain. He was serving notice on the world that Brad Tantrall was still his friend, daring any man to say something about it. It brought a lump into Brad's throat. Not until this evening had he realized

29

how much a friend meant.

Looking slightly sheepish, Canby Jack, Slim Parks, and Tom Dorsett moved forward, too. These closest friends were still all with him, and a finer bunch of men had never ridden together.

Brad thanked them with a look and then, raising his voice, addressed the room. "Men, there's been a hold-up over at Coyote Pass. Number Seventeen, that just pulled into the station, was held up and her express safe robbed of sixty thousand dollars in bar gold. I was riding through there and tried to stop the outfit that done it. But they were too many. Six at least. They got away. I want a posse quick to go after them. It'll mean hard riding, and shooting if we catch up with them."

Ben Picketts, a stocky, powerful rider for Wallace Morgan's Ladder U outfit, spat on the floor and said audibly: "Then what do you want to go along for?"

Brad walked over to Picketts. "I spoke plain," he said coldly. "I want a posse that can fight. Are you volunteering?"

"Not for no posse you lead," Picketts sneered. His hand dropped to his belt, just over his gun.

Brad's hand did not go near his own weapon, which he had gotten from the sheriff's office as he came up from the station. Instead, it flashed out and caught Picketts's gun wrist so he could not draw. With his other fist Brad slugged Picketts in the jaw.

A vacant look came over the stocky waddy's face. His knees sagged. He pitched to the floor, out completely.

Glory Pat heaved an audible sigh of relief. "I knowed someone was gonna get it afore the night was over," he muttered joyfully.

"Get your guns and plenty of ammunition and gather down in front of my office," Brad said to the rest, as if nothing had happened. "Roust out anyone else you can, men. I'll deputize everyone, and we'll ride."

"Any man who stays behind is a yaller belly," Glory Pat said loudly. "An' when I git back, I'll tell him so to his face."

IV

"THE BLOOD TRAIL"

Dawn was just pushing up over the Cristo range, forty miles to the east, when the eighteen horsemen of Brad's posse trotted into Coyote Pass where the hold-up had occurred. They found the spot easily enough, and the places where the horses had been held. Brad's belt gun was still on the ground, trampled into the earth. Fritz was nearby. He stopped long enough to remove his saddle from the horse and cache it. Then they again took up the trail.

It led easily west through the pass for half a mile, then turned north, and began to climb the steep slopes of the mountain. Slim Parks, who was as tall and thin as an *ocotillo* cactus branch with a gaunt freckled face and an infectious smile, exclaimed disgustedly after half an hour of climbing: "Those buzzards must've been a mess of ornery-eyed *orejano*s to leave their trail so plain. They knowed they was comin' up thisaway an' did it a-purpose to lead us on till we give out an' rolled off our bronc's."

Tom Dorsett, short, thin and lively, snorted. "Ef you give out an' roll off your bronc', I'm gonna take that quart you snuck in your saddlebags an' ride on. No lowdown long-legged son of sin is gonna spread hisself in the sun an' guzzle likker while I'm doin' his hard work."

"The only hard work you ever done was to lift yourself in the saddle, an' let yore hoss wear hisself out," Slim grumbled. "An' fer them unkind remarks I'll keep the bottle corked up a while longer."

The bandits seemed to be heading for the inaccessible crests of the range where the heavy forest and great tangled bushes still lay under many feet of snow. Back in there, ridge after mighty ridge rolled off into the west. There were great hulks of fallen trees, thick forests, hidden valleys that had never known cattle, and deep slashing cañons that had never been trodden by the feet of white men. The only doubtful thing about it was, as Brad said to Glory Pat: "There's too much snow now. They'd leave a trail a kid could follow soon as they hit the snow. Near as I can see, their only hope is to lose the trail and ride hard and fast."

"Looks that way to me, too," Pat agreed.

Up above the piñon and juniper growth, where the pines and bush thickets were just beginning, the closely bunched trail they had been following split. Seven horses went six different ways. There was only one thing to do then. Brad split up his men into six bunches.

"It may be a scheme to break us up and bushwhack as many as possible," he said. "We'll have to take the chance. It's every man for himself now. We probably won't get together again until we meet in Vaca Prieta. Good luck, boys."

"I'll go with Slim and keep an eye on his bottle," Tom Dorsett said enthusiastically, and did so.

Brad and Glory Pat rode on alone, following the trail left by two of the horses. It angled up the mountain for a short distance, and then began to cut evenly across the slopes. It angled down again, the far-spaced tracks indicating hard-ridden horses.

Since leaving Vaca Prieta, Brad had ridden more or less silently. No one had noticed it, for the pace had been hard, and they had scattered out. But now Pat said abruptly: "You

33

look like you've got a heap of trouble on your mind, Brad."
When he got no reply to that, he added casually: "Now that
little ruckus last night don't amount to a whistle on a skunk's
back. Jared was soused to his big ears." Pat coughed, then
mumbled weakly: "I think you done just right."

Brad smiled. "You're a good-natured liar, and you know
it," he accused. "You still think I should have taken his dare
and made him eat all the trouble he started."

"Well, what of it?" Pat asked defiantly. "That's the only
way to settle a thing like that. I know you wasn't afeerd of
him. But *he* didn't."

"He's an old man, and bitter, Pat. I feel sorry for him. I'd
like to be friends. I wouldn't want to look at my face when I
shave if I took that excuse to throw some lead into him. Jared
needs a son, not a bullet." Brad's voice dropped soberly. "A
son the Black Tantralls took away from him. The only one he
had."

"You better stop worrying about it."

Brad took a deep breath. "I'm not worrying about that,"
he said slowly.

"Huh? You ain't? Then what? You can't run a blind trail
on me, Brad. You've been studying a heap since it got light
enough for me to see you."

Brad nodded.

Pat waited a moment, then asked bluntly: "What is it? I'm
your friend, Brad. That goes fer anything."

"Pat, what would you think if you were told the leader of
that bandit gang was my brother, Luke?"

"Jeehosephat and little crickets!" Glory Pat gasped. "Am I
supposed to laugh at that?"

"I don't feel like laughing," Brad confessed unhappily.

"It can't be your brother. I never knew him, but he's locked
up tighter'n a cow tick in a bottle."

34

"He could be out about now, allowing for time off. Or he might have escaped."

"Did you see him?"

"No."

"Huh . . . jest havin' nightmares like? 'Course, that wasn't your brother. He'd have let you know if he was out."

"No," said Brad. "We were never close. Luke has become surly like my uncles. Prison changed him for the worse. I visited him once. He said he didn't want to see me again. Told me to go back home and not be a damned fool. He was like a man who'd jumped in quicksand, and was warning another away from it."

"That ain't no grounds fer thinkin' he was tangled up in this business."

"Here's what happened," Brad said. And he described the scene by the train, finishing: "That fellow who asked me so many questions, and then made 'em turn me loose, called me *kid*. Luke is the only one whoever did that. I'm not a kid, now. A stranger wouldn't think of it."

"You said they called him Slash?"

"He was using another name," said Brad flatly. "His voice sounded familiar even before he spoke to me and, when he called me kid, I was sure. If I hadn't been his brother, I'd probably have stayed there with a bullet in my back."

Pat argued no more. But after a moment he said doubtfully: "You're ridin' out to catch your brother?"

"I swore to uphold the law, and I'll do it, no matter how close it strikes. If Luke has come back and turned outlaw, I'll treat him like any other outlaw. And he knows it."

"Then God help you both," Pat said devoutly. "Tantrall against Tantrall. It'll be something this range'll talk about till the kids grow white beards."

"It has to be," Brad said heavily. "But that isn't all of it."

He told Pat about the girl on the train. "Because I'm one of the Black Tantralls, I'm damned before I start. I was there on the spot. What good does it do people to tell 'em I was riding out that way, not paying any attention where I was riding? All they'll see is that I was there when the train was robbed, and got away without any trouble. That girl put it plain enough when she same as accused me of helping them, without even knowing my brother was in it. When folks find out who he was, my best friends'll wonder if I hadn't thrown in to help him. The Black Tantralls riding again, with one of them sheriff."

"Your friends won't believe that!" Pat snapped.

"Wait and see. And if I meet my brother and have to . . . to kill him. . . ." Brad shivered slightly at the prospect, then finished tightly: "They'll not be above saying we had a falling out, and I killed him in cold blood under the protection of my badge."

Glory Pat Malone shook his head silently.

Brad's youthful face suddenly looked old. "If I have to kill my brother . . . ," he whispered.

An hour later Brad and Pat Malone reined in their mounts at the upper falls of Maverick Creek, staring down the drop of Maverick Cañon and out over the rolling mesa country beyond. They were silent for a moment as their eyes searched the rocky banks to the edge of the falls, where the water slid glassily over into the fifty-foot plunge to the rocky pool below.

Pat spoke first, disgustedly, as he fingered his short, black beard. "Them two lobos never passed here. A rock squirrel couldn't claw himself down around them falls. I'll be a wall-eyed tarantula if they ain't given us the slip."

Back of them Maverick Creek was all of ten feet wide, as it roiled and rushed its flow of cold snow water through the rocky channel that snaked down out of the mountain. Maverick Cañon was no more than two hundred yards wide, its rocky walls worn and eroded, split into smaller rocky cañons and narrow fissures that twisted back to unknown distances.

Three miles back, the trail they followed had led into the beds of Maverick Creek, heading downstream. And, though they had ridden those three miles with their eyes glued on the creek banks, they had found no sign that the two horses ahead had emerged. Now they were stopped by the falls, and Pat was right. No horse could have advanced farther, or its rider afoot, either.

Brad hoisted himself around in the saddle and stared reflectively back up the cañon. "We missed them," he decided. "Somewhere back there they got on the rocks and out of the cañon. There's places back there where they'd have had clear rock for a long way. And any water they dragged out of the channel would have evaporated long ago."

"Uhn-huh. An' it'd take us a week to sashay up all them side fissures an' cracks. Brad, they hornswaggled us."

"Looks that way," Brad agreed. He slowly rolled a smoke, flicked a match alight, and inhaled deeply. "Whoever we were following knew this country like a book," he said abruptly.

"I've been noticing that," Pat Malone said dryly. "They know where they're goin' an' how to get there."

Brad nodded at the far-flung sweep of mesa land, unrolling down beyond the mouth of the cañon. "That's the upper Bar X lease down there. Luke punched cattle for Jared Jines and rode these hills plenty."

"Uhn-huh." Pat's very unwillingness to argue the matter showed how his mind was running. They both were certain now they had been following Luke Tantrall and a companion.

Pat suddenly placed both hands on the saddle horn and leaned forward, peering beneath the sagging brim of his sombrero. "What's that dust out there?"

Brad looked, too, saw a tiny column of dust, drifting up far out on the mesa, and by looking hard he was certain he saw through the clear air small black dots at the head of it. Even as he looked, they dropped down out of sight into lower ground.

"That's not cattle, Pat."

"Nope. Somebody's ridin' hard. Must be a dozen of 'em anyway."

"Can't be our men," Brad said instantly. "They're scattered back up the mountain."

"Jared Jines ain't sendin' a passel of riders like that out on ranch business."

Their eyes met, and for a moment they were silent.

"I reckon we better look into this," Brad said evenly. "They're cutting kind of north. That would bring them out somewhere near Dead Horse Flat where the Bar X peters out into the mountain."

"Yep. I know the lay. Jines has had a line cabin there for years, an' keeps a rider there sometimes to throw his cattle back off of the mountain."

Brad neck-reined his horse around. "We can take that cut about a quarter of a mile back and get around the falls," he said.

Two horses were waiting on a rise beyond a dry arroyo when the hard-riding bunch of horsemen topped the opposite rise and suddenly saw them. Dust and small stones flew as sweat-lathered horses were abruptly reined in. Rifles leaped to shoulders and covered the two riders. Then a huge white-bearded figure waved an arm at the men around him. His bull-like bellow drifted across the arroyo.

"Hell, that ain't Luke Tantrall!"

38

And the rest followed as he spurred down into the bone-white arroyo sand and rode up the other slope. Pat Malone was bristling in his saddle. Brad was smoking calmly, one hand resting easily on the saddle horn, as Jared Jines reined to a halt before him. Back of the old patriarch of the Bar X crowded Wallace Morgan and Buck Rogers of the Ladder U, Ben Picketts and four other Ladder U riders, and five men at least from the Bar X outfit — all that Jared Jines could get together in a hurry, Brad guessed.

Jared Jines laid a huge hand on the stock of the rifle, projecting out of his saddle boot, leaned forward belligerently, and demanded harshly: "What brings you here on Bar X land, Mister Sheriff? Where's your posse?"

"Back on the mountain," Brad replied without seeming to notice Jared's manner. He wasn't even looking at the old man. His eyes were riveted on the last rider who had galloped up. And a low flush crawled into his cheeks as she rested her big, panting roan a few yards away and met his glance with a disdainful lift of her chin. It was the girl who had questioned him so scornfully on the train, clad now in riding boots, smart trousers, and a soft leather jacket.

Wallace Morgan pushed his snow-white sombrero back on his head and showed gleaming teeth in a smile under his small black mustache. "You didn't send them back in the hills on a wild goose chase, so they wouldn't see what you were doing, did you, Tantrall?" he questioned mockingly.

Brad's glance shifted to him. "Meaning?"

"Meaning just this!" old Jared Jines broke in angrily. "We're wise to yuh, Tantrall! Wonder someone didn't ketch on when you got your posse together. I seen it all as soon as my niece, Laurette, got off the train an' talked to me. Sixty thousand dollars in gold was took off the limited last night. That was a Black Tantrall job, an' you was there."

"What makes you so all fired sure it was a Tantrall job, you old whiskered goat?" Glory Pat Malone drawled, dropping his hand to the gun at his hip.

Jared Jines ignored the challenge. "Callin' names ain't gonna help your friend none, Malone. We've done wired the penitentiary an' found out that Luke Tantrall busted out four days ago. An' long before daybreak this morning Jim Blake, who's been riding circle, heard two men ride by his camp, goin' slow an' talkin' clear. One of them was Luke Tantrall. They was planning to bed up fer the day at the head of Dead Horse Flat, wait fer some friends, an' catch fresh hosses there. Jim rode in with the news before breakfast."

"And you figure I was mixed up in that business, too," Brad suggested. "Your niece hinted at it last night on the train."

"Figger? We know!" Jared roared. "It's as plain as daylight between a burro's ears! You couldn't wait until you was in office two days before you turned rotten like all the Tantralls. Last night you crawled dust, an' then slunk out an' met your brother an' his men, an' the lot of you held up that train. Then you come back with a cock an' bull story to lead the posse that was bound to go out, to make sure nobody caught up with them."

"You lie in your whiskers, Jared!" Pat Malone barked. "I've been with Brad since the posse left. He's done his damnedest!"

"Where's your posse?" Wallace Morgan queried slyly.

"The men we were following split up, and I split the posse to follow them," Brad told him evenly.

Morgan flashed his teeth again in an amused smile. "An' now you're tryin' to head us off from Dead Horse Flat, I suppose?"

"Damn your dirty, mud-slinging face!" Brad flared violently at Morgan. "I'm not trying to head you off from anywhere. We saw your dust and knew something was up, so we rode

40

out to see. But I'm reminding you now, Morgan . . . and you, Jared Jines . . . that I'm sheriff of this county. You'll all take orders from me in this business."

"And your orders are?" Morgan taunted.

"Hell, don't stand here wastin' words!" Jared shouted. "The Black Tantralls are ridin' this range again, an' we come out to clean house. That goes for this lily-livered sheriff as well as his murderin' brother."

Brad roweled hard, and his startled pony crowded suddenly in against Jared Jines. Hardly an eye in that group saw Brad's gun move, but suddenly it was jammed against Jared's side. One look into his blazing eyes stayed the old man's hand. He sat rigidly while Brad threw his belt gun to the ground and did the same with the holstered rifle.

Pat Malone had acted almost as swiftly. His gun flashed out and swept threateningly over the others. "I'll take at least three of you misguided wildcats with me, if you get rambunctious an' call me!" he threatened.

The men growled among themselves, but no one made the first move. Only Laurette, Jared's niece, dared push her roan horse in to Brad's side. Her eyes were flashing, and there was contempt in her voice as she cried: "A Black Tantrall would do that to an old man. Take that gun away from him." She lifted her quirt and slashed Brad across the face.

Brad's cheek muscles crawled around the livid line that the braided leather thong left. "If you do that again," he warned coldly, "I'll kill him. Get back." It was the only way he knew to stop her. And it worked.

"Oh!" she gasped. "You're worse than I thought even a Tantrall could be."

"Get back, girl," Jared ordered thickly. "He's a snake an'd probably do it. He's bent on giving his brother a chance to get away. I shouldn't have let you tag along."

Laurette reined her horse away, and her face was pale and anxious, the small, determined chin quivering slightly. "Can't any of you men do something to him?" she appealed.

Ben Picketts growled apologetically: "He's got the drop on Jared, miss. We can get him, all right, but he can get Jared first."

"And there would be a bloody mess before it was over," Wallace Morgan told her smoothly. "Better get back and stay back."

"Well?" Jared glared at Brad. "What are you goin' to do about it, Tantrall?"

"Tell your men to ride ahead of us."

"Where to?"

"Dead Horse Flat. Come in from the north side, in the cover of the piñons."

IV

"BROTHER AGAINST BROTHER"

Dead Horse Flat was a quarter-mile-wide tongue of grassy mesa, thrusting back into the foothills for at least half a mile. It narrowed at the upper end, petering out finally in the rolling rise of the mountainside, covered thickly with piñon trees. The foothills, cloaked with piñons, also came down on either side of the flat, like a natural boundary that was yet not a barrier.

At the upper end, hard by the mountain slope, a small spring welled out of the ground, and there was a low, weather-beaten log cabin with one room inside and a few yards away from it a small corral. The cabin commanded the whole sweep of the flat. On the far fringe of the Bar X holdings, isolated, it was seldom visited from one year to another, save by the men who took turns at watching this upper end of the ranch.

Old Jared was riding closely beside Brad and still muttering in his sweeping white beard as the group of riders came in from the north and stopped a full half mile from the flat at Brad's low-spoken order.

Pat Malone had scouted on ahead of them, and a few minutes later he met them. "They're there," he said coolly to Brad. "Hosses in the corral, all saddled, ready to make tracks. No one in sight, but I reckon someone's watching."

Brad nodded and holstered the gun that had been resting on his thigh. "Now, you jaspers," he said, "I've brought you here. You didn't bring me. I'm telling you again I'm sheriff, legally elected and running the law in Lode County. Somebody

43

held up a train, and I'm going to do my duty, the same as I have been trying to do since it happened. I'm going to swear you all in as deputies, since my posse is scattered, and I'm reminding you that makes you liable to my orders. Are you willing?"

"There's a trick in it!" Jared said violently.

"Not for you," Brad replied calmly. "You'll do no revenge killing under the protection of the law. Pot one man, Jared Jines, and I'll take you in for murder. If the rest of you see any outlaws making a break, you can open up on 'em."

"You ain't goin' to make me stand around helpless, damn yuh!" Jared choked in his beard.

"You are hobbled, hamstrung, an' hog-tied, Jared," Pat Malone said with grim humor. "Now take it to yore bosom like a man an' don't founder from your own bile. Move back. You are obstructin' the law."

The men hesitated, eyeing one another questioningly.

"Are you all goin' to let him pull blinders over your eyes?" Jared demanded.

Wallace Morgan bit his lip, and then shrugged. "There's a legal side to this, Jared. We aren't the only ones in the county. We can't shoot the sheriff they elected, even if we are sure he's crooked. He's out dealt us. We're here, and he's talking law. The best play I see is to call his hand. If he can deal from the bottom with all of us watching him, he's a smarter man than I think he is. An' if we're convinced from the evidence we see that he's helping them to get away, then by his own law we'll stop him. Swear us in, Tantrall, and watch your step."

Brad did that, and gave his orders swiftly.

"Pat, take five of the men and ride up even with the cabin. Tie the horses and place your men on the hill back of the cabin, as near as possible, with rifles. That ought to be enough to pick off anyone trying to make a break back onto the

44

mountain that way. Morgan, you and the rest ride down to the edge of the flat and stop just inside the piñons. If anyone rides out toward you or across the flat, you can drop them, or ride fast after them."

"And then what do they do?" Jared sneered. "You got 'em split, half without their hosses. Do they stand around an' wait? I tell you, boys, there's a trick in it. Rush the blasted cabin an' get it over with!"

"And get picked off," Brad pointed out harshly. "That place is like a fort. They could hold off a posse all day and night. Do what I say. I'll give you half an hour to get your men in place, Pat."

"What do you do?" Wallace Morgan questioned shrewdly.

"Whatever I feel like," Brad replied shortly. "I told you I was giving orders here. Get in your places, men. And don't move from there until I tell you to. Jines, watch your niece."

"No Tantrall is going to hurt me!" Laurette flared.

Pat Malone reined close to Brad. "You aren't going to do anything foolish, *amigo?*" he asked anxiously.

Brad's face was pale and haggard, and the smile he gave Pat was mirthless. "Go on," he said. "Let me handle this."

Pat shook his head dubiously, as he turned his horse away and vanished among the trees with his men.

Brad looked at his watch, rolled a cigarette, and waited silently, smoking. Morgan's men had drawn away from him and were eyeing him furtively as they inspected their guns and talked low among themselves. When twenty minutes had passed, Brad jerked his head at Morgan.

"All right," he said briefly.

And with no more word than that he rode away from them, angling to the left on a line that would bring him out on Dead Horse Flat some distance farther away from the cabin than the point to which they were going. He heard Jared say resentfully

45

as he left: "He's going to put something over. I'll bet he hightails an' keeps goin'."

Brad didn't look around, and none of them made a move to follow him. Short minutes later Brad reined in among the last trees at the edge of the flat. Half a score of horses were grazing well out in the open, and Bar X cattle were scattered well beyond them. Brad Tantrall's face was set and expressionless, as he looked to his rifle and belt gun, making sure they were ready for instant action.

Brad was not ashamed of the tears he dashed from his eyes with the dust-covered back of his hand, as he rode forward into the open, and turned toward the head of Dead Horse Flat and the squat little cabin that rested there with a faint curl of blue smoke, seeping from the rusty stove pipe. He had sworn to uphold the law. Luke had broken that law, willfully and cold-bloodedly. There was only one thing to do. Brother against brother.

Peace lay over Dead Horse Flat as Brad loped toward the cabin. He could see their horses in the corral, and he knew that eyes must be watching him through the cabin window. He knew also that many other eyes were on him, too.

The horses in the corral lifted their heads and moved to the bars, watching. The little tufts of bunch grass muffled the loping hoofs of his own horse as it drew near the cabin rapidly. Then, suddenly, without warning, the cabin door opened a crack. A rifle barrel poked out. The sharp crack of a shot split the silence.

Brad's pony stumbled and went down in a tangle of legs and flying dust. Brad fell clear, rolled over, and came to his feet. The horse was badly wounded, unable to rise. Brad drew his gun, gave it a mercy shot, then holstered the gun again, and turned his face toward the cabin once more. On foot he took up the advance.

The rifle barked again. The bullet smacked the ground in front of him, kicking up a little fountain of dirt — plain warning that he wasn't wanted at the cabin. Brad kept on.

The rifle spat again, and once more dust kicked up near him. Then a third bullet whined viciously past his head. Grim warnings, each more threatening.

"Luke!" Brad called.

An instant later the door opened. Luke loomed in it, bareheaded, rifle in his hands. Dark stubble covered Luke's face. He wore old clothes and looked surly and desperate, as Brad stopped. For an instant they eyed each other, not more than a hundred yards apart.

"So you knew me, kid?" Luke called gruffly.

"After you let me go."

"What are you doing here?"

"You know," said Brad evenly. "I'm sheriff, Luke."

"Yeah?"

"You played the wrong hand."

"I didn't know you were sheriff, kid."

"You know now."

"Yeah."

"I've come for you, Luke. And the others."

"Get out of here, kid," Luke called grimly. "I ain't going back to that hell hole. Not if you were a dozen sheriffs."

"I'm coming in there and get you, Luke."

"I'm warning you!" Luke shouted. "Get back, kid. I let you go once. If you were anybody else, I'd drop you now, since you know me."

Brad drew his belt gun. "I'm coming, Luke." He started forward.

Luke raised his rifle. His voice was suddenly hoarse with emotion. "Kid, this is the last warning. Get back! Get back, you young fool. I don't want to kill you. Not my brother."

"No more than I want to arrest my brother," Brad answered in a choked voice. "But you asked for it, Luke. I'm coming in there after you. You're surrounded. You haven't a chance."

For a long moment Luke stood rigidly in the doorway, the rifle steady at his shoulder, covering Brad's advance. A grim, surly, menacing figure. And then suddenly Luke lowered his gun and stepped back into the cabin. The door swung shut.

Brad heard voices, shouting inside the cabin, as he plodded forward. There was a sickish feeling in the pit of his stomach. He didn't care much whether Luke shot or not.

A gun exploded in the cabin. An instant later the door jerked open again. Another figure, not Luke, leaped into view and swung a rifle up. Brad knew that this time the bullet would not miss.

He threw himself forward on his face as the rifle barked. A cold shock struck his left shoulder. He felt the hot rush of blood under his shirt and numbness creeping down his arm. Taking aim from a prone position, he fired twice at the doorway as the man, standing there, pumped the rifle lever rapidly and fired again. The bullet kicked dirt in Brad's face.

A moment later the man was shoved out of the doorway by other figures, dashing out, shooting wildly in his direction, as they raced toward the corral. Rifles suddenly began to bark from the hillside behind the cabin. One of the four men stumbled, pitched forward on his face, lay still. A second lurched and began to hobble, as he reached the corral.

Bars were hastily thrown down. Two of the men swung up on horses and spurred out, slashing madly with the romal ends and emptying six-guns at Brad as he leaped to his feet. Shouts came from behind. A swift glance over his shoulder showed Morgan and his men, spurring their horses out.

One of the riders went down in a cloud of dust, rolled out, and ran, limping, toward the opposite trees. The other rider veered toward them also, without stopping for his companion. He had almost reached them when he suddenly toppled out of the saddle, hit the ground hard, and lay where he fell. Morgan's men thundered past Brad, toward the lone man, running and firing as he went.

Without stopping to see the outcome, and ignoring the wound in his shoulder, Brad ran for the gaping cabin door. Luke had not been one of the four.

The cabin was still. He saw booted feet, and then Luke, lying face down on the floor inside the door. Luke did not move when Brad dropped to his knees beside him. Tied to a chair at the end of the room by a lass rope was one of Jared Jines's men, who had occupied the cabin.

"Ain't no use," he said as Brad dashed the back of his hand across his eyes. "They plugged him in the back when he jumped in an' swore he wouldn't shoot his brother. They was a tough lot. Cut me loose. I'm damned near paralyzed."

Brad did that dully. He was leaning against the door when running horses slid to a stop before the cabin, their riders swinging down. Jared Jines's niece stepped in and, after her, Jared. A moment later Pat Malone and his men crowded in also.

Brad faced Pat bitterly. "He's dead!" he said harshly. "He wouldn't shoot his brother, so they killed him." He swung on Jared Jines and his niece. "You hear that? They killed him because he wouldn't shoot. He was a man. A better man than a lot of you."

Laurette made no attempt to hide the tears in her eyes. "We saw it all," she said unsteadily. "And heard it. It was magnificent . . . and heartbreaking. I was crying. And Uncle Jared was swearing. And sniffling, too. I'm sorry. I didn't know about you. I'd only heard things that had been said."

Jared Jines was fingering the end of his patriarchal beard.

"Son," he said, "I don't know as you'll want to shake hands. But I'm telling you . . . and all the rest here . . . that your brother was the last of the Black Tantralls. An' he went out white. Pure white, by God! And I, fer one, am right proud to have you sheriff."

BITTER VALLEY

"Bitter Valley" was the ninth story T. T. Flynn wrote in 1935. It was completed on April 8th, a week after he had finished "The Wolves of La Cogulla" which was sold to *Star Western*. Popular Publications, because of the success of *Dime Western*, had launched *Star Western* with the first issue dated October, 1933. Blazoned across the middle of the cover of that first issue was "Hell's Half-Acre" by T. T. Flynn. It was regarded as a more prestigious magazine than *Dime Western* as reflected by its cover price of 15¢. From that point on Flynn's Western stories customarily appeared in both magazines where his rate per word was 2.5¢. At Popular Publications only Walt Coburn was paid more. However, Flynn still could not be regarded as exclusively a Western writer. Only three of those first nine stories in 1935 were Western stories. Rogers Terrill bought "Bitter Valley," and it appeared under the title "Renegade of Bitter Valley" in *Dime Western* (8/15/35). In late 1934 *Dime Western* had become biweekly and remained so for a time. It still carried the logo "All Stories New. No Reprints!" In 1951, when Mike Tilden was editing *Dime Western*, the magazine did carry reprints of stories that had appeared many years earlier in Popular Publications magazines. Not having a new T. T. Flynn story to run in the January issue, Tilden reprinted "Renegade of Bitter Valley."

I

"A NECK FOR A NOOSE"

Blood oozed down Donnigan's arm, as they held him on Buff Creed's horse and lowered the noose around his neck. Buff Creed stood on the ground in the firelight and looked directly at the prisoner.

"If you care to talk, Donnigan," he said harshly, "before we swing you off to hell, spit it out!"

Creed's sharp, stubble-covered face glistened in the wavering light of the hastily built fire. Creed had climbed the tree, tossed the rope over the limb, and slid down, yelling for the men to get the prisoner on the horse. Now Creed wiped his red bandanna across his face and scowled, as he waited for a reply.

Donnigan ducked his head and wiped blood out of his left eye with his shoulder. More blood seeped down from the crease through his black hair. The bullet, ricocheting from the side of the cabin window, had come close to killing him. Not that it mattered much — with this hanging following it. From the saddle Donnigan looked down at the men who had come with Buff Creed. They stood uncertainly, holding their rifles. Only Dave Greenwood was on his horse a few yards away. The end of the hanging rope was dallied around Greenwood's saddle horn.

Greenwood wasn't looking as if he particularly enjoyed the job. His own rope hung on his saddle. Buff Creed's rope ran over the limb and down to Donnigan's neck. And Creed himself had tied the crude hangman's knot which bulked under Donnigan's left ear.

Creed had yelled: "I been in at the fixin' of half a dozen hoss thieves an' killers no better'n this one! Here's my rope to hang him . . . an' I'll tie the knot! Get it over quick before some smart lawyer has him ridin' out a free man, thumbin' his nose at us!"

Creed's rasping voice had swayed them with that. Now they stood with the firelight dancing on their faces, intent on the moment when Greenwood's horse would snatch the body into the air.

Donnigan visualized it clearly. If he was lucky, his neck would be broken in the first savage jerk. If not — he'd have a bad time of it for a few minutes. Any way you got it, the end was the same.

Donnigan's hands, with the cutting rawhide thongs about his wrists, were resting on the saddle horn. Creed had evidently not thought it worthwhile to tie them behind. Numbness was creeping above the thongs. In a way the numbness was welcome. It dulled the pain of the bullet wound, high in Donnigan's left arm.

Creed had fired that bullet when he first kicked open the door of the log cabin and saw Donnigan, jumping from the table with his gun coming out. Creed had fired and dodged back. Donnigan had knocked over the candle, dived to the door, and slammed it against the storm of lead that had blasted at him a moment later. They would still have been laying siege to the cabin if that other bullet had not ricocheted and creased Donnigan. Now the bright stars were winking overhead, and the noose was around his neck.

Creed spoke again: "Last chance, Donnigan! You got anything to say? Not that it'll help you any. You're guilty as hell, an' you're swingin'."

Donnigan grinned mirthlessly. Some of the men there on the ground looked away from his face in that moment. Donnigan knew them. Lariat Jenkins, who owned the small Circle L spread down the valley, Nat Thompson, who drove the stage now and then, when old Henry Hicks took time off to go fishing. There were others, too. Once they had been friendly. Now blood hunger darkened their faces.

Donnigan drew a deep breath. Lord, how good the crisp night air felt! He'd never paid much attention to it before. Donnigan spoke to Creed. His voice had a bitter lash. "I reckon you'll hang me, Creed. You'll hang me up and leave me here for buzzard bait. I don't know what's behind this. Today I got back from the pen, where I spent three years for the dirty rustlin' some low-down skunk wouldn't admit. I came back to find my partner dead, my cows run off, my fences down. And while I was sittin' in there under my own roof, tryin' to figure it all out, you kicked the door in, Creed, an' cut loose with your gun. Why do you want me dead, Creed?"

"Hold on!" Creed replied angrily. "Don't make out like I got it in for you, Donnigan! I never liked you . . . but I let it go at that. But when it comes to a man like Deacon Tetweiler, gettin' shot down in cold blood, then I'm takin' the lead in swingin' the killer to the first handy limb. Any decent citizen'd do the same. Ain't that right, men?" Creed looked around for confirmation. His manner was aggressive.

Behind him a quick voice backed him up. "You're right, Buff. We're all with you. Hang 'im quick . . . an' men'll be able to ride out after dark without gettin' their heads blowed off!" That was Bert Willis, who owned the small XT spread above Creed's land.

Donnigan gritted: "So Deacon Tetweiler's dead? An' you're hangin' me for it? How come you didn't ask me any questions? After I'm buzzard bait, I won't be able to deny it."

"What's the use of talkin'?" Creed snapped impatiently. "Plenty of folks seen Deacon Tetweiler stop Donnigan on the street in Bitter Fork this afternoon an' warn him the better folks didn't favor his brand of orneriness back in the valley again. Plenty of 'em heard Donnigan tell the deacon there'd be trouble if he was bothered. An' Donnigan was seen galloping down the Crippled Spring road a little after the deacon drove his buggy that way. Donnigan, you killed old man Tetweiler, took the money he'd drawed outta the bank, and cached it somewheres. You was busted an' had to get a stake. Swing him up, boys! Ride off with that rope, Greenwood!"

Creed looked at Dave Greenwood. The others looked also, to see the jerk of the rope. And Donnigan, who had been sitting, bitter and watchful, whipped his bound hands to the left side of his neck. The fingers still had enough life to grip the bulky hangman's knot and shove it up on the rope. As Dave Greenwood spurred hard, and his horse leaped forward, Donnigan ripped the noose up over his head and let it fly freely into the air.

With a mighty lunge forward Donnigan caught the ground-tied reins, brought them up on one side, and drove his heels hard. The horse bolted forward through the watchers.

"Look out, boys!" Willis squalled.

Creed whirled. The horse struck his shoulder and knocked him to one side. The other men scattered, too astonished to think of their guns. Past the leaping fire, Donnigan drove Creed's big bay horse, and on into the black shadows beyond. Yells rose behind him. A gun barked. The bullet whistled closely as Donnigan crouched forward. Other guns blasted against the night back there. But the fire glare was in their eyes. Donnigan and the horse were only a bolting shadow, vanishing into the darkness.

Past the cabin Donnigan rode, catching one rein in his teeth,

56

flipping the other before the horse's head to its rightful side. Lead was still whanging through the darkness after him. He swung the horse over, put the cabin behind him, and sent the animal slashing through the thicket behind the cabin into the Tumbleweed Trail.

They followed, of course. One man would be afoot — but it wouldn't be Buff Creed. He would be in at the kill. Donnigan's lips drew apart in another mirthless smile. There would be no kill tonight. Matt Donnigan, ex-convict, bankrupt rancher, outcast of Bitter Valley, would go on to throw the lie in their teeth.

A mile up the side of Tumbleweed Mountain the pines rose thick and straight, and the silver aspens gleamed like ghostly rods in the white moonlight. Donnigan heard the pound of pursuit not far behind on the trail. Creed was leading them furiously in the chase.

Donnigan could leave the trail, but the noise it would make would bring them fast. He needed distance, and he wasn't gaining. Two miles more and the trail rounded Squaw Rock, angling south up Squaw Cañon. Donnigan hitched the reins on the saddle horn, swung his leg over the horse's neck, and made a flying drop.

Creed's big bay raced on. Donnigan shouldered down the Squaw Cañon slope in great leaps, fighting through the tangled growth. He was crouching silently far down the slope, when the pursuit rounded Squaw Rock and kept on up the trail.

Once the last man had passed, Donnigan smiled thinly and went on down to the tumbling waters of Squaw Creek. He plunged his swollen wrists into the cold current, wetting the rawhide thoroughly. He drank quickly and waded hastily down the rocky bed.

Donnigan waded for a quarter of a mile, then struck up the opposite side of the cañon through the pines again. He traveled slantwise across the mountain's face, bearing upward steadily through the virgin forest. The wind soughed overhead. Unexpected noises in the dark gave notice other life was astir also. A bobcat screamed eerily nearby. Far down toward Bitter Valley coyotes raised shrill, yapping clamor against the stars.

Miles farther on Donnigan struck the upper reaches of Copper Creek. He went down on his stomach and drank deeply, then squatted by the water, and soaked his wrists again. After a bit he got the thongs off.

He was tired. His head had stopped bleeding, but warm blood still trickled down his arm. Creed's bullet had torn a big hole through the upper muscles. Constant movement was keeping it open. Pain was there, too, but Donnigan ignored that as he splashed across the six-foot width of Copper Creek and went on with long, space-eating strides.

In all the Bitter Valley country there was only one place now where he was certain of safety. He had to get to that spot before the new day brought eyes abroad which might spot him.

Hour after hour, mile after mile, Donnigan strode on, gaining altitude steadily. The air thinned, grew colder. His chest heaved to the hunger of his pounding heart. Fatigue blotted his strength. Blood still trickled down his left arm. Three years in the state prison did not fit a man for a grueling, night-long walk up slopes that never ended. Nor did a lifetime of saddle work build legs for this sort of travel.

The true gray dawn bloomed overhead. Gold and scarlet streamers of sunrise thrust over Tumbleweed Peak. A buck deer sprang out of a covert and streaked away. A turkey called nearby. Later, an outlaw steer that had wandered high up, away from its kind, surged to its feet and snorted away.

The blazing sun was sliding over Tumbleweed Peak when the sharp report of a rifle not far ahead brought Donnigan to a sudden stop. He listened. Just that one shot was fired. But a dog began to bark, and a slow smile of weary satisfaction broke across Donnigan's face. He stumbled on.

Donnigan was walking without regard for noise when a silent figure materialized uncannily ahead of him. The man carried a rifle. Long, uncut hair hung from under a battered old hat. The face was seamed, weathered, impassive. A lank, spotted dog came forward stiff-legged, questing the air with its nose. The dog suddenly barked once, sharply.

Donnigan called thickly: "Your eyes going back on you, Joe?"

"By damn!" Indian Joe replied, shifting his rifle to the crook of his arm and coming forward. "I don't know you, hey, Donnigan? My eyes, she ain't so good, eh?"

Indian Joe was grinning broadly as he put out a lean, hard hand. But concern appeared on his face, as he looked at Donnigan's blood-caked arm and stared into Donnigan's gaunt, weary face.

"Where you hoss?" Indian Joe demanded quickly. "You have trouble, hey?"

Donnigan grinned while the dog sniffed at him and wagged an approving tail. "Hard to tell where my horse is now," Donnigan replied. "I walked here, Joe."

Indian Joe clucked unbelievingly, patting his rifle barrel with a questioning look.

Donnigan nodded. "That's right, Joe. I'm in a heap of trouble. I got back from the pen yesterday, and before I could get some sleep, I was shot up and hightailing it ahead of guns. They're looking for me now, Joe. I figured, if I could make it here, I could lay up a day or two and get my breath."

"Wait," said Indian Joe. He strode off silently in his buckskin moccasins. In a few minutes he was back, as silently, carrying a huge turkey gobbler over one shoulder. "You want help for walk?" he asked.

"I got this far. Reckon I can make it to the cabin." Donnigan grinned. "You're sure a sight for my eyes, Joe."

"She's be plenty lonesome without you, Donnigan," Indian Joe said simply.

And so, walking together — Indian hermit, spotted dog, wounded fugitive — they covered the last mile to the little grassy mountain valley where Indian Joe's log cabin had stood for twenty years.

Here in the high country where men seldom came, Indian Joe, gaunt, aged stalker of mountain trails, lived alone. Joe trapped in the winter, killed wolves and cougars for the bounty, shot his meat, caught his fish, and now and then sallied down into the lower country to eye with disapproval the crowded range where men were hemmed in by neighbors as near as five miles. Joe's neat, clean, pine-log cabin had two rooms. At the foot of the grassy slope before it a small trout stream brawled swiftly from the snow reservoirs among the peaks.

Indian Joe tossed the turkey on the clean-swept dirt before the front door and pointed inside.

"Home," he said.

Donnigan had known it would be like this. But yet, as he sat on the rawhide seat of a homemade chair and watched Indian Joe make coffee, fry bacon, set out sourdough bread, and open a can of hoarded peaches, Donnigan's heart grew full with the welcome. Life held nothing better than such a friend.

While Donnigan drank hot, black coffee and recounted the events of the night before, Indian Joe took off the bloody shirt, washed the arm, examined it carefully. The bone had not been touched, but the flesh was torn badly.

"This Buff Creed," said Indian Joe stolidly, "one tam in Bitter Fork he shoot at my feet. I have promise some day I kill him, maybe."

"Creed isn't worth the trouble you'd get into, Joe. Lordy,

I never tasted anything better'n this bacon. Seems like I walked all night with my mouth set for it."

"Don't eat much," Indian Joe cautioned. He put a finger on the swollen, feverish flesh around the wound. "Maybe you plenty sick man."

Donnigan looked down at his arm and nodded. "I began to figure that just before dawn, when fever started in it. I can feel the blood pounding now. Maybe I'll have to go down to a doctor and give myself up?"

"No dam' good," Indian Joe said. "You wait."

Indian Joe went into the next room and came back with a handful of dried leaves and a clean flour sack. He set a tin cup of water on the sheet-iron wood stove, crumbled leaves in the warming water until he had a thick, hot mash. With a hunting knife he ripped the flour sack into lengths, plastered the paste over the wound, and bound it there with strips of the sacking.

"She good by'm'by," Indian Joe promised. He went into the next room again and came back with a clean shirt.

Donnigan put it on and grinned at the tight fit across his chest. "Good thing I don't have to wear all your clothes, Joe. I'd look like a skinned dogie. Now I got to get some sleep. Somebody may come looking for me. Folks know we're friends."

Joe chuckled. "I fix that, too. You come with me."

Taking a blanket from a bunk against the wall, Indian Joe motioned Donnigan to follow him out of the cabin. He led the way onto a rocky, tree-sprinkled slope at the upper end of the little valley. A hundred yards up the slope he stepped around a great boulder, disappeared into a low entrance of a cave that was all but invisible unless a man came to this spot.

Following, Donnigan found the cave opened up inside. The roof was somewhat higher than his head. It was at least fifty feet deep with an upslope to the floor. The cave was dry, airy, and would have sun in the entrance later in the day. One could look past the great rock in front over the tops of the lower trees to Indian Joe's cabin. Pine needles and leaves had been carried in to form a thick, comfortable bed. Indian Joe tossed the blanket over it.

"I come back by'm'by," he said, and left in the silent, abrupt way he had of coming and going.

Donnigan lay down and slept at once, despite the throbbing pain of his arm.

Late that afternoon Donnigan struggled up, a sick man. His arm felt like it was on fire. The pain was shooting clear to his head. His face was dry, hot. He staggered weakly to his feet, lurched to the warm sunshine, pouring in the cave mouth. His swimming eyes focused over the tree tops to Indian Joe's cabin. Half a dozen horsemen were gathered before it.

Men had remembered his friendship with Indian Joe and had come to this high mountain valley looking for him. A figure on foot faced them before the cabin door. Donnigan reeled back to the blanket. He lay for a while staring at the cave roof — and dropped off to sleep again, burning with fever.

From that time life became a black stretch through which grotesque nightmares whirled. Shorty Simmons, Donnigan's partner, grinned from the shadows as only Shorty could — roundup nights when lightning flashed and the cattle were boogery — gray days in the state prison with drab lines of prisoners, marching in lock step — the hurt, stricken look of a woman's face, staring from the front row of the courtroom — imps, clawing at the swollen arm.

There were short, lucid stretches when the whirling shadows rolled back, and Donnigan found Indian Joe there in the cave, spooning broth through Donnigan's fevered lips, working on the throbbing, swollen arm with hands, gentle as a woman's. Indian Joe, muttering words of reassurance, and then the blackness rolling back, and hell again.

And then, abruptly, the afternoon sun was shining warmly, cheerfully into the cave mouth, and Donnigan's brain was clear — a great hunger was gnawing in him. Donnigan turned his head. Indian Joe was sitting, cross-legged, beside him.

"I . . . I must've slept sound today," Donnigan muttered. He was surprised at the weakness in his voice. "Seems to me I've been dreaming a heap," he recalled.

"Five days," said Indian Joe. "I say you be plenty sick. Some tam you holler so I think she hear you down in Bitter Fork."

Donnigan tried to sit up — and barely made it. All his strength had gone. But the fever had left, the pain was out of his arm, and his head was clear.

"Five days," he said wonderingly. "You've been running up here, looking after me for five days, Joe?"

Indian Joe nodded. "I think maybe I have to tie you down some tam," he said, smiling with the corners of his eyes. "You plenty mad. You loco in the head!"

"Must've been delirious," said Donnigan, thinking. "Seems to me I recall something about some riders down at your cabin. But I'm not sure about that."

"Creed come first day," said Indian Joe. "Want to know where you are. Look all around." Indian Joe spat. "Good thing I burn your shirt."

So Creed came looking for me?" Donnigan mused. "He must want me bad."

"Uhn-huh," said Indian Joe. "How you walk?"

Donnigan tried to stand up. Indian Joe had to help him. But by gritting his teeth and leaning heavily on the old man, Donnigan got out of the cave, down the rocky slope, and across the grass to the cabin. He collapsed on the bunk while Indian Joe made a bowl of turkey broth — and topped it with a slab of warm turkey meat.

Then, while Donnigan had his first smoke for days, Indian Joe examined the arm. It was healing.

"Good," Indian Joe grunted. "But dam' bad for time. Plenty poison. Now you sleep."

Lazy days followed. Days when Donnigan sat in the sun before the cabin and talked with Indian Joe, days when he moved about and began to tramp the hills nearby, gaining strength rapidly. Under Indian Joe's constant attention and use of strange herbs the wounds healed miraculously. No more riders from the lower country appeared. Up here on the high slopes the world was far away.

Evenings they sat by the stove, smoking, yarning. Indian Joe could tell Donnigan no more about Shorty Simmons's death than Donnigan had heard in Bitter Valley the day he had returned. Shorty had been dead weeks before his body had been found, back in the mountains. By then it was too late to tell what had killed him. The remains had been buried where they were found.

"Shorty was the best partner a fellow ever had," Donnigan told Indian Joe soberly. "He didn't die natural. Nothing'll ever make me believe that."

Indian Joe nodded silently.

"Three years ago," said Donnigan bitterly, "I had half a ranch, half a sweet bunch of cows, money in the bank, folks I thought were friends, a girl I used to lay awake at night planning to marry. I had all a man could want. I was happy. My head was up with the best of them.

"Look at me now, Joe. On the run from a killing I didn't do, and a stretch in the pen behind me. Folks look down on me as a rustler and warn me I'm not wanted in Bitter Valley.

My cows are gone, my partner's dead, my dreams are busted, and I'm a renegade. Sometimes I wake up at night, wondering if it isn't all a nightmare. All that couldn't happen to a man who never harmed anyone."

"You got friend here . . . home here," said Indian Joe placidly.

"Don't think I don't appreciate it, Joe. If we both live long enough, I'll try to pay a little of it back."

At daybreak the next morning Indian Joe left for Bitter Fork on one of his fat ponies, riding Indian style, bareback and using a hackamore. His spotted dog followed him.

Donnigan wandered around restlessly all day. He had a hot supper ready at dark when Indian Joe rode a weary horse up to the door and slipped soundlessly off on moccasined feet. Something had happened down below. Donnigan saw it at a glance. Indian Joe was grinning broadly.

"Tomorrow," said Indian Joe, "you go to Bitter Fork."

"I ain't a fool, Joe."

"Bitter Fork," Indian Joe repeated with a broader grin. "Las' week one man, she hold up stage an' get shot. Before she die, he say kill Te'weiler. They don' want you now."

Donnigan stared for a moment, then let out a yell, and threw an arm around Indian Joe's shoulder. "I could kick like a spring colt on green grass!" Donnigan laughed. "Lord, what a load off my mind! Come in and get your grub. I'm too wild to eat."

Indian Joe gave Donnigan a questioning look as he entered the cabin. "What you do now?" he asked.

Donnigan sobered. His face drew into hard, bleak lines. "I reckon I've known all along what I'd do, if I could. I've still got money in the bank. Shorty and I kept our pile together, so if one ever got killed, the other'd have it. I'm going down in the valley, buy cattle, start up the ranch again, and show

65

every son in forty days' ride I can still hold my head up." Donnigan paused, then added bitterly: "And I'm going to try to find out what really happened to Shorty."

II

"A RENEGADE RIDES BACK"

Donnigan left the next morning, taking one of Indian Joe's
ponies and an old saddle and bridle Joe never used any more.
Just before he swung into the saddle, Joe brought out a worn
cartridge belt and an old single-shot pistol.

"Better take," Indian Joe said impassively.

"I don't need a gun now."

"Best time kill deer when she not afraid," said Indian Joe.

Slowly Donnigan reached down for the gun belt.

"You're right," he admitted. "Good bye, old-timer. You
know how I feel about all this. I'll bring your pony back myself,
soon as I get my feet on the ground down there."

"Plenty time," said Indian Joe. "Watch your feet."

Bitter Fork looked the same as ever, sprawling there beside
the shallow, sandy channel of Bitter Fork River. And yet, to
Donnigan, it was different as he rode in on Indian Joe's sleek
pony. It was strange. He was a man coming back from exile,
a man who now rode free of the noose's shadow.

Donnigan stopped first at the red brick building that housed
the bank. Miss Sue Gibbons, rated the best gossip in Bitter
Fork, was just turning away from the teller's window when
Donnigan entered. She gave him a startled look, sailed past
him with her nose in the air, ignoring Donnigan's faint grin
and lifted hat.

Lem Whitaker, the cashier, looked through the teller's window with his usual jovial smile. It vanished. His jaw dropped. "Why . . . why hello, Donnigan."

"Hello, yourself," said Donnigan "I want a hundred in cash and a checkbook. You look like a ghost has walked in on you."

"Well . . . er . . . I wasn't expecting to see you," Whitaker stumbled.

"Why not?" said Donnigan, smiling calmly. "Isn't my account here?"

"Yes, but I thought you were. . . ."

"Whatever you thought . . . I wasn't," said Donnigan. "Give me my money. You don't know of a nice bunch of cows for sale, do you?"

Lem Whitaker was superintendent of the Sunday school. He had been a bosom friend of Deacon Tetweiler's. His pudgy face grew sharp with disapproval as he slid three gold pieces and four bills under the wicket and slapped a checkbook down after them.

"I don't know of any cows for sale," Whitaker said. "You'll find cows hard to buy this time of year."

"What you mean," said Donnigan with a crooked smile, "is cows'll be hard for *me* to buy any time. Just to make your dinner set better, I'll tell you I'll get cows if I have to ship 'em in. You can spread the word around that the S D ranch is on its legs again and'll be shipping beef as usual. I can use cowhands, too."

Whitaker pressed his lips together tightly and said nothing to Matt Donnigan.

Donnigan was grinning as he walked outside. The grin vanished when the first person he met outside the door cried: "Matt!"

Donnigan went pale. Lia Brady was pale, too. Donnigan was twenty-nine, Lia twenty-three. Donnigan just missed being six feet, and Lia's brown curly hair barely reached his throat.

Lia Brady's face was oval, finely-shaped, and her tip-tilt nose was saucy, her lips red, shaped for laughter, and her gray eyes usually merry. But now those eyes held pain.

"I . . . I didn't think I'd meet you here in town," Donnigan said lamely.

Lia wasn't smiling. She had the look of one who saw old wounds opening up. She spoke uncertainly. "I wrote you two letters, Matt. You didn't answer them."

Donnigan nodded. "I thought it was best, Lia. There wasn't any use in your writing to a man in the pen."

"Was that all?"

"I reckon that was enough."

A flush of indignation crept over Lia's first pallor. "How dare you get ideas like that, Matt Donnigan! You were hurt, bitter, but you had no right to take it out on me. I hadn't done anything to you."

Donnigan clenched his fists, grew whiter. He saw people on the street, stopping, staring at them. Most of Bitter Fork knew how they had been. Miss Sue Gibbons was across the street with two women friends, eyeing them avidly.

"Maybe it isn't so good for you to be seen on the street with me," Donnigan muttered. "I don't rate well with folks these days. Deacon Tetweiler led off the circus . . . and Lem Whitaker just spoke his piece. I'm a renegade, Lia."

"Matt Donnigan," said Lia Brady in a choked voice, "I could slap you right here in front of everyone! Do I have to beg you to be decent to me? Have you forgotten all the nice things you used to say to me?"

"Forgotten them!" Donnigan choked with sudden fierceness. "What kind of a man do you think I am, Lia? I've thought of 'em days and nights till it seemed I'd go crazy over what I'd lost. Why . . . why, dear Lia, I surely loved you then, but I didn't know just how much. It took losing you for that.

There'll never be another woman for me . . . but I'm not the man for you any more. I'm a renegade. I'm not wanted. Until folks want me, I . . . I can't ever tell you the things I feel. I don't have that right."

Lia was smiling. Her eyes were wet. "That's all I wanted to know," she said. "Matt, you big goose, did you think I could ever stop loving you? What do you think I've been doing these last three years? Waiting for you . . . praying you'd come back . . . hoping you hadn't forgotten. Just now you made the sun shine for me again. Nothing else can ever matter."

"Oh, Lord!" Donnigan groaned. "If folks weren't lookin', I'd kiss you right here on the street . . . even though I know it'd be a fool stunt, and . . . and what I've told you has got to stand."

The bank door slammed behind Donnigan. An oath of anger reached his ears. Shattuck Brady, Lia's father, planted himself firmly in front of Donnigan and the girl.

"If I'd knowed this was going to happen, I'd have stopped it before it started! Lia, get along to the buggy! Donnigan, I didn't think you'd have the nerve to speak to my daughter again."

Shattuck Brady was a huge man, standing half a head taller than Donnigan. His weathered face had the handsome traits he had given to Lia. Those gray eyes of Shattuck Brady's could be merry as hers. But now the eyes were cold. Shattuck Brady's brown mustache could not hide the hard anger around his mouth.

Donnigan answered softly: "According to your way of thinking, maybe you're right, Mister Brady. This was an accidental meeting. I was telling Lia I wouldn't see her any more."

"And I wasn't listening!" Lia burst out. "I'll not be a target for Matt's foolish ideas or your wrong ones, Dad!"

"You heard me, Lia!" Shattuck Brady said harshly. "Get in the buggy!"

White-lipped she answered: "I'm of age! I'm afraid I'll have to do what I think best."

"Please, Lia!" Donnigan begged.

Shattuck Brady growled deep in his throat. His coat was open. He brushed it back so the gun he wore was clear. "Don't put me to the trouble of drawin' a gun on this man an' runnin him away from you, Lia!" Shattuck Brady warned with anger that was now more ominous because he did not raise his voice.

"Lia," said Donnigan miserably, "don't make him. For if he does, I'll have to defend myself. There's no man in the world who'll make me crawl from this day on."

"Oh, dear God, not that!" Lia cried. "I'll go to the buggy. Please get away from each other until you cool off and can think sensibly."

She hurried on along the sidewalk. When she was out of earshot, Shattuck Brady wheeled to Donnigan.

"Stay away from her," he grated. "I want no prison whelp disgracing my daughter with his attentions. If I catch you runnin' after her, I'll hunt you down with a gun and save the hangman the trouble. That's my final word." Shattuck Brady turned on his heel and stalked away after his daughter.

A score of people had watched it. Donnigan's face was red with anger, and his mind was whirling as he left Indian Joe's pony before the bank and cut across the street to the saloon.

A dozen men were in the Big Deuce bar. A tense hush was over the room as Donnigan walked in. He saw the reason. Halfway down the bar Buff Creed was standing with a sneering grin on his face. Bert Willis was just beyond. With a quick glance Donnigan recognized two cowpunchers who had been with Creed in the hanging party.

A tense silence held everyone in the room as Donnigan

ordered and poured a drink, and took it neat. Then, as Donnigan picked up his change, Buff Creed spoke to Willis with a sneer. "I didn't think he'd have the nerve to come back."

Donnigan pocketed the change, turned deliberately, and looked along the bar at Creed. "Referring to me?" he asked slowly.

Creed looked at him with exaggerated surprise. "Why not, Donnigan?"

"Just so you won't start wondering about other things," Donnigan said, "I'll let you know now I'm stocking the S D ranch again. And Creed, I'm givin' you public warning never to be caught inside S D wire again. That goes for you, too, Willis . . . and the men working for both of you."

Bert Willis grinned nervously and said nothing. He had never been noted for his personal courage.

Creed snorted. "Puttin' your roots down again, Donnigan? You've got a nerve, tryin' it! Folks don't want you in the valley. If I know anything about 'em, they won't stand for it. I reckon it'd've been a good thing if that hangin' had gone off on schedule."

Donnigan nodded slowly. "Maybe . . . for you, Creed. I've been asking myself why you led that bunch of weak-willed blood-sniffers to put a noose around my neck. I reckon I'll find out if I look long enough."

Creed's face was truculent. "I don't care to be a neighbor to jail bait! I ain't got any more use for you than Shattuck Brady had a few minutes ago, when he caught you there in front of the bank."

Several of the men grinned at that.

Donnigan began to tremble. "Creed," he said in a thin voice, "you're egging me on to start trouble because you know I don't want it. But, Creed, you're stepping close to trouble. I'm getting away before you crowd me. My warning about S D land stands."

Donnigan walked to the door with his hand well away from his gun. As he went out, Creed's sneering voice followed. "He ain't only jail bait . . . he's yellow. Drink up, boys, an' wash the taste of him outta your mouths. He won't last long."

III

"COWARD BRAND"

Donnigan had trouble getting his cows. The range was dry, drought-threatened, but nobody would sell. Old Whisker Bill Inman came out bluntly with his reason.

"I'd be glad to take your money, Donnigan. Fact is, I need it like hell. But Lem Whitaker has put the Injun sign on yuh. When I went into the bank to see about time on my note, Whitaker dropped a hint he didn't favor no man who'd help you get started again." Whisker Bill fingered his ragged gray beard and nailed a wandering beetle with a stream of tobacco juice. "It ain't right. I'm all fer you, Donnigan. It riles me to have a curb bit jammed in my teeth by a sanctimonious note-shaver like Whitaker. But he's got me hawg-tied with my note. I got to look out for myself. All I can do is wish you plenty of luck."

"I understand," Donnigan said. "Thanks for the luck, Bill. I need it."

Donnigan got his cattle in small bunches from outfits outside of the valley. He hired two hands.

Jigger Jones was a short, bandy-legged cowboy with a cast in his left eye and a cheek always bulging with a huge quid of tobacco. Roaring Bill Quinn, taller than Donnigan and broader, had a voice like a foghorn, a hair-trigger temper, and a love for trouble. Roaring Bill had just been fired from his last job over beyond Crippled Spring for beating up the foreman.

"The wages are small, and there'll be plenty of work,"

Donnigan warned. "I'm not wanted in the valley. We'll be playing a lone hand. And I won't stand for fighting. I'm trying to live peaceful."

Roaring Bill grinned hugely and boomed: "Keep my belly full an' try to swamp me with work. I'm a lone wolf myself, an' I'm peaceful as a pet calf. When do we start?"

"Right now," said Donnigan. "I'm heading for some cows."

Once more life stirred on S D land. Cows grazed on the lush flats, calves frisked in the sunlight, horses moved against the horizon, and the men tramped in the cabin. Indian Joe appeared silently, stayed overnight, left with his pony. Other visits followed that. Indian Joe helped where he was needed, said little, vanished without farewell when he was ready to leave.

Hard work filled the days. Fences had to be repaired, new wire strung, water holes cleared, stray cattle hazed off. Grass was high on S D land, and cattle had wandered in or been thrown in. Most of the banked money had gone into the place. Donnigan had bought, at bargain prices, a few young steers to fatten. The calves were coming along. With luck there would be enough salable stuff in the fall to carry on comfortably until next year.

There were times at night when the memory of a girl's troubled face stayed close to Donnigan. He tried to forget Lia, and couldn't. The place was lonesome without Shorty Simmons, too. Donnigan hunted up Shorty's remote, unmarked grave in upper Squaw Valley, four miles from the cabin. Shorty had evidently been up here, sifting the brush, when death overtook him. Donnigan stood a long time by the weathered mound of dirt, then soberly turned his back on the spot for good.

Jigger Jones and Roaring Bill did the town errands. Donnigan seldom went to Bitter Fork. When he did, there was no change. He was still the renegade of Bitter Valley. People eyed him askance.

Roaring Bill Quinn brought the first hint of trouble. One noon he galloped in, entered the cabin, and boomed: "The wire's down in the south pasture, an' there's a hundred head of Brady cattle workin' on our grass. They must've been in for two, three days, by the way they've et it off."

"Grab a bite, and we'll ride over and haze 'em out," Donnigan said. "Brady's grass must be gettin' almighty short for them to bust through the wire that way."

Roaring Bill snorted. "Bust, hell! That wire was pulled down. I found a frazzle of rope on one of the barbs. Old Shattuck Brady's got more tricks than a one-armed hoss thief."

Donnigan's face darkened. "We'll stop that," he said curtly.

It was a hot sweaty job that long afternoon, combing the brush and draws and throwing Brady cattle back across the wire. Donnigan satisfied himself about the frazzle of rope. The wires had been dragged from the posts for a hundred yards and left on the ground. The staples on this section of fence were on the Brady side. The pulling had been done from that side.

Roaring Bill ran some of the last cows well over on Brady's land. Donnigan was studying the fence when he heard Roaring Bill's voice raised in a bellow of anger. Donnigan galloped toward the spot, knowing suddenly trouble was here.

Bill was in the saddle, facing four Brady cowhands.

"What's the matter?" Donnigan demanded, riding between them.

Bill yelled: "These ory-eyed grass-snatchers come steamin' up, accusin' us of monkeyin' with their beef! They are lookin' for rustlers, an' they figger we fill the bill. One more word outta 'em, an' I'll clean up the whole bunch."

A red-headed, sour-visaged man who sat stiffly in his saddle moved his hand menacingly toward his gun. "If you pine fer trouble, big mouth, lead off!" he barked. "We got our orders about you S D men . . . an', when we find you on our side of the wire, hazin' our beef, you better come through with somethin' more'n loud talk."

"You'll get it!" Bill yelled. "If you're honin' to draw that pea-shooter on your leg, drag it quick!"

"Wait a minute!" Donnigan rapped, turning angrily to the red-headed man. "The wire was pulled down from this side of the fence. Your half-starved critters were cutting down on my grass fast. We've been running 'em back. If you need a warning not to try any dirty tricks like that again, you're getting it now. Tell Shattuck Brady to buy his feed."

A short, thick-chested man with a scar on his left cheek and a rattlesnake band around his sombrero pushed forward, answering with cold anger. "I reckon you're Donnigan. If you claim Tumblin' L men have been pullin' down wire to get at your grass, it's a damned lie. Tumblin' L beef is gettin' awful scarce on this side of the range. Brady has give out orders to find out why. If he knowed the wire was down an' you was hazin' his cows near it, he'd argue with lead an' talk about it later. No one from Tumbling L pulled that wire down. You hear me? I'm callin' you saddle tramps liars!"

"Stand back, Donnigan!" Roaring Bill bellowed. "No man can call me a liar an' git away with it!"

Horses swerved. Guns came out. Roaring Bill's face was black with anger as he flipped out his gun and tried to ride around Donnigan.

Donnigan drove his horse against Roaring Bill's horse, so that he blocked the big man. "Put that gun up, Bill!" Donnigan rasped angrily.

The big cowhand sawed on the bit and tried to ride around Donnigan. They clashed together hard. Donnigan yanked out

77

his own gun. Before Roaring Bill knew what was happening, steel clubbed his head.

Roaring Bill Quinn slipped forward in the saddle. Donnigan grabbed him and heaved the heavy figure over before him. Roaring Bill lay limply, blood showing at the edge of his hair. His gun was down in the dirt.

Behind Donnigan the red-headed cowpuncher uttered an oath of scornful disbelief. "Slugged his own man to keep outta a fight."

Donnigan reined around, facing the Brady men. "Listen to me, you misguided fools," he gritted. "I don't want trouble. My men have got orders to keep out of it. The wire was pulled down from this side. The rope marks are still on it."

The man with a scar on his cheek sneered truculently. "Rope marks don't tell us who dragged it down. You served time for rustlin', Donnigan, an' you've just showed that you're yellah as a bullfrog's gizzard. If we catch you on this side of our wire again, monkeyin' with our beef, we won't waste talk on you. We'll rope you off your hoss an' pistol whip you. Now get the hell off Tumblin' L land . . . an' stay off!"

Donnigan began to tremble as he held Roaring Bill across the saddle and looked at them. "You can't push me to draw!" he said hoarsely. "I'm staying peaceable, damn you. I'm ridin' wide."

Leaving Roaring Bill's gun there on the ground, Donnigan caught the reins of the riderless horse and rode back toward his own land, with Roaring Bill's limp body across the saddle before him.

"I've heerd about men bein' that yellow, but I never figgered I'd see one," a Brady man said loudly as he went.

Through a red haze Donnigan felt Roaring Bill's pulse. It beat slowly but strongly. Roaring Bill would come out of it all right.

Donnigan was near the wire, and Jigger Jones was a quarter mile away, pushing three steers toward him, when a clear whistle rang out. Donnigan looked up. Lia Brady was galloping toward him. Her face held swift concern as she came up.

"What is it, Matt? Have you had trouble?" Lia asked, casting a worried look at Bill's limp figure.

Donnigan grinned weakly. "I've just been keeping out of trouble," he told her. "Bill, here, had a little accident. He'll come around all right."

Lia's face was flushed with sun and exercise. She was pretty. Too pretty. Donnigan felt the sinking feeling in his middle that came these days when he thought of her.

"I'm glad it wasn't anything serious," Lia sighed with relief. "Seeing you on this side of the fence, carrying that man, I . . . I didn't know what had happened."

"Nothing'll ever happen on this side, as far as I'm concerned," Donnigan replied grimly.

Lia smiled sadly. "I'm beginning to believe that, Matt. I've ridden this way time after time, hoping to see you. But I never do. I saw you in Bitter Fork one day, but you hurried away and disappeared."

Donnigan replied miserably. "I've been trying to keep away from you, Lia. I don't come to this side of the ranch if I can help it . . . for fear I'll see you."

Lia colored, stiffened. "What am I to think when you talk to me like that, Matt? You make me feel like a little fool."

"Don't you turn on me today," Donnigan begged. "It's hard enough, as it is, Lia. Don't you know that you're never out of my mind?"

"You show it in strange ways, Matt."

"I'm showing it the only way I know how," Donnigan said heavily. "You haven't forgotten your father, have you? There'll be trouble sure, if I'm fool enough to give way. He still looks on me as a renegade. I won't hurt you by getting you mixed up in my troubles."

Her face shadowed. "Matt, can't I make you see your troubles are mine? But . . . I love Dad, too. I don't think I could stand trouble between you two . . . maybe one of you, killing the other. And Dad won't change. He's stubborn. His mind is made up, Matt. What's going to happen to us?" Lia cried. "Must I go on waiting . . . always afraid?"

"There won't be any trouble, honey."

"Are you sure of that, Matt? Can you promise me?"

Donnigan forced a grin. "Sure I can promise. I just dodged trouble before you rode up. After what just happened, nothing can make me fight your folks."

"What happened?"

"Some of the Tumbling L men pulled the wire down and ran cattle over my grass. Your range is getting pretty thin, and I reckon my grass looked too good to pass up."

"Dad never did anything like that, Matt."

"He won't shed any tears about it, anyway." Donnigan grinned. "He's an old fox."

Lia's cheeks were flaming as Donnigan finished. "I'll report it," she said. "You can be sure, Matt Donnigan, no Tumbling L cows will get on your land again. We don't run our ranch that way."

Lia quirted her horse and galloped away.

Donnigan looked after her with amazement. "I put my foot in it," he said aloud. "No matter which way I turn, it's wrong."

Donnigan glumly rode to meet Jigger Jones.

Roaring Bill was lying on the ground when his eyes opened. For a moment he looked stupidly around — then remembered. He surged to his feet, cursing. Glaring at Donnigan, who stood soberly smoking a cigarette, Roaring Bill choked: "Donnigan, yuh bent a gun over my head. I'm through. Gimme my pay."

Jigger Jones shifted his big quid of tobacco to the other cheek. "Donnigan's told me what happened, Bill," he said. "He was right to his way of thinkin'. Calm down and talk reasonable about it."

"Reasonable, hell! I was fightin' for Donnigan hisself, wasn't I? An' he turned on me. I'm ashamed to be drawin' his pay. Donnigan, I've heard tell you was yellow . . . an' now I know it. You clubbed me when I wasn't lookin' so you could crawl outta trouble."

Donnigan met Roaring Bill's glare calmly. "You were warned, when I hired you, I'd stand for no fighting, Bill. And the first time trouble sneaked up on you, you rared to meet it. In another minute we'd've been killed."

"What of it?" Roaring Bill shouted. "Didn't you hear what he said?"

"I don't give a damn what Shattuck Brady's cowhands think of my ways," Donnigan said. "If there'd been gun play, we'd've been pitchforked into a range feud. The word would have gone out that I'd been caught with Brady's cows."

"You're yellow, Donnigan! I hate to say it, but you are! I'm huntin' me a boss I can respect."

Donnigan smiled thinly. "Maybe we can settle that here, Bill. Put up your fists, you over-grown leather-walloper, and let's see how much of a man you are yourself."

Donnigan unbuckled his gun belt, tossed it aside, stepped in swiftly, and drove a fist into Quinn's middle.

Bill grunted, staggered back, looked pained, then angry as he got his breath back. "I'm gonna wipe up the ground with you, Donnigan!" he bellowed, and rushed, flailing huge fists.

Roaring Bill was a head taller, a good twenty pounds heavier, all beef and muscle. Donnigan slipped aside from that bull-like rush and snapped a fist to Roaring Bill's cheek. Quinn bellowed again as he whirled around and came back.

"Stand up and fight!"

Donnigan grinned, dodged the second rush, and smashed another blow to Quinn's cheek. The skin split. Blood appeared. Quinn shook his head, came back warily, ready to dodge, too. Donnigan met him flat-footed, driving straight-arm blows. Roaring Bill rocked back on his heels, then settled himself, and traded blow for blow.

A smashing fist caught Donnigan over the heart. Life seemed to stop for a moment. Roaring Bill crowded in, pasted Donnigan over the eye, spinning him half around with a mighty smash on the shoulder.

Donnigan weaved back out of a clinch. His eye was already beginning to close. Roaring Bill's fists were like sledge hammers when they landed. But hard work had put whipcord and steel in Donnigan's body once more. He stepped back before Quinn's next rush — and suddenly leaped in savagely, smashing straight-arm punches, uppercutting, hooking a storm of blows that did not stop.

Roaring Bill bowed like a mighty pine before a gale, set himself, and traded blow for blow. Science was forgotten in that wild mêlée of slugging. Jigger Jones was jumping up and down, yelling and cursing.

Human flesh could not long stand such wild fighting. Gasping, blood-streaked, they slowed down, began to stagger.

Roaring Bill suddenly stepped back with a grin on his bloody, battered face. "I'm satisfied, Donnigan. You're a ten-clawed grizzly from the bobcat country. If you're willin' to call it quits an' shake hands, I'll be proud to go on with you."

Gulping air, Donnigan grinned, too, as he met Quinn's grip. "You're plenty man, too, Bill. I'm proud to have you."

That fight welded them together. Donnigan, Roaring Bill, and Jigger Jones rode three abreast now, friends. But Donnigan was still a pariah in Bitter Valley.

IV

"FROM NOW ON IT'S US"

There were ominous reports of cattle missing. Jigger Jones came back from Bitter Fork with news that Shattuck Brady was threatening publicly to kill any man he caught fooling with Brady cattle. Buff Creed was claiming the loss of at least a hundred head. Cattle were working high up the mountain slopes where feed was better. Line fences seldom ran in that tangled high country. Ranchers began eyeing one another with suspicion.

"You'd think Roarin' Bill an' me was pizen, the way folks look at us in Bitter Fork," Jigger Jones complained. "I was asked three times how much beef we'd lost. How come, Donnigan, all this rustlin' is passin' us up?"

"I've been wondering that myself," Donnigan confessed. "I've been putting two and two together, though, and getting four, if it means anything."

They were standing in front of the cabin after supper. The full moon was a placid silver disk overhead. Fireflies winked in the darkness like drifting sparks. An owl hooted behind the cabin as Donnigan struck a match and lighted a cigarette. In the yellow glare his face was lean, brooding.

"I been asking myself," continued Donnigan, as he flipped the match away, "why Buff Creed was so damned anxious to get me hanged when I first came back. And what really happened to Shorty Simmons?"

"I hear his hoss was never found," Jigger Jones said.

"What happened to it?" Donnigan asked. "Who ran off all the stock after Shorty died? Who tore down the fences? And why has Buff Creed got such a hate ag'in' me?"

"Ask me somethin' easy," said Jigger Jones.

"That's not all," persisted Donnigan. "Who was behind that rustling deal I did time in the pen for? Buff Creed was deputy sheriff then. He was one of the bunch who found the cows on my land with their brands freshly worked over. Bert Willis, who licks Creed's boots, found a green hide belonging to Lariat Jenkins back up in the brush. A fool wouldn't have left that green hide around to stink, if he was guilty. Both Buff Creed and Bert Willis were ready to hang me as soon as I got back."

"You think Buff Creed had a hand in double-crossin' you into the pen?" Jones asked with interest.

"I'd like to know."

"What'd he want to pick on you for?"

"I don't know," admitted Donnigan. "Creed wanted to buy this land once. We wouldn't sell. That didn't set well with him. His land touches the S D on the south, you know."

"That ain't much to nail Creed with."

"I'm not figgering on nailing Creed. That all happened too long ago. Shorty's dead. It won't help him to go poking into old dirt. I've served my time in the pen, and I can't undo that. If I can build my life like I want it, I'll be satisfied."

"Marry and raise kids, I suppose."

"None of your blasted business."

The owl hooted again.

Roaring Bill Quinn, joining them, spat audibly on the ground. "That goggle-eyed pigeon reminds me of the old owl-hoot trail," he observed. "Hear him moanin' . . . who-who-who? I've been askin' myself where'd all this missin' beef go? It ain't in the valley. It ain't been shipped out. There ain't been no strangers around. And if there's any *hombre* slick enough to rustle cattle over the mountain, he can tie leather on my back an' take his ride. How about it, Donnigan?"

"It could be done," Donnigan said. "Squaw Cañon leads up into Little Skeleton Cañon and that takes you to Big Grizzly at the top. From Big Grizzly there's a dozen ways to get down the other side."

"Then what?" Roaring Bill argued. "The mountain busts straight off on that side. The rains all stop here at the valley. There's a hundred an' twenty miles of dry hills an' desert over there. No water on it, not much feed. Nobody but an outlaw on the run or a crazy Injun ever crosses it. There ain't a cow built that could make it that far without water."

"If they did make it, they'd be within strikin' distance of the border," Jigger Jones mused. "If I could figure how to get a cow that far without water, I'd go over there an' have a look."

"You figure," Donnigan chuckled. "And when you get the answer, I'll go over with you."

The next afternoon Donnigan heard three faint gun shots in the direction of the cabin. He galloped back in. Indian Joe was there with his spotted dog.

"Did you fire those shots, Joe?" Donnigan asked, swinging down.

"Want see you," said Indian Joe, nodding. "Dead man up Squaw Cañon."

"Who is it?" Donnigan asked, startled.

Indian Joe shrugged. "Don't know. Shot in head."

Roaring Bill Quinn and Jigger Jones now came racing in. "What's the shootin' about?" Roaring Bill yelled.

Donnigan gave them the news.

"That ain't far from where your partner got his," Jones said.

"No," Donnigan agreed, his eyes narrowing.

Indian Joe pointed up the mountain. "Cows go that way."

"Cows up there?"

"Tracks," said Indian Joe.

Donnigan looked at Jigger Jones. Jigger was chewing furiously. The cast in his left eye gave him a quizzical look. "I ain't figured how to get cows across the dry stretch yet," he said. "But I bet there's an answer."

"Damned if I don't think you're right!" Donnigan suddenly agreed. "We'll look into it when I get back with the sheriff. You boys go up the cañon and have a look at the body. See if you can nose out anything. Better put the rest of the remuda in the corral. I'll be needing a fresh horse when I get back."

Donnigan rode hard to Bitter Fork. Darkness was just closing in when he got to the sheriff's office. The door was locked. A man standing nearby volunteered the information that the sheriff had ridden out in the afternoon, saying he'd be back by dark.

Donnigan rode to the Big Deuce saloon, racked his horse in front, and stepped in for a drink. A dozen men were inside. Donnigan saw only one — Buff Creed, wearing chaps and gun. Creed's face twisted in a sneering smile when he saw the newcomer. Donnigan went to the bar, ignoring Creed.

"You're layin' right low these days, Donnigan," Creed said, still smiling.

"I'm minding my own business, at least," Donnigan replied curtly.

"Must be queer business to keep you undercover so much."

Donnigan tossed off his drink, took the chaser, ordered another. "I don't like you, Creed," he said, turning his head. "Keep your mouth out of my affairs."

"Maybe it's time someone looked into your affairs."

"Meaning what?" Donnigan snapped.

"Once a thief, always a thief about hits it, I reckon."

"Damn you, Creed!"

Creed laughed. "You're yellow, Donnigan. Don't waste your breath. I'll. . . ."

Creed broke off as a horse rushed to the front of the saloon, and the rider ran to the Big Deuce entrance. The swinging doors burst open. Donnigan knocked over his glass as Lia Brady appeared there in the doorway, where few women ever stepped. She wore a divided riding skirt and had a six-gun strapped to her waist.

"Matt! Come outside, quick! It's important!"

Behind Donnigan, Buff Creed chortled loudly. "It'll be a damn' sight more important if old Shattuck Brady catches 'em."

Donnigan drew his gun as he whirled toward Creed. Instead of shooting, he slammed the heavy weapon broadside into Creed's face. The man dropped like a falling tree, nose broken, blood spouting from his smashed features, gun clattering from his hand. Donnigan crouched, sweeping the room with his gun.

"Anybody here want to take it up?" he demanded harshly.

An uneasy silence had fallen. No man was smiling now.

From the doorway, Lia begged frantically: "Matt, for God's sake, hurry! They're coming!"

As Donnigan turned toward the door, her words were borne out. Other riders raced up and leaped down. The dust flew.

"Who's coming?" Donnigan turned and asked — and stopped short as a long arm plucked Lia back. Shattuck Brady lunged into the room.

The big cattleman's face was a mask of fury. Men crowded in behind him. "Donnigan!" Shattuck Brady blared, "you ain't even goin' to get a rope around your neck this time!"

Shattuck Brady's gun was out. Lia pushed in behind him

and caught his arm. Men scattered, some vaulting over the bar. The barkeep yelled: "Don't start nothin' in here, gents!"

Backing off a step, Donnigan demanded: "What's the matter with you, Brady?"

Shattuck Brady roared. "Matter enough, you damned bush-whackin' cow thief! You're caught cold this time. My men found where you eased some of our cattle through onto your land."

"You're a liar, Brady!"

"One of them critters had a twisted hind foot, Donnigan. Two of my men followed it across your land, up the mountain into Squaw Cañon. And there, by God, you an' your murderin' cowhands bushwhacked 'em! Killed one of 'em and damned near killed the other. He laid there all night, come out of it this mornin', an' took most of the day draggin' himself back to the ranch. You didn't even give 'em warning, Donnigan. You cracked 'em from cover."

"Brady, we had nothing to do with that. Indian Joe found the dead man this afternoon. I rode in here to get the sheriff."

"Come for the sheriff, did you, Donnigan? And I find you loafin' at the bar! They let you off once with the pen, and you dodged a hangin' when you got back. But your luck is over. We went to your cabin, found that damned Indian there, heard you had sneaked off here to Bitter Fork, an' come for you. Throw down that gun an' come along, or I'll kill you where you stand!"

Lia was sobbing. "Dad, please! I know you're wrong!"

"Pull her away!" Shattuck Brady ordered his men. "If I'd knowed she was going to ride ahead to warn him, I'd 'a' locked her up."

Tight-lipped, Donnigan said: "I've taken everything off this valley I aim to! Call off your men, Brady, or I won't be responsible."

89

The men in the doorway were pulling Lia outside as gently as they could. Donnigan saw her face, white, tortured. And then she was gone, the door blocked with Brady's men.

Shattuck Brady demanded harshly: "Are you coming, Donnigan?"

"Damn you, no! Don't make me kill you, Brady."

Shattuck Brady yelled: "Let him have it, boys!"

Donnigan knew he couldn't kill Lia's father. He whirled, vaulting across the bar. Guns blasted. Men shouted. Donnigan felt a bullet graze his left leg. He landed on a man who had sought shelter behind the bar.

The barkeep's scatter-gun shot out a big hanging lamp over the bar as Donnigan crouched and lunged toward the back, past the men who had ducked down behind the bar. The barkeep's gun roared again. The second lamp went out, throwing the room into blackness.

"He's behind the bar!" Shattuck Brady bawled. "Don't let him get away. Run around back and watch for him!"

A door to the outside was at the back end of the bar. Donnigan yanked it open and dodged outside. The moon was not yet up. He ran through blackness to the rear of the building and cut to the left behind the other buildings.

Horses stamped out ahead of him. As Donnigan lifted his gun, Lia Brady called out: "Matt! Are you back here?"

Donnigan limped forward. "What is it, Lia?"

"Here's your horse, Matt."

Donnigan swung into the saddle. "Thanks, dear," he said hoarsely. "Good bye."

Her voice had been heard. Men were shouting Donnigan's location as he galloped to the first cross street. Lia swung her horse into the street beside him.

"Go back!" Donnigan called to her.

She answered as they rode. "I've had all of this I can stand!

I'm going with you, Matt. From now on it's us . . . against everybody!"

"You can't do it," Donnigan called as he pushed his horse hard. Already pursuit was fast behind them.

"I'm doing it," Lia cried.

Donnigan could not draw away from her. Bitter Fork fell behind. They rode across open country. The moon began to show.

"Where are you going, Matt?" Lia called.

"Cutting over to the ranch road. I'm getting my men, if I can, and riding up Squaw Cañon, past the big burn and down to the dry sands. I think that's where your cattle went."

They raced across country with pursuit closely behind them and darkness about them. Donnigan didn't spare his horse. If he could make the ranch in time, he could get a fresh horse out of the corral before pushing on. Lia kept even with him.

They thundered along the ranch road. Five miles from the ranch Roaring Bill Quinn's voice suddenly boomed off to the right. "That you, Donnigan?"

Donnigan turned toward the voice. "Brady's men are coming!" he shouted. "I'm heading for a fresh horse!"

"This way! Indian Joe told us Brady an' his men was after you. We were headin' for Bitter Fork with hosses when we heard you comin'."

Roaring Bill led the way into a brushy hollow. Indian Joe and Jigger Jones had horses there. As he hit the ground and tore his saddle off, Donnigan heard the distant thunder of hoofs, coming along the ranch road. He hurled the saddle on a fresh horse. Roaring Bill transferred the bridle. Donnigan talked as he worked. "Brady's convinced we got his cows and killed his man. We've got to keep ahead of them."

Donnigan turned from the freshly saddled horse, drew his knife, flipped the blade open, and reached Lia Brady's panting horse in two steps. He caught the reins and severed them close to the bit.

"Why did you do that?" she cried angrily.

Donnigan vaulted into his saddle. "It's the only way I can protect you, Lia. There's sure to be more shooting. I don't want you hurt or killed."

Tears of frustration came to her eyes. Donnigan leaned forward and pulled her toward him, trying to kiss her.

"Damn you!" she exclaimed, pushing him away.

"I love you, Lia," he said, then reined around and led the men at a gallop toward the mountains.

Through the long night they rode — up into the timber, up Squaw Cañon, up Little Skeleton Cañon, and high into the chill thin air to the roof of the world. They had lost the pursuit quickly in this wild country.

On the other side of the mountain they dropped precipitously down steep, rocky slopes, sparsely covered with trees. Far below spread out the dry sands, barren and desolate. Indian Joe's spotted dog was following the trail of cattle that had come this way. He led them out into the dry country, running before them like a spotted ghost.

Sometime before dawn, Roaring Bill said: "I just seen a little light a way back there, like somebody struck a match."

"Bugs in your eyes," said Jigger Jones. "There ain't nobody back there. We've come too fast."

An hour after that the dog suddenly turned his head and whined softly. Indian Joe spoke under his breath. "Not far now."

"Get your guns ready, boys," Donnigan said. "Ride as easy as you can."

They rode forward a quarter of a mile, half a mile. Dawn was just graying the eastern horizon when Donnigan topped a rise of ground and reined in sharply as a horse whinnied ahead of him. A dog barked ahead.

The road broke away sharply down to a small, barren flat. Down there a small fire was burning beside a big wagon. Restless cattle were being held in place by two riders. Men were harnessing horses to the wagon.

A shout rang out. "That you, Creed?"

"There's Brady's cattle and the men who bushwhacked his riders!" Donnigan rapped out. "It's a toss up, boys. Shall we hit 'em?"

"We're damned if we do, and damned if we don't," Roaring Bill said grimly. "Let's go!"

Donnigan spurred down the steep slope and raced toward the wagon, raising his voice in a wild yell. The others spread out behind him, yelling, too.

A gun cracked at the wagon. Other shots followed. Donnigan fired at dim, running forms. With a roll of hoofs the cattle stampeded in a wave across the flat. The wagon lurched, rolled forward as the four-horse team, being hitched to it, ran away.

Lead whined past Donnigan. He saw a man swing on a horse and race off ahead of them after the cattle. Donnigan fired through the faint light. The man fell forward, hung onto the horse's neck, and kept going. A bullet ripped through Donnigan's hat. He saw the shot flare near the campfire. A man was standing there with a rifle, frantically pumping another shell into the breach. He swung the rifle up again.

Donnigan ducked, hearing the bullet scream just over his head. He emptied his gun at the man and missed. The rifle was coming up a third time when Donnigan bore down on the man.

The man leaped aside. Donnigan swerved the horse, crashing into the bearded stranger as the rifle went off. The man went down. Donnigan's horse staggered, plunged to its knees. It had been shot. Donnigan hit the ground, rolled, staggered up with the breath knocked out of him. But he still had his gun. The man he had ridden down was staggering up, too.

Donnigan thumbed in two fresh cartridges and snapped the cylinder back as the man turned toward him, drawing a hand gun. It blasted, missing. Donnigan aimed carefully, firing once. The man pitched forward.

Roaring Bill's wild tones rose a hundred yards ahead, where he was following a rider. Guns barked. Roaring Bill turned back.

Jigger Jones galloped near. "They're high-tailin' it," he yelled.

Far behind a nearby plunging, picketed horse a rifle cracked, and Jigger Jones pitched from the saddle. Cursing, Donnigan ran toward the frantic horse, thumbing fresh shells into his .45. Lead screamed past him. The horse broke free. The man stood there in the open, blasting shots as Donnigan charged. Lead struck Donnigan's shoulder a terrific blow. He staggered, spun around, stopped, gritted his teeth, recovered, aimed carefully, and drove in three shots. The third one was not needed. The man was already going down.

Turning dizzily, Donnigan looked for more trouble. But the firing had died away. The wagon had overturned on the steep side of the nearest hill. The team was kicking in its harness. A shrill Indian yell came from the other side of the flat where Indian Joe was turning back.

Roaring Bill Quinn galloped toward the fire, shouting: "Two, three of 'em rode south! Let's go after them!"

"Stay here!" Donnigan ordered as Roaring Bill came up. "Jigger is down. I'm wounded. We'll be lucky if they don't come back and wipe us out. See about Jigger. He's over there by his horse."

Donnigan limped to the spot after Roaring Bill. Jigger was

lying on the ground, breathing heavily. He was shot through the chest.

"Boys, I reckon I'm done for," he gasped weakly.

"You'll come out of it all right," Donnigan encouraged, bending over him. But he lied. Jigger didn't have a chance.

"I rode by that wagon over there," Roaring Bill said. It's full of water barrels. There's a couple of water troughs tied to the side. They been gettin' small bunches of cattle across this dry stretch by hauling water in from the other side."

A moment later Jigger was forgotten as a mass of riders poured down into the flat from the direction of Tumbleweed Peak. Roaring Bill grated: "It's Brady and his men. Here's where I do some killin' before they get me."

"Take it easy," Donnigan said, pulling down the rifle Roaring Bill had lifted.

The sky had brightened enough to show Shattuck Brady, leading the men. No shots were fired as they rode up. Shattuck Brady threw himself off his horse. Behind the riders Donnigan saw Lia.

"What's come off here?" Shattuck Brady demanded harshly as he stared about him with a scowl. "We heard the shootin' back there."

"Your cattle just stampeded out on the flat here," Donnigan answered coldly. "Some of the men who bushwhacked your riders are there on the ground. Several more rode south. They've been running Bitter Valley cattle through here on water they hauled from the other end. Creed was mixed up in it. I reckon that's why he wanted to keep Squaw Cañon clear. To be sure of that he had to get me out of the way. If any of the men we shot down can talk, you'll probably get something out of them. Tell them Creed got caught and confessed."

"Boys, look around an' see what you can find out," Brady

barked at his men. "Donnigan, what are you doin' here, fightin' for my cattle?"

"Damn you and your cattle!" said Donnigan thickly, standing on spread legs with blood soaking his shoulder. "I tackled the job to get peace at my ranch."

Some distance away one of Brady's men shouted for him. Shattuck Brady turned on his heel without a word and strode there. Lia's face was pale and tired as she came to Donnigan's side.

"Matt, I told them where you'd gone, after I made Dad promise to keep his head when he caught up with you. He wouldn't believe you were following his cattle. Oh . . . your shoulder!"

"Lia," said Donnigan, placing his good arm around her, "it isn't my shoulder that's worrying me right now. It's my heart. You shouldn't be here."

"Well, I am! No thanks to you. Don't try to keep me away from you again."

Shattuck Brady strolled back toward them. His manner was strangely different. "Donnigan . . . it was Creed. That fellow over there talked. This has been going on for years. Maybe there's been a mistake about you for a long time."

"There's one mistake that's not going on any longer, Dad," Lia said firmly. "Matt and I are going to be married . . . !"

"Don't expect me to stop you," Shattuck Brady growled at his daughter, "not no more . . . though even a fool has some rights." He looked solemnly at Matt Donnigan and said no more. He was trying to smile, but was uncertain, until Matt smiled at him.

BULLETS TO THE PECOS

According to the journal he kept, T. T. Flynn did not title this story. It was the fourth one he wrote in 1949, completing it at the beginning of May. Mike Tilden, who by this time was editing *Dime Western*, *Star Western*, and *Fifteen Western Tales* for Popular Publications, read and bought it the day it arrived on May 25, 1949. It was published as "Bullets to the Pecos" in *Fifteen Western Tales* (11/49). It was Mike Tilden who titled it, and that title has been retained for its inclusion here.

I

"WATCH YOUR BACK TRAIL!"

Trouble broke so fast there on the Jackknife Flats in South Texas, where the trail herd was making up, that Bob Kenny was dazedly slugging big Red Wallace with both fists, for his life perhaps, before he quite realized what was happening. His gun had been deftly jerked from his holster as he had turned away from bawling out Red Wallace for loafing on the job. He'd swung around fast and met the terrific smash of Red's big fist. Steve Creel and Bo Creel had just happened to be standing there between the branding fires. Or so it seemed. They hadn't been standing there a couple of minutes before. Neither had Blackie Fenner nor Hi-Low Jack Bristol. But there they were when the mule-kick punch on the side of his jaw drove Bob Kenny, reeling, into the Creel boys. He caught a confused glimpse of the group of four. Bo Creel's hand steadied him upright and shoved.

"Get the red-headed skunk!" Bo Creel's husky voice had urged in his ear.

In the same instant a second terrific blow had struck the back of Bob's head, under the wide, dusty hat brim. No fist that. Wood or metal had done it. Bob Kenny was all but paralyzed. Knees buckling, he lurched back to meet big Red's rush. It was all confused, mixed up, whirling in front of his foggy eyes. Then Red Wallace, hatless now, gun belt shucked aside, wide, muscular face stone-hard with purpose, jumped in close. Red's fist exploded from nowhere, and this time Bob

Kenny spilled flat and sprawling.

He rolled by instinct, a great sickness in his belly and wild, helpless rage battling the fog in his head. The rage brought him up, dodging the furious kick of Red's high-heeled boot. Red had jumped in to stamp him. Red meant to finish him. Bob Kenny came up, staggering, lurching away, trying for extra seconds to get the fog out of his head, the drag out of his body — that tall, corded, solid body that had never failed him, until now.

Riders came galloping out of the dust cloud their horses raised. Other men were running close to watch, to hear the panting, scornful yell Red Wallace loosed: "Stand an' take your lickin', Kenny!"

A stumbling dodge eluded Red's rush. But it didn't help. The hard-baked alkali ground seemed to be weaving. Everything stayed blurred. Red was coming in again. Bob stood and slugged at him. It was like a bad dream. With movements slow and weak he hit Red, and it did no good. He drove a fist against the hard, muscular face. Red Wallace walked right through the blow, smashing his right fist, his left, his right.

Bob Kenny was reeling back again when he saw the colonel's big, jet-black horse rein up close from a full gallop. He saw the colonel's pinned-up, empty left sleeve, the trim and military set of the colonel's shoulders, and the blazing disbelief on the thin, proud, imperious face. All that in a glance — and then Red's fist smashed it away into a dizzy haze.

Bob rolled on the ground again, finished this time, and he knew it. Red's stamping boot heel grazed the side of his head. Red meant to stamp him unconscious. Wasn't much he could do about that, either, except put his arms up as a guard. Red's boot toe got through with the next kick and split his cheek and drove his head over on the dirt, and the day seemed to be darkening into night.

Colonel Stillman's shout of command cut through the heat and dust. "Hold that, Wallace!"

Red Wallace obeyed.

"Get Kenny on his feet!" The colonel was not a big man, but his blazing, imperious pride was high and wide.

Bob Kenny was trying to crawl up. Steve Creel and Bo Creel grabbed his arms and hoisted him roughly upright. His loose knees would have dropped him if the Creels hadn't held him. Blood spattered his arms and hands, and it was his blood, from his ripped cheek and pounded mouth. There wasn't much pain, only that feeling of being half paralyzed in every inch of the corded, solid body that always had been lithe and quick.

The colonel stayed there, fifty yards away, on his big black horse. His raspy voice carried quickly enough, angry, scornful. "Kenny! You got whipped! You're not the man to trail my cattle to Colorado! Wallace gets your job! Can't even use you as a hand. It would make trouble along the trail. You've got a week's pay coming. Stop by the house and get it on your way out."

Bob Kenny spat red. "Damn your pay, Colonel!" he gasped, but the colonel was already wheeling his horse away. The Creel boys let go, Bob staggered, and almost fell down again.

Red Wallace was grinning. "You two watch him pack an' line out. I'll be busy. If he makes a move with that gun, shoot the son-of-a-bitch. He got licked, but it'll eat at him."

A man's world could crash like that. Men who had been friendly could cast side glances of pity. Men who'd resented him could grin with satisfaction. The Creel brothers, with their wide cheekbones and swart, dark skin, had that satisfied look as they loitered near the chuck wagon while Bob Kenny washed his head in a leather bucket of water and old Gus, the cook, limping badly, gave him some stickum tape for his face.

"How'd you git that cut an' big lump on the back o' your

head?" old Gus demanded. He was leathery and wrinkled, with pale gray eyes, shaggy gray hair, hunched shoulders, a gimpy leg, and one cheek always bulging with a big chew of black plug.

Bob gingerly touched the back of his head. He was steadying a little. "Red must have stamped on it," he said.

"Don't see how he done it! Would've bet a year's pay he couldn't!" Gus snatched off his flour-sack apron. "I got enough of a fool outfit run by a stiff-necked old sidewinder who still figgers he's chargin' into battle an' damn the men who ain't chargin' to suit him."

"Climb down, Gus. The colonel's all right. So's the 5 X bunch."

"The hell it is! Not with that Red Wallace bossin' on the trail."

"He'll let you alone. When the colonel gets his 5 X brand settled on that long grass up north, you'll be set right, Gus. It's fine country. The ranch buildings will be up before snow, and you'll be bedded purty for life."

"Who wants to bed down for life?"

But Gus was wavering a little. A man all broken up inside, barely able to limp around his chuck wagon, wasn't one for the long trails any more. He couldn't even be sure of a cook's job all the time. "Where you goin'?" he asked.

"I'm not sure where I'm going. It'll be a far piece," Bob said.

"Don't want an old gimp like me along, huh?"

"I won't have you quittin' on my account. Take it bristlin' if you want to, you cantankerous, stiff-necked old hellion."

Bob said it, grinning, and got a glare back. Gus stamped to the back of his wagon and started rattling pans. Bob roped his own top horse out of the rope corral and switched saddles at the bed wagon. He lashed his bedroll on another horse while

102

the work of road-branding the last of the great herd went on in the heat and eddying dust. The last thing he did was fill a saddle canteen at the water barrel on the chuck wagon.

Old Gus limped over to him with a gunnysack. "Grub," Gus said. "Where you heading?"

"Send word to you when I get there."

The Creel brothers had stayed nearby and close together. Two stocky, flat-faced men who never talked much. The colonel had hired them for the drive west and north. Bob had noted that the two men had a way of sauntering off when strangers appeared.

He stopped now beside his saddle horse, touched the swollen back of his head, and turned for a long slow scrutiny of the Creel brothers. One of them had slugged him from behind. They'd been waiting evidently to do just that after Red Wallace started the fight. Everything had been planned neatly. The trick had worked. The trap had snapped — and Red Wallace was taking the Stillman 5 X herd to Colorado.

The Creels drew closer together in a kind of stiff watchfulness, hands ready to snatch guns. They knew what he was thinking.

Bob Kenny smiled thinly, swung on the horse, and gathered up the pack horse rope. "So long, you two," he called. "Don't forget me."

Bo Creel gave a flat, unsmiling answer. "We'll look for you."

They stood watchfully as Kenny rode off. He guessed the two brothers were thinking the same thing he was. Somewhere they'd have a meeting, a settling. The Creels might even come after him today to have it over with.

He was probably alive because the Creels and Red Wallace had lacked a good excuse for a shooting. A killing might not have put Wallace in as trail boss. Colonel Stillman wasn't one to hire cold-blooded killers. Red Wallace had known what he was doing. So had the Creels. Everything planned, carried out neatly. But why?

In the south a fast-riding figure topped a roll of the brush-dotted land, riding to cut him off. The distant rider became Carol Stillman, the colonel's daughter, and Bob Kenny waited for her. He'd been glad Carol wasn't with her father to watch the beating he took. Now he could almost guess what Carol was coming to say.

Riding sidesaddle, Carol wheeled her blowing horse along-side and burst out heatedly: "Father told me! He was wrong, Bob. Wrong like he usually is when his temper takes hold."

Bob Kenny differed calmly. "He was right. All the men saw me take a whipping. After that, I wasn't the one to give orders."

"Why not?" Carol demanded with the same heat.

"Every man who saw it would have it in his mind each time I bore down on him."

Carol was slim and dark, a lady to her fingertips, though with her father's fiery nature. But Carol could be level-headed where the colonel was apt to explode in temper.

"You can whip that Red Wallace!" Carol burst out.

"I didn't," Kenny reminded dryly.

"I don't understand it." Carol was troubled. "The trail won't be the same with Wallace in your job." Her forehead knit in thought. "Bob, if you'll stay another day, father might change his mind."

Kenny said — "No!" — much shorter than he meant it to sound. He added: "I wouldn't take a job that a woman had to beg for me. And I wouldn't have this job back if your father begged me."

"You hate him now, don't you, Bob?"

"No."

"You couldn't help it," Carol decided unhappily. "What are you going to do?"

Kenny started to answer and shrugged instead.

Carol smoothed her skirt and held the horse in. For once, her face gave no hint of what she was thinking. She gathered the reins and said quietly: "Good luck, Bob."

"The same, Carol. We might meet in Colorado one of these days."

Carol nodded, but her manner suggested no belief that they would. She lifted a gloved hand and shook her horse into a high lope back toward the ranch.

Kenny rode on, looking soberly after the receding horse and rider until they were out of sight. He felt worse, and he felt better, too, because Carol had made the hurried ride out to talk with him.

The dropping sun was a blaze ahead when Kenny's frequent scrutiny of the back trail was rewarded. A thin dust lifted back there and became another rider coming fast along his tracks.

Kenny dismounted, drank leisurely from the saddle canteen, and built a cigarette. He pulled the carbine from the saddle scabbard and sat comfortably on the ground, waiting. He recognized the reckless cant of the weathered old black hat when the rider was still distant and put the carbine back. Baldy Emerson saw him, waiting on foot, slacked off the long run, and came up at a blowing trot.

"Hell of a note!" Baldy called. When he stepped down, Baldy's brown mustache had a bristling look. "Let a red-topped bag of wind whup you!" he snorted. He was a thick-torsoed man, bald and mustached, with squinting eyes. "We brought the last hosses from Hawk Creek past the ranch house an' heard the news from Miss Carol." He spat expressively and jerked a thumb at the blanket roll tied on his saddle. "I quit right there. I'll git my other stuff if I'm back that way. Where we heading?"

"Can't use you, Baldy."

"Who asked you to use me? I can ride along, can't I?" Baldy spat expressively. "I ain't takin' orders from Wallace."

"Want to help me, Baldy?"

"I'm here, ain't I?"

"Go back and hit the trail with the colonel like you planned."

Baldy smoothed one side of his mustache. His squint deepened. "That help you any?"

"Might."

Baldy thought it over as he rolled a cigarette. "You got whupped. It's tracked all over your face. You got fired, too."

Kenny smiled at the puzzled look on Baldy's face. "That's right."

"Somethin'," Baldy decided, "ain't right about it. I thought so when I first heard. Red Wallace is tough, but he ain't that good."

"Tackle him and see," Kenny chuckled, and then turned wry. "Baldy, this is just for you to see. Never mind talking about it later on."

Kenny pulled off his hat and turned the back of his head. "Red could claim his boot heel did that. But one of the Creels buffaloed me on the sly, right after the fight started. They were standing there, waiting. Had it all planned, I think."

Baldy was scowling. "Damn them dirty two! They never acted that friendly to Wallace. Show your hand, Bob. What good does it do anyone if I make the drive with that bunch . . . an' you farther away every day?"

"It's a long trail to the Pecos and north, Baldy. The colonel is pulling out of Texas for good. Taking everything. Making a new start."

"Everyone knows that."

"He's not a cattleman at heart," Bob mused. "His brother,

Tom, ran the ranch until he died three years ago. The colonel was the Army man, the fighter."

Baldy snorted.

"But never a dirty fighter," Bob Kenny said. "The colonel's kind rush out front with the flag, ride at the guns, and never look back at who gets shot."

Baldy snorted again. "Injuns'll teach him not to gallop around in the open, wavin' a sword. He ain't learned what dirty fightin' can be."

"White men fight trickier and dirtier than Indians when they're minded." Bob Kenny was thoughtful. "The colonel's driving through wild country. Dry and rough. Anything could happen."

"You tryin' to say something?" Baldy demanded.

"I'm not sure, Baldy. In Colyville about six weeks ago Doc Ring bought me a drink and offered me a job."

"The nerve of that tinhorn, duded-up, crooked cattle swapper!" said Baldy explosively. "If that peaked-lookin' little skunk had banked a dollar for every blotted brand an' rustled beef he's traded in, he'd own half the pesos in South Texas! It's only pure luck he ain't been hung or shot long ago. A job? Hell! Takes jail bait to ride for Doc Ring."

"You're guessing about most of that," said Kenny. "Anyway, Doc Ring is heading north. Told me he'd be along with his drive most of the way, but he needed a good man he could trust to boss the drive. I told him I was taking the 5 X drive to the Pecos and Colorado. He said he'd heard so, but if my plans changed to ride over and take his job. Remember that trip to Colyville? The Creel brothers hit the colonel for a job there and rode back with us."

"Damned if they didn't."

"Couple of years ago in San Antonio I saw Red Wallace and Doc Ring with their heads together over drinks and talk.

Didn't mean anything then. I didn't even think of it there in Colyville. Might not mean anything now."

Baldy was pulling hard at one side of his mustache and squinting ferociously. "Now Wallace is in your job. The Creels helped him. An' Doc Ring is headin' north about the same time the other bunch heads west."

"I'm curious about all that, Baldy. Curious about why Ring wanted to hire me. You ride with the colonel. Keep your mouth closed and your eyes open."

"While you head north with Doc Ring?"

"If he hires me. If he doesn't, I'll be over the horizon, a way from your drive."

"Why?"

Bob shrugged.

Baldy pulled off his weathered old black hat and rubbed a callused palm over his sunburned, bald pate. "Somebody's a damn' fool," he decided. "Either a fool fer havin' such hunches or a fool to get tangled with 'em."

"You're right, Baldy."

"Me, I'm a fool twice. I'm havin' the same kind of hunches, an' I'll make the Pecos drive under that red-headed blowhard, Wallace. Look, Bob, on night herd I'll sing a lot of 'Oh, Susanna.' On a dark night it'll locate me if you happen to drift around. And if I do any scoutin' out, I'll try to keep north of the drive, or ahead of it in that quarter. Make it easier to run across me that way." Baldy clapped his hat back on. "A man can get shot in the back mighty easy," he reminded ominously.

"Watch your back and I'll watch mine," Bob Kenny said as they shook hands. "Baldy, I'll feel a lot better knowing you're with the colonel."

"Don't start feelin' until we see what happens. I quit the 5 X. The colonel may git his back up an' tell me to stay quit."

"If he does, make for Doc Ring's place on Mesquite Creek."

Baldy was stepping back on his roan horse. He said — "Uhn-huh." — and wheeled again onto the back trail.

II

"BULLET STORM"

Doc Ring's skimpy herd of eight hundred head, road-branded Bar O, pulled out from Mesquite Creek with scant ceremony. Bob Kenny was trail boss over eleven drovers and a giant, silent, black cook called Jimp.

Doc Ring had meant to boss the drive himself. "Had to hire what I could get. They aren't much," Doc Ring had complained when he hired Kenny. "I'd given up hoping you'd take the job. So Stillman fired you over a measly fight?"

"He fired me because I got licked."

"Any man can get licked now and then, and not be licked inside. I know that Red Wallace. He's tricky in a knockdown fight."

Doc Ring was a small man, thin and hollow-chested, with a weakness for fine broadcloth, linen shirts, hand-tooled boots, and gold-wire braided around the crown of his pearl-gray Stetson. The two guns he wore in the holsters under his armpits were gaudy with silver and fancy with ivory handles. But the man was dangerous, and he was shrewd. He coughed often, deep in his reedy, hollow chest, like a man who belonged flat in bed. But Doc Ring could outride men of twice his bulk and muscle, and often did.

Doc had stood in front of his two-room adobe ranch house in the Mesquite Creek chaparral, when Bob Kenny had arrived. Sunlight never seemed to tan his pale, thin face. The ivory handles of his guns had been visible inside his open broadcloth coat. He had held a brown paper cigarette between thin, supple fingers and looked Kenny in the eye.

"I met that Red Wallace in San Antonio a couple of years ago," Doc Ring had said. "He told me he liked to get a man off guard in a fight. Made it easier. That stiff-necked ass, Colonel Stillman, handed you a raw deal to my way of thinking. I'll give you a better one, Kenny."

"I'm here," Kenny had said. "I'll run the men my way."

"Deal your orders like they're needed. I'll tell you where to point your drive. The rest is up to you." Doc Ring had pulled hard on his cigarette and flipped it away. He had been smiling. He had sounded sincere. "Takes a load off my mind. You'll see why when you get a look at the men I've hired. Best I could do. They're road-branding now. Dutch Ike is in charge. I'll side you down the creek and turn the men over to you."

Two miles down Mesquite Creek, on another flat handy to water, the confusion, dust, and bawl of nervous cattle had been spiced with the rank stench of burning hair and flesh from hot branding irons. Doc Ring had ridden to the fires and beckoned men to the spot while Kenny had dismounted. On his magnificent bay stallion Doc Ring had looked smaller and more dandyish than ever as he lifted his voice. A thin smile had been on Ring's pale face.

"This is Bob Kenny. Some of you may know him. He'll boss this drive. His orders go."

They had been surprised. No man had showed a welcoming look. They had shuffled around, sizing him up. Bob Kenny had weighed them quickly. A tough bunch, he had decided. Every man packed a gun while working. But then, Doc Ring used men like these.

A bowlegged, young-old man, dusty and sweating, had said: "You was ramroddin' the 5 X, wasn't you? Over on the Jackknife range?"

"I'm ramrodding here now," Kenny had said mildly. "Where's Dutch Ike?"

He had known the man without asking. Dutch Ike had been shouting an order as they had come up and had stalked to the fires, hat pushed back off his unshaven, dusty face. A big man, muscular and stolid looking, with bunches of muscle at the points of his cheeks that lumped and eased as he munched on a wad of tobacco.

Dutch Ike had a sour look as he had jerked a thumb at his deep chest inside his greasy hide vest. "Me," he had said.

"Keep 'em moving while I look around," Kenny had ordered.

Dutch Ike had spat. The moment had drawn out while he had looked the new ramrod over. Doc Ring had watched in silence. Kenny's eyes had begun to narrow. Ike had turned away.

Doc Ring had sat on the big bay, grinning maliciously. "Keep a hard bit in the Dutchman's mouth, or he'll throw you."

"Kind of looking for it then, weren't you?" Kenny had asked as the men had dispersed and he stood alone beside Ring's horse.

"If you can't handle Dutch Ike, you can't handle the rest of them," Doc Ring had said. "Might as well find out fast."

That was the way it started. Three days later the weathered chuck wagon and bed trailer lurched slowly out of the Mesquite Creek bottoms, heading north. The remuda followed, then the bunched, uneasy herd strung out after the point men.

"Damn' poor stuff I'm starting with, and not much of it," Ring remarked, looking almost contemptuously at the strung-out, plodding herd. "Best I could do. Money's tight." Doc Ring's smile broadened. "I tried to make some deals to fill out my herd with other brands and sell up north for them. The

112

tight-fisted fools wouldn't have it. They'd rather wait and hope for a little sure cash from the hide and tallow markets than gamble with Doc Ring."

"Some men hate to take a chance," Kenny murmured.

A spasm of coughing shook Doc Ring's reedy chest and brought a red flush to his pallid cheeks, but his eyes stayed on Kenny while he was coughing. He seemed to be looking for something. His glance had held this weighing look more than once since Kenny had appeared at Mesquite Creek.

Kenny had marked that furtive glance at the handkerchief each time Doc Ring coughed and wiped his mouth. It told a lot. Doc Ring was a sick man, knew it, and was afraid. Bob Kenny himself could almost call the future. Some day, red blood would spot the handkerchief, and Doc Ring's days would begin to run out.

"Stillman gave you a raw deal," Doc Ring said bluntly. His glance was weighing Kenny again. "You can't have much use for Stillman now."

"How would you feel?" Kenny asked evenly.

A wolfish edge came on Doc Ring's smile. "I'd feel like peeling off some of the blatherskite's hide. I'd show him. I'd have my try at the fellow who licked you. And them two who helped him."

Kenny had told Doc Ring about the Creel brothers, as frankly as Doc Ring had admitted knowing Red Wallace in San Antonio. Now Kenny looked at the plodding herd. "Most men would feel that way," he agreed.

Doc Ring was not satisfied. "That the way you feel?" he pressed.

"I'm human, I guess. It came to mind."

Doc Ring chuckled. "Keep it there. A man never knows what'll turn up."

It was that kind of an outfit, that kind of a drive, beginning the long plod north out of the mesquite country. Nobody seemed to care much what was ahead, but the men were studying the new trail boss. Kenny felt it on the first day, sensed it in the way voices trailed off around the night campfires when he stepped close. Dutch Ike was one of them. The big, thick-chested man had evidently expected to boss the drive, and the sourness stayed with him. The men evidently were with him, too, for what it might mean in the weeks and months ahead.

Bob Kenny had his own puzzle — why Doc Ring had hired him over Dutch Ike. The Frio River was behind. They were heading for the lusher bottoms of the Llano. The drive was shaking down. They had almost too many men for the small herd. Doc Ring rode out each morning, grub in his saddlebags, and returned at night on a dead-beat horse, saying nothing about where he'd been. The weather was good. The cattle began to bed easily at night.

In the long hours alone in the saddle Kenny thought of the 5 X drive, making its slow and ponderous advance toward a crossing of the Nueces and pointing on into the rugged, parched Devil's River country. Colonel Stillman had chosen that route rather than risk his rich outfit on the buffalo plains where outlaws and cattle thieves infested the buffalo hunters working out of Fort Griffin. Red Wallace and the Creel brothers, Carol Stillman, and Baldy were moving west. And Doc Ring's poor outfit was heading north. The bunch had evidently been wrong. Kenny struggled with the feeling he should be riding west. He might have misjudged Doc Ring. But not Red Wallace. Not the Creel brothers, or any friends they might have among the 5 X men. A man like Red Wallace didn't scheme and fight bloodily for a chance to boss a Pecos drive without a reason.

They were still short of the Llano River bottoms the next

night, when Doc Ring rode up to the campfire and climbed stiffly down. He was dust covered. A fit of coughing caught him as he stood at the edge of the wavering firelight. On the other side of the fire, on a box against the chuck wagon wheel, in shadow, Bob Kenny watched talk stop and the sitting and sprawled men eye the reedy, hollow-chested figure, choking and shaking.

None of them showed pity or amusement. Doc Ring and his ivory-handled guns wasn't one to laugh at. The men watched with cold detachment while Doc Ring coughed it out and looked furtively at his handkerchief before putting it away.

That told a lot, too. It fitted in with all that Kenny had been watching. Doc Ring was no closer to his men than Kenny was, except for Jimp, the giant cook, who jumped to serve Doc Ring at every chance and seemed to like doing it.

Doc Ring stepped into the firelight and looked around. "I made a deal today. Not going to Kansas. In the morning we'll swing west toward the head of the Llano. Anybody want to cut loose now?"

It caught them by surprise. Bob Kenny was sure of it by the way the men looked at each other. His own pulses began to pound harder as he sat stiffly on the box, watching from the shadows.

The hunch was working out. Doc Ring was beginning to show his hand a little. Even Dutch Ike, getting up heavily, seemed to be surprised.

"How far do we go?" Dutch Ike demanded.

"As far as I say," said Doc Ring. His shoulders seemed to hunch in a little. He watched Dutch Ike fixedly. "Suit you?"

"Yah," said Dutch Ike after a moment.

"Suit the rest of you?" asked Doc Ring. A trace of the thin, malicious smile came on his face. "Hard riding ahead."

"Hell, no!" It was the bowlegged, young old-looking one

115

who had recognized Kenny the first day. Kid Frio he called himself. Or the Frio Kid. No one cared. He had a jumpy temper and had crossed words several times with Dutch Ike. "I started for Dodge City. The hell with headin' west. Pay me off."

Doc Ring's eyes began to look yellow and luminous in the firelight. "Where you going from here?"

"None of your business. Pay me off. I'll get going in the morning."

"You quit," said Doc Ring. "Saddle and get going now. I don't like a man that quits with dry country ahead." Doc Ring did not turn his head. "Kenny, send a couple of the boys riding out a few miles with the kid, well beyond the horse herd. We don't want to come up a few horses short in the morning."

Kenny was on his feet before Ring finished. So were other men around the fire. That was dangerous talk with a hot-tempered one like the kid.

The Frio Kid's rage keened in a loud, brittle challenge. "You callin' me a horse thief?"

Doc Ring's malicious smile did not change. "Aren't you the damnedest horse thief who ever jumped the Nueces ahead of a noose?" he asked. "And a yellow, loose-mouthed talker to boot . . . I've heard down in Live-Oak County."

The kid choked an oath and grabbed for his gun. Bob Kenny was almost in the line of fire. He stood there with eyes fixed intently on Doc Ring. He had a flash of wondering whether the kid realized Doc Ring had goaded him deliberately. Then one of Doc Ring's silver-mounted guns crashed flame and smoke twice. The kid jackknifed, spun half around, and fell hard at the very edge of the fire. One of the men grabbed a foot quick and jerked him away from the coals.

A quarter of a mile away on the bed ground cattle lunged up in fright that quivered and shook the star-bright night. The two men, riding night watch, began to sing loudly, and every man around the fire stiffened a little, listening, waiting for the first pounding thunder of a stampede.

Doc Ring spoke through the tension — mildly, with his gun back in his holster. "They're holding. The kid ain't going to Kansas, after all. Bury him tonight or in the morning, Kenny. Whichever suits you."

"Put him on a tarp, boys, and carry him out a way. We'll take turns digging," Kenny ordered. He was rolling a cigarette. He was steady and casual, and the men were shrugging it off, not too concerned about the kid.

Kenny guessed most of them knew what he had been watching for. The flash of Doc Ring's pale, supple hand inside his coat, almost too fast for any eye to mark it. Doc Ring was a wizard with a gun. It was Kenny's first actual sight of the reedy little man's threat in trouble.

Doc Ring was calmly eating grub that had been kept warm in a Dutch oven when they carried the tarp-wrapped bundle and shovels out into the night. Bob Kenny was thoughtful. It had been a good hunch. One man dead already. More would die, Kenny's next hunch was certain, before Doc Ring's wandering trail herd reached its destination. He was glad Baldy Emerson was out there on the Pecos trail. And anxious too, about Baldy. Men could get shot in the back.

They moved a little faster now, toward the upper reaches of the Llano River, pressing west. Grass and water were fair. Doc Ring had stopped riding out. He seemed in good spirits, except when the hard spells of coughing shook him. Then Doc Ring grew moody. There was a mystery about all this, too. A puzzle. Uncertainty. A man would think Doc Ring would be close to his gun riders. Most of them, Kenny guessed, were wanted by sheriffs. Dutch Ike was their man. Dutch Ike would have been a good trail boss.

Kenny sent men over toward the Llano River bottoms on a hunt. They brought back two deer and three wild turkeys. Game was plentiful over along the Llano. It was a good land — a vast, empty, lonely country, not yet taken up for grazing, but getting dryer each day now, as the stolid, plodding advance of the strung-out herd reached farther west.

Dutch Ike rode point most of the time. Doc Ring began to ride out again. The men loosened up with Doc Ring gone. They laughed more, talked more around the open fire at night. There was even some singing and harmonica playing that drifted out over the bedded herd and faded against the bright, blazing stars.

Long Jack, a lank and mostly silent man with a full, hooked nose, lowered the harmonica he was playing. "Where's Ring headin'?" he called across the fire to Kenny on his usual box by the chuck wagon wheel.

"Ask Ring," said Kenny.

Long Jack spat. It sizzled in the red coals. His thin mouth, under a drooping mustache, turned down in an open sneer. "You're bossin' the drive an' don't know?"

"That's right."

"How'd he come to hire you?"

"Ask Ring."

"Hell!" said Long Jack. He spat again, contemptuously, and cupped the harmonica back to his mouth.

Kenny sat without expression. He noted Dutch Ike's surly grin. Often at night, around the fire, Kenny had caught Dutch Ike's eyes on him. Sometimes they seemed to be glowing — like cat eyes, watching patiently.

Kenny had the tight-nerved feeling that trouble was shaping. He couldn't put his finger on it. Too many things he didn't know himself. Jimp, the big black cook, cleared his throat on the other side of the wagon, where he hunkered, alone and silent, most evenings.

Kenny rolled another cigarette, and rolled his ideas up into a decision with the movements of his fingers. He'd seen enough of the drive — and of the men — to guess that Doc Ring had hired him because Dutch Ike was too thick with the men. They formed a close-knit company. Doc Ring would have been on the long trail alone with them. They'd have had the drive to themselves when Doc Ring was riding off. They were a hard bunch. Doc Ring, in his reedy, hollow-chested way, was just as hard. But he was only one man. Kenny stood between them. Dutch Ike had no authority, but he held his surly resentment at Kenny, bossing the drive. Doc Ring could be sure Kenny wasn't going to become one of the bunch.

That was it, Kenny decided, as he drew deeply on the cigarette. He was in the middle. And the men were tightening up against him, with or without Dutch Ike's prodding. If they'd been the usual trail crew, it wouldn't have meant much, but these men were different.

Doc Ring was not back the third day. The weather had been good. Dry, in this drying land. They brought the herd early to a broad, shallow water hole with a wide belt of sun-cracked mud around it. There was no wind. The sun was setting a sullen red. The cook-fire smoke rose straight up, and the day's heat and the herd dust lay heavy.

"Weather tonight," Kenny announced after the remuda was rope-corralled and night horses put on short picket ropes near the wagon. "Hold 'em tight, men. Double guard out when those clouds hanging to the north begin to move in."

Long Jack, his tin plate piled with grub, just missed a sneer as he turned off to sit cross-legged on the ground and eat. "Hell! A few clouds ain't got you jumpy, have they?"

"Doesn't come often through here, but it comes hard, with plenty of lightning and noise," Kenny said calmly. "You can taste lightning in the air now."

"You taste it," said Long Jack. "My mouth's full of dust an' set for grub." Long Jack grinned loosely as several of the men laughed.

Kenny ate in tight-lipped silence, then saddled a night horse, and rode out around the bed ground. The gaunt, big-horned steers were restless. He was glad it was a small herd. As night marched in, the clouds were banking higher, blacker in the north. Streaks of livid lightning were beginning to thread the sable night beneath them.

The electricity building in the silent, heavy night might have engendered the wild and lonely feeling in Kenny, a sort of leashed violence that carried his thoughts, winging over the long miles to the Stillman herd.

There, too, Baldy was alone, and trouble was building. It could not be otherwise. In that frame of mind Kenny stopped back at the wagon for coffee. Most of the men were already in their bedrolls. Black Jimp, with a lantern, was lashing his chuck wagon tarp snug.

"Mistah Doc gonna be out in this," Jimp's soft rumble observed. "Dat li'l' man oughtn't get so wet an' col'. Ain' good fo' him, sah."

"Think a heap of him, don't you, Jimp?"

"He kilt a white man what aimed to kill me," said Jimp simply. He came to the back of the chuck wagon, where Kenny was standing with the tin cup of hot coffee. Jimp's eyes rolled white in the lantern light. He was a giant, and he had at times the soft simplicity of a child. "He been good to me, sah. Man saves yo' life, owns yo' life, ain' hit so, sah?"

"A man could think so, Jimp."

"I thinks so, sah. Mistah Doc say maybe some day I save his life. Jes' stay with him an' watch close." Jimp's deep breath was like a soft whispering wind in advance of the storm. "That's

120

whut I do, sah. Stay close an' watch."

So Doc Ring had one faithful friend. One pair of eyes and great hands and arms, watching, waiting for trouble. Kenny understood about Jimp and Doc Ring now. It was more proof that Doc Ring's mind was keen and sharply weighing everything. Doc Ring couldn't buy or hire the faithfulness he had in Jimp. That devotion deserved a better man than Doc Ring, Kenny thought wryly, as he smoked a cigarette and watched the sky to the north. The picketed night horses were restless, too, in the hushed night.

Second guard was riding the bed ground when Kenny called the other men out. Wind was rising, thunder rolling. A few miles to the north great livid streaks of lightning were slashing from clouds to earth.

There had been a period when Kenny had thought the storm might miss them. It was not one storm, but several. They seemed to change course, to halt for a little, each storm taking its own erratic way. Now the camp was threatened.

Sleepy, cursing men grabbed slickers, tested cinches, and made for the herd. The wind was coming sooner than Kenny had expected, picking up dust and heavier sand already, tearing red sparks out of Jimp's dying fire.

Bad lightning. In the brilliant, blue-white flashes the riders could be seen starting their circle, singing, chanting soothingly. The cattle were up, hair roaching with fear as they jostled in a mass that turned away from the storm. Then the wind broke. Kenny rode to the head of the herd, the collar of his canvas jacket up against the dust, pelting the back of his neck. The wind was trying to tear his hat away from the chin strap. This was a stampede storm. The men ahead of him knew it. Their figures, ghosts seen in the flashes of lightning, were keeping clear of the tossing, clashing horns of the lead steers.

The rain was a rumble, a roar, now rushing close. It hit

121

them in sudden, solid sheets of water and sand. The lightning was more fiercely on them, around them, on all sides. Then one stunning, blinding bolt struck into the herd itself. It was a blaze so brilliant that the world seemed to dissolve in glare. It was a thunderclap that left ears useless. It tore the night apart. Kenny's horse reared wildly and plunged away, trembling, and the herd broke in a panicky stampede, but not in a forward rush from the wind. It scattered away from the lightning bolt in all directions.

A senseless, earth-shaking wave of crazed steers charged toward Kenny's horse. The riders ahead of him were in the path, too. The stampede was around Kenny in a moment, his horse running with it. He heard the faint, futile pop of gunshots as men tried to turn a portion of the stampede. Lightning flashes showed the fear-crazed steers all around. One of the ghost riders was some fifty yards to the left of Kenny. The bellow of his gun was audible. It sounded as lightning flashed. Kenny felt rather than heard the sodden blow of the lead, striking the base of his saddle horn. He heard the shrill ricochet of the misshapen bullet. He slapped a hand down and found a third of the horn cut off.

The tar-black storm blotted all sight in the second it took Kenny to draw his own gun. All the leashed violence that had been building in him two hours ago came unfettered. That screeching ricochet was no accident. Murder had been tried. The shot, made from a full, wild gallop, had been meant for Bob Kenny or his horse. Either target would have dropped Kenny under the pulping drive of stampeding hoofs.

Lightning flared. The dimly seen rider was looking at him as Kenny's hand gun spewed its muzzle flare twice. Then the tarry night closed in again. His horse broke stride. Kenny thought the horse was going down. Maybe wounded. But the horse recovered and took up the wild gallop over ground getting muddy and treacherous. The stampede plunged into a dip, swept up a steep slope. When Kenny looked through more lightning glare, the other rider was not there. He'd been dropped, or had hauled back a little.

It was a wild, dangerous ride while the storm swept on and outdistanced the stampede. Lightning drew off into the distance. Thunder rolled in receding peals. Kenny managed to ride up ahead of the lead steers, draw off to one side, and rein up his blowing, steaming horse. The stampede would run out in the aftermath of the storm. After daylight they could count the losses and start rounding up.

It was bad enough next morning. Eight head had been killed on the bed ground by the one searing strike from the sky. Some of the herd had broken back and mired and snapped legs or drowned in the big, shallow water hole that was larger and deeper now. Other crippled or dead ones were scattered out over the prairie for miles. But none of the men had died.

Doc Ring had ridden in some time around the chill, damp dawn, soaking wet, exhausted from a long, hard ride. He was coughing. He looked peaked, unhealthy, when Kenny came into camp after carefully retracing in the first gray light the way he had gone with the stampede.

"Round 'em up!" Doc Ring ordered. "Never mind if you miss a few." Doc Ring noticed the bullet gouge at the base of Kenny's saddle horn. He stepped close and stared at it. "Lose any men last night?"

"Haven't counted noses yet," said Kenny briefly.

That was all. But when the men straggled in for fresh horses and grub in the early brilliance of clear fresh sunlight, Doc Ring watched closely. He was counting noses as Kenny was counting, and listening to the talk.

Two riders headed in from the north while part of the men

were already eating and gulping Jimp's scalding, strong coffee. Kenny faced the eating men.

"Somebody took a couple of shots at me last night during the stampede. Almost shot my saddle horn off. You all know what almost happened to me," he said.

They knew. They'd stopped eating. One by one tin plates of grub were set on the ground. The men eased up on their feet, eyeing one another and Kenny's tight, hard face.

Doc Ring stood off to one side. The faint, malicious smile touched his haggard face. He stood loosely, watching, fresh dry coat unbuttoned, one ivory-handled gun visible in its shoulder holster. He had unbuttoned the coat when Kenny started talking.

"The man who did it want to speak up?" asked Kenny.

Not a face showed guilt. They were uncertain about Kenny and about each other. Mostly about Kenny. He'd been an untried man so far. He'd taken talk that suggested he wasn't so dangerous. He might have been relying on Doc Ring's authority to back him. But here it was without warning — a showdown.

Kenny said softly, slowly: "The man who did it is a yellow dog. A snake. I wouldn't wipe my boots on him. He's a liar because he's not admitting it now."

Silence. Faces were getting hard. Some red. Tension was stretching out and out.

"None of my business what any of you men have been," said Kenny in the same soft, slow voice, "but I took it every one of you was a man."

Dutch Ike growled: "If I did it, I'd tell you, mister. Don't let any of that come at me."

"It's for the man who tried to coyote me. Can't I make him step out and say so?"

"We ain't all here," said Dutch Ike.

124

"It was to the north, where they've been," said Kenny. "Anyway, I shot back at the man. Over there in the wagon, hidden down under the driver's seat, is a hat the stampede ran over, near where I was shot at. It's got a bullet hole in the crown. The yellow dog can go get it."

One man had come in hatless. All eyes swung to him. Men moved hastily away. Stubbled face contorted, mouth working, he was already snatching at his gun. Kenny had called him, knowing who he was, ready for it. His first bullet struck Long Jack above the belt, his second high up in the chest.

Doc Ring spoke coolly as the blasts died away, and Kenny stood with cocked, smoking gun, looking for more trouble.

"One skunk less, an' nice shooting. Jimp will plant him. Grub up and round up. Dry country ahead and I'm in a hurry."

III

"THE TRAIL WOLF'S FANG"

West, over the divide between the Llano's headwaters and the Devil's River country, the heat began to come down. The land roughened up into cañons and draws, and the gray sage began to be seen. Water holes became scarce and would be bone dry a little later.

Near the headsprings of Devil's River they found the first dead, bloating steer. It bore the great 5 X on the left side, the Stillman home brand, and the small Rafter S of Colonel Stillman's road brand. They located other steers that had gone over cutbanks. One cañon prong had a dozen dead steers that had charged blindly over a fifty-foot drop.

"Stampede," said Doc Ring. "Looks like company ahead, and Stillman is having his worries." A malicious grin was shading Doc Ring's mouth.

They came on the trail Colonel Stillman's big herd had left. The wheel marks of the heavy wagons were there also. Bob Kenny, scouting out ahead of the remuda and Jimp's chuck wagon, was strangely moved by the sight. There over the hoof-churned earth had passed Baldy Emerson, Carol Stillman, Red Wallace, the Creel brothers, and Colonel Stillman with his empty sleeve and fiery, imperious ways.

5 X strays were sighted. "Throw 'em in the herd," Doc Ring ordered. He was trailing Colonel Stillman's drive like a half-starved wolf, following fat cows and calves. "He's in a hurry," Doc Ring said. "Not stopping to clean up his stampedes

or strays. Or his men don't give a damn."

It was the gray dawn. The men were gulping Jimp's grub and coffee. Doc Ring had had a bad spell of coughing. He looked thinner and more hollow-chested than ever, as he stood with a tin cup of steaming coffee and looked around at the men. "If this keeps up, we'll have a bigger herd," Doc Ring said, "and a fat bonus for every man . . . depending on how well we do."

The men looked at Doc Ring and at one another. They understood that kind of talk. Several of them grinned. Cinch Spalding, a lanky, close-mouthed man with reddish hair and mustache and a blotchy spatter of freckles on his face and the backs of his hands, chuckled with a new kind of friendliness.

"Maybe you knew what you was doing when you turned away from Kansas," Cinch decided.

"I do business where I find it," said Doc Ring. The malicious smile touched his face. "From here to the Pecos, it gets worse every mile for a cattle drive." He took a swallow of hot coffee. "The bigger the drive, the worse it gets," he said, "and better for doing business the way I like to do business."

It told a lot Kenny hadn't been aware of. It told that Colonel Stillman's herd was being bled of sound cattle for Doc Ring's benefit. It proved that Doc Ring and Red Wallace had an understanding, a plan. A man could look into the hazy distance ahead and see death and destruction moving west with Colonel Stillman's drive.

They found a grave — a lonely mound of fresh, drying earth on a little rise near an old camp site. It had been there about two days, Kenny judged. There was no headboard on the grave.

"Dig it up," Doc Ring decided. "Let's see who they buried."

While a man was riding after the wagons for shovels, and the herd was plodding past, Kenny said evenly: "Might be Red Wallace."

Doc Ring dismounted, smoking a cigarette and looking at him closely. "Or old Stillman himself," Doc Ring said finally, and the way he said it was like a cold-deck ace, showing briefly.

With Colonel Stillman dead, Carol, his daughter, would own the rich 5 X drive. If something happened to Carol . . . ? One man — one girl — between Doc Ring and a fortune.

Kenny prowled the camp site while the drag dust of the herd went by. He found where tents had been pitched, where a narrow-tired buggy had rolled. He found the marks of small boots in the floor space where one small tent had stood. Half covered by scuffed dirt he found a woman's small tortoise shell comb. It was a small and fragile object when Kenny dusted it off and held it in his hand, and it brought Carol into vivid memory, as he'd last seen her on the long gallop across the prairie to head him off.

Two short days ago Carol had slept here under tent canvas and faced another day. How had she faced it? What had she been thinking? Or fearing? Death had struck at this camp. Kenny lifted the comb to his nostrils. It seemed to him some of the clean, fresh fragrance and sparkle of Carol herself still clung to it. She had ridden on, but she was here, too.

Kenny shoved the comb in his pocket and turned back to the grave where Doc Ring waited with four of the men. The bodies had been wrapped in canvas. Two of them, buried in a common grave. Doc Ring had never been more poker-faced than Kenny was as the bodies were laid beside the open grave and the canvas opened.

"Latigo Raines and Tex Jones," Kenny said without expression.

He thought Doc Ring looked relieved. Latigo and Tex had been shot. Nothing else to tell what had happened. They were put back in the ground again to rest forever, forgotten in this great sweep of dying desolation, just two more men who had died heading toward the Horsehead Crossing of the Pecos. How many more men were buried back toward the Nueces crossing? Baldy himself? — although two tents erected at this camp spoke against that. But men the colonel could depend on were being whittled away. The colonel still might not realize it. Kenny did as they galloped on to overtake the herd.

Time was running out fast, and Kenny knew it with hard certainty as Doc Ring rode closely beside him with a thin smile of satisfaction.

"Not Red Wallace or the Creel brothers," Doc Ring said, jerking his head back toward the grave. "Or that stiff-necked ass, Stillman. They're still ahead . . . especially Stillman."

"Then what?"

Doc Ring looked over at him. It might have been the drag dust they were entering that set Doc Ring off into a violent spasm of coughing and choking. Kenny had never seen it worse. Doc Ring doubled over. His face grew purple. He was gasping when it ended. He reached for a fine linen handkerchief, wiped his mouth, and looked furtively before putting the handkerchief away. Kenny, watching from the corner of his eye, as he always did now, saw a fresh red stain on the white linen. Doc Ring dabbed the handkerchief back with a fierce and frantic movement. A second stain was there when he looked. He was licking his lips and swallowing as he shoved the handkerchief away and glanced toward Kenny's uninterested profile.

"Then what?" repeated Doc Ring. His voice was thin, harsh, as it had never sounded before. "Business is business, where you find it. A man only lives once . . . and not too long at that. He's a fool if he misses any chances."

Doc Ring ate a hearty supper. The herd was bedding down as he saddled the best horse in his own fine string, took a filled canteen and saddlebag grub from Jimp, and rode on ahead into the twilight. Jimp's great black figure stood motionless, watching him go. There was a soberness about Jimp that suggested some animal-like premonition that all was not well.

Kenny rode out a little later, as he often had, no man particularly curious about what he was doing. He was trail boss. His business was his own. Tonight he had an idea they were glad to see him go. It was only a thought. His mind was on the 5 X drive, far ahead. Doc Ring had sparked new ideas in the men. Easy profit. A broad hint of money outside the law. Easy money with which they all were familiar. He guessed they were going to talk about it tonight, around Dutch Ike. He thought again that Doc Ring had shrewdly planned far ahead when he put a stranger rather than Dutch Ike bossing the drive. Doc Ring was not alone against them now, with easy wealth in sight.

The moon was in the quarter. A man could almost reach and pluck the bright cold stars. Coyote clamor wailed and sobbed across the drying world of sand and sage as Kenny pressed his fine horse west. *There were human coyotes and wolves, too,* Bob Kenny thought, as he rode hard on the dim-sighted swath of the 5 X's passing. He might overtake Doc Ring at any time, and that might mean a showdown between them. Kenny loosened the gun in his holster. Doc Ring was a sick, savage man now.

It was along in second guard, sometime before midnight, when he sighted the far glint of campfire light. A little later, when he pulled the horse up for a blow and then an easing walk, the drift of cool night wind brought the distant bawl and mutter of the restless herd.

Kenny swung off, circling out. He had the wind with him. He was an unseen figure out in the star-hung night when he heard the distant, muted singing of the night guards, circling the bed ground. He dismounted, tightened cinches, walked in

130

closer, leading the horse, and sat relaxing on the ground, waiting, listening. He was there when a few sparks from the stirred campfire marked coffee and the guards' changing. The camp was on the other side of the bed ground. There would be a small tent there, with small boot marks in the earth, and Carol, dreaming perhaps of a kinder land of running water and rich grass.

The whispering wind brought the slow sad singing of a third guard rider: "Oh, Susanna, don' you cry fo' me. . . ."

The great uncertainty rolled from Bob Kenny. Only one man could sing so lugubriously, so badly. Baldy Emerson was still alive! Kenny drifted closer in the saddle, a silent shadow. The rider came, circling the herd. A cautious match flared as he lit a smoke and came on.

"Baldy?"

"Who the . . . ?"

Kenny sang cautiously: "Oh, Susanna. . . ."

The rider came toward him at a slow trot. "Bob?"

"Yes."

"My God, I'm glad to see you. Let's ride out. Look sharp. Red Wallace is somewhere on a horse tonight."

"Doc Ring's drive is back over the horizon. He changed his mind about Kansas and turned up the Llano. Had it planned all along, of course."

"I oughta knowed it," Baldy cursed. "One damn' thing after another has hit us."

"The colonel and Carol all right?"

"So far. The little gal's lookin' peaked, though. Like she had an idea somethin' was bad wrong. Her old man's gittin' that look, too, now'n then. I've nigh sung myself crazy on that song, nights, an' grabbed excuses to scout out. I'd give up hope you'd show up."

"Ring had Latigo and Tex dug up to see who it was."

131

"The damned body snatcher! Figgered it might've been one of his friends, I reckon. Tex got in a fight with Steve Creel. Leastways, that's what was told. Latigo dragged his gun to take it up. They say he cut down on Steve Creel from the back. Bo Creel shot him."

"The damned liars," Bob Kenny said past set teeth.

"Red Wallace swore it was so. He was there an' seen it. Told the colonel it was pure self-defense on the Creels' part. Red said he'd stand by the Creels as good men. It's all six-gun law in these parts, anyway, an' most of the men'd stand by him on it." Baldy spat. "Hell! He had the colonel, an' the colonel knowed it! This ain't the Army. Red's trail boss with part of the men backin' him up openly. The colonel didn't have a good man to take Red's job. Maybe Red was tellin' the truth, anyway. I think the colonel wants to git over this last dry stretch to the Pecos before he tries a curb bit on anything. He's been stampeded an' rustled until he swears a curse is on him."

"Add it up, Baldy. Since the colonel planned to pull out of Texas, Doc Ring's sights have been on him. Why deal in shady stuff in a small way, when a man could get a whole big trail herd and supplies to set up a ranch? Doc Ring had about run out his rope in South Texas, anyway. Too many men watching him. The colonel was heading this way beyond the law. Just him and Carol. No one ahead or behind, worrying about him. A fortune in good beef, an outfit to start a ranch, all ripe for rustling. All it needed was the right man planted among the colonel's men, and Doc Ring with help close. No law to worry about, everyone ahead strangers to the colonel and his outfit."

"Means the colonel would be kilt," said Baldy.

"Yes."

"His daughter, too," Baldy guessed harshly.

"Or worse," said Kenny more harshly.

"An' I was worryin' about my own hair." Baldy was past cursing. "It shapes up, Bob . . . all but you bossin' Doc Ring's bunch."

"If I don't track right, I can be killed," reminded Kenny. "Ring thinks I hold a grudge against the colonel and Red Wallace and the Creels. He's planned it like a stacked deck."

"Figgered on everything, didn't he?" said Baldy.

"He rode this way ahead of me tonight, rigging everything for his jackpot play somewhere between here and the Pecos," guessed Kenny. "Red Wallace moved out to meet him, I reckon."

Baldy was silent a long moment. His comment had a savagely helpless sound. "What do we do, Bob? Even if the colonel knowed, an' believed, which I doubt, he's in a corner. Ain't no law. Ain't no help."

"How many men can the colonel trust?"

"Four, includin' Gus, the cook. Then the colonel an' his daughter. An' you."

"Not enough against Red Wallace, Doc Ring, and the men who'll do as they say." Kenny sat thinking. They had pulled up behind a rocky fold of the land, beyond any earshot.

Baldy said uncertainly: "Two days to the Pecos from here, an' no more water. Whatever happens, comes quick now."

"Doc Ring and Wallace must be planning it tonight," guessed Kenny. "Easiest way would be to get the colonel first. Make it look like an accident. The rest would be easy. When the 5 X beef hit the Pecos, it would be Doc Ring's. Anyone who didn't agree could be floated down the Pecos. Bodies don't come back from the cañons downstream."

Baldy's growl held a promise. "Them cutthroats won't Pecos me!"

"They'll have the 5 X. Baldy, I've heard of snakes fangin' themselves to death with their own poison. If we could make

133

Wallace's bunch think Doc Ring's bunch was aiming to double-cross them, which they probably are, and make Doc Ring's bunch think Wallace and his men were trying to cut them out. . . ."

Baldy whistled softly. He grunted. He chuckled. "Snake ag'in' snake. Fangin' each other."

"Take a chance on getting killed tonight?"

"Takin' it, anyway, ain't I?"

"Light a shuck on the back trail then, and try what I tell you. . . ."

IV

"PECOS SIXES"

The two tents were well away from the chuck wagon, the picketed night horses, and the sleeping trail crew. The three big freight wagons, tassel-topped buggy, and a buckboard cut off the tents from the crew, giving Carol and the men their privacy. Baldy had said the colonel's tent was the north one, the larger, and the colonel was a sound sleeper.

The campfire was a yellow point beyond the wagons when Bob Kenny eased on foot to the back of the colonel's tent. A picketed horse stamped and snorted. The colonel was snoring gently as Kenny eased through the tent flaps, gun in hand.

"Wha . . . what?" the colonel demanded sleepily as a hand jogged his shoulder. The canvas camp bed creaked as the colonel reared up in his white nightgown.

The jabbing gun muzzle emphasized Kenny's low, cold order. "Not a sound, Colonel. Sit quiet and listen. This is Bob Kenny."

"With a gun? You scoundrel . . . !"

"Last warning, Colonel. I'm here to help you."

The colonel subsided, muttering. He was brave enough. Kenny started to explain the situation, fast, low. The colonel snapped: "I don't trust you, Kenny!"

"Don't trust you, either," said Kenny bluntly. "You're a hot-headed fool. I'm thinking about Carol. I want you two out of here."

"I'll not sneak away from my own cattle drive like a thief

in the night. A damned coward."

"Tell your daughter to ride out with me, then, where she'll be safe."

"Ridiculous! What scheme is this, Kenny?"

Kenny was in a cold and quiet rage by now, even though he'd known it would probably end like this. And you couldn't take a man and his daughter from under the noses of all that trail crew at gunpoint. There wasn't time to handle them anyway. He might have wasted too much time as it was.

"I've told you, Colonel. Let Carol know. She has more sense than you'll ever have. And if you aren't a hot-headed idiot, keep quiet while I leave."

A moment later Kenny was outside again, turning back between the tents, gun in hand. His mind was on Carol, in the adjoining tent, when he halted abruptly, gun muzzle flipping up.

It was close. He was challenged. "Who are you?"

Carol's voice. She had on some kind of a dark wrapper and at first sight had looked like an overcoated man, standing there, gun in her own hand. Close. Carol would never know how close she'd been to getting shot.

"It's Bob Kenny," he told her under his breath.

"W-with a gun?" Carol's voice strained thin. "You were in father's tent. I knew you hated him. B-but not like this. So you've been near us all along. And we've had trouble and more trouble."

"Go talk to your father, Carol."

"I. . . ."

Colonel Stillman's rasping whisper came through his tent canvas. "Come here, Carol."

She hurried, still upset, uncertain. Kenny went on with long, quiet strides. He'd done all he could now and perhaps was too late for what had yet to be done.

136

He tried to guess where Ring and Wallace might have met, if they had met, and to keep between that point and camp. He was some miles out, listening, when his horse's ears pricked toward the south. Kenny wheeled that way and rode fast, stopped to listen, heard nothing. He started on, and suddenly, half a mile away, a match flared to a cigarette, clearly seen.

Kenny came quartering from the direction of the camp, calling as he closed in: "Red Wallace?"

"Who is it?"

"Baldy Emerson! Trouble at camp!" Kenny said, and hoped it worked as he came in alongside the suspicious rider. It did. He sighted a hand shoving a gun back into its holster.

"What trouble?" Red's rough voice demanded.

Kenny had him covered an instant later, as they paused there side by side. "Unbuckle the belt and shuck it, Red."

Hands went up shoulder high. "Kenny," Red Wallace ground out. He could see Kenny's own gun gesture menacingly. His belt and holstered gun slipped off and thudded on the ground. Wallace's hands lifted again. "You been trailing me clean to the Pecos?"

Doc Ring hadn't told him. More proof Doc Ring was planning deeply. Kenny chuckled. "You didn't think Doc Ring trusted you, Red? Or Bo and Steve Creel? Or the others? Doc promised you to me after he got the size-up tonight."

Red Wallace choked on it. "You mean that smooth-talkin', double-crossin' . . . ?"

"Shut up," Kenny said, and he was chuckling. It was easy — for who could come like he had, knowing everything, save at Doc Ring's orders? Red Wallace would wildly believe anything he heard now.

"Doc," said Kenny, "knows a crook like you and that bunch you're heading. Doc's got the men he needs. With you out of the way Doc means to ride in and take over while you're strung out on the trail. But you won't be there, Red. Or the Creel boys. Doc don't want 'em. Too crooked. I got Baldy Emerson tonight, thinking he was one of the Creels. Too bad. I liked Baldy. I'll get the Creels tomorrow."

"He said go on to the Pecos. The lyin' little dog," Red gritted. "Going to cold-deck me. . . ."

The drive of Kenny's offside spur made his horse jump. Kenny yelled at the horse. Swore. His gun spewed a shot as Red Wallace ducked low and drove his own spurs and rode for his life, wheeling sharply away.

Kenny fired again and again as the race stretched out across the plain. He missed each time. His horse dropped rapidly back. Red Wallace got his saddle gun and started firing back. He drew away. He escaped.

Kenny circled away, smiling grimly. It would have been a pleasure to shoot it out tonight with Red, even terms, but Red was needed to ride back to camp with his rage. He'd find Baldy gone, as Kenny had said.

Bible oaths stacked high would never convince Red Wallace now that Doc Ring wasn't a mortal enemy. Taking over the Stillman herd would wait until the matter of Doc Ring was settled. A man could figure it that way in his mind. Red Wallace was a mad dog. Could you be sure a mad dog would act like you thought? Kenny was troubled as he rode south. He had to take the risk. And if Baldy failed . . . ?

At sunset a low butte had been visible off in the southwest. From the 5 X camp it was a cloud-like shadow some distance off in the southeast. Kenny rode to its north base in the starlight and dismounted on the talus slope above the level of the plain. He unsaddled and made himself comfortable. From this higher point he could look across the rough sweep of the land and see the 5 X campfire stirred to brightness, far away. Seated on a flat rock, pulling on a cigarette, Kenny thought of the war council Red Wallace must be having. Red would be giving his own version of what had happened, making sure every gun in the outfit was ready. If there were only some way of making sure the colonel and Carol would come through this safely. There was no way to make sure. He tried. It had to be like this. The uncertainty nagged and drew out.

The horseman came toward the butte from the east while dawn was still hours below the horizon. Kenny's rifle was on the sound, then on the final cautious approach across the talus slope. A whistle. Kenny whistled back and lowered the rifle.

Baldy came on and dismounted. "How'd you do?" he inquired.

"Had luck. Red Wallace is primed."

"I dern near missed my little weasel," said Baldy. "Got ahead of him an' rode close to his camp afore I turned back. About three mile out I was settin', wondering if it was all bad luck, when he come slopin' along, ridin' easy an' coughin' like a sawmill exhaust gone wild. Never did hear his hoss. Would've missed him. Knowed it had to be him, so I fogged right out after him, callin' . . . 'Doc Ring!'" Baldy chuckled. "Wonder he didn't catch on. He pulled up, an' I hollered . . . 'Red sent me! He fergot to warn you!'"

"If he hadn't seen Red tonight, that would have been a spot," said Kenny as Baldy hunkered beside him.

"Uhn-huh. I was sure hopin' he had," agreed Baldy. "It settled him, though. I was right in beside him when he unloaded some coughin'." Baldy spat. "So I reaches over an' helps him stop it with my gun barrel. I yanked him over an' spilled his guns outta them shoulder holsters while he was still foggy. 'Red sent me to kill you, friend,' I says pleasantly, 'which I aim to do. You're too greedy. An' just to make you feel good about it, Doc, I'm headin' into your camp with word you an' Kenny an' Red Wallace want half the boys to move up fast an' help take over the 5 X. They'll be met an' took care of. I met Bob Kenny, scoutin' out, an' fixed him. With you dead, too, Doc,' I says, 'we'll ride an' git your cattle, an' be fat as a Christmas goose when we hit the Pecos.'"

"Doc and Red will never stop shooting long enough to talk it over," said Kenny, chuckling. He sobered. "Baldy . . . we've had too much luck tonight."

"When do you reckon they'll tangle?"

"Quick as Doc Ring can get his men riding," guessed Kenny, standing up. "Doc will try to surprise Red Wallace as much as possible . . . if I know Doc. Waiting won't help him any now."

"You see the colonel?"

"He stayed in camp. God knows what he'll do, with that temper." Kenny was saddling. "We'd better move in closer. I asked the colonel to pass word to Gus, the cook, and the few men Gus knows can be trusted. Baldy, it's going to be a day."

"Somebody," said Baldy with dry understatement, "will get hurt."

They had chuckled with a certain macabre humor over what they'd done, but as they rode off the talus slope, they were sober. Any way you added up what was ahead, this was a day of guns, of slaughter.

The lone rider found them in the first mile. It was Carol Stillman, dressed like a payroll hand, riding a black horse, with booted rifle and a cartridge belt and gun. Kenny took all that in, barely seen, as Carol sat her stock saddle between him and Baldy. He had asked the colonel to send her to the butte. A great relief filled him as Carol said hurriedly: "Red Wallace came in like you said he might, Bob. That convinced father."

"What did Red say?"

"He said you surprised him, Bob, and were going to kill

140

him. Before Red got away, you admitted Doc Ring was going to raid us and had planned it back home, before we left. Red said you were Doc Ring's right-hand man, because Father fired you."

"What's Wallace going to do, Carol?"

"Father took charge," said Carol.

"Wallace let him?"

"He didn't object. Father was issuing orders when I left. Just like he was back in the Army."

"Riding into battle again," said Kenny. His touch was reassuring as he reached out and pressed Carol's hand. "He's a great old war dog, Carol. What are his plans?"

"There's a long rock dike about a mile on the back trail," said Carol. "He's going to ambush there. Surprise them. Even in daylight the men and horses can be hidden behind those rocks."

Kenny said thoughtfully: "Doc Ring isn't a fool. He's been told Red's men will be waiting. Doc will try some kind of a surprise."

Carol was worried. "Father quietly arranged to have the men he can trust stay close to him, where they can get his orders and act together."

"Used his head there," Kenny approved.

"I'm a fool," Baldy muttered. "You kilt me tonight an' put me safe outta it, Bob, but I reckon I better raise up from the dead an' move in with the colonel. He'll need another hand he knows he can trust."

"Doc Ring," decided Kenny, "can use a dead man, too. I'll try to cut in with his bunch and earn my pay by helping Doc kill off as many of Red Wallace's outlaws as I can."

"Snaky," said Baldy, "purely snaky, ain't we?" A thought struck him. "Listen. I'll be in front of your sights. Be dern careful who you're shootin' at!"

"Don't get cross-eyed yourself," suggested Kenny. "Carol, ride on to that butte. Get up to the top of it, if you can. If it's daylight, you can see what's happening. If Doc Ring should have luck and take over. . . ."

That was all Kenny could say. All he could do. He doubted that Carol would watch from the butte. This might be their last talk. Carol knew it. She was calm.

"Ring won't, Bob. We'll see the Pecos together. And Bob . . . Bob. . . ."

"You fool!" Baldy snorted. "Kiss her like you both want! Or ain't either of you got sense enough t' know what you want?"

Baldy reined his horse aside, and from the saddle Bob Kenny leaned over, arms hungry, mouth dry, until it met the warm, yielding gift of Carol's lips.

She held his hand for a final moment, tightly, and spoke to Baldy. "Thank you. I've had sense a long time."

"Knowed it," said Baldy.

"Tonight we'll be in camp, talking it over," said Carol.

That was her *good luck* — her promise. She sat silently on the black horse, fading back into the starlight as they rode away.

There was a great quiet in the fading night. Dawn had not yet brushed the horizon, but it was near. Coyotes yapped and clamored across the distance, as if wise in the ways of men and death.

Doc Ring was later than he should have been. It made Kenny more certain of Doc Ring's craftiness. Kenny was between the ambush and Doc Ring's camp, holding the horse quiet for long moments now, listening intently.

He heard it first like the pulse in his own ears — then as a tremor of the night itself, hammering faster, nearer, louder.

Hoofs. Many hoofs. They came in a long, pounding run, toward him, toward the ambush where Colonel Stillman's men waited.

Kenny pursed his lips, frowning. It would take all Doc Ring's massed men, spurring hard, to come with such a pounding rush. And yet there they came riding furiously to overwhelm the 5 X camp.

He barely glimpsed the mass of running horses as they stormed through the near dawn, and then he lifted into a hard gallop that swept into the dust of Doc Ring's advance and pulled up toward the last riders. He was close before he began to be puzzled, closer before doubt grew mightily. In the starlight it was hard to see clearly. Kenny was almost at the heels of the last horses before he guessed the truth.

Several riders made up that pounding rush. The rest were led horses, running on ropes to right and left of each man. They made a great pounding rush that would spring any ambush before dawn. And Doc Ring and the bulk of his gunmen were elsewhere in the night. Doc was crafty. Very crafty.

The rough rock dike lifted to the left, funneling them in against higher ground on the right. Kenny bore over to the right, knowing what was coming, bending low. He was a target, too.

One gun signaled with a lance of flame. The dike erupted with gunfire. A led horse plunged down with a scream. The riders pulled up sharply, wheeling back, and the mass of led horses rushed on, and the gunfire followed them.

The men had swung down from their blowing horses as if shot. Three men. Four men, when Bob Kenny called his name and joined them. He recognized Cinch Spalding's voice.

"Kenny? We heard you was dead!"

"Not quite! Where's Doc Ring?"

Cinch Spalding laughed. "We flushed 'em for Doc. They're

fannin' them led hosses right toward their camp with guns. Look!"

Stillman's men had hit saddles and spurred after the rush of hoofs, too eager to notice they were doing all the shooting. Red Wallace, crazy mad, was probably behind it.

But on beyond that, gunfire stroked the night. Even here, where they talked, one could feel the earth's unease, as thousands of heavy steers stampeded off the bed ground toward them.

"All Doc wanted," said Cinch Spalding, "was to know where they was hid, so he could point the stampede. It'll break 'em up. Get yore handkerchief up over your face, Kenny! Every man that ain't got a handkerchief acrost his face is gun meat. Doc and the others'll be ridin' in a bunch in the dust of that stampede, cuttin' down any man they find scattered out in daybreak without his face covered. Hell! By sunrise there won't be enough of them to bother with. Doc says get 'em all. He's wild." Cinch climbed his horse. "We better ride up on them rocks an' let the worst of the fuss git past."

Behind the handkerchief mask Kenny's mouth was a hard, bitter line. The 5 X men were outfoxed. They'd be overwhelmed, hurried back, scattered, and confused by that wave of crazed hoofs and horns driven off the bed ground by the guns and yells at their flanks.

Half an hour later would have given enough light to see what was happening, Kenny thought bitterly, as he rode with the other three up among the rough dike rocks. Already the first gray of dawn was lifting to the east.

They topped the rocks, Cinch Spalding bragging: "There'll be a two-year drunk for every one of us in that 5 X herd. An' I mean to have my cut."

"Fire!"

That crisp military command sent Kenny ducking low on

the off side of his horse as guns crashed. His horse gave a great leap, staggered as Kenny flung himself off. A riderless horse bolted past him. Another was down.

The gasping rattle of a dying man came off the rocks as Kenny flattened. They'd been in clear silhouette against the starlight. Good targets. And Colonel Stillman and some of his men hadn't been flushed toward the stampeding herd.

Kenny was alone, six-gun in hand. The thunder of the stampede was sweeping closer as Kenny yelled: "Baldy?"

"Hold it!" Baldy's shout came back. "That's Bob!"

"Handkerchiefs over your faces! Everyone else gets shot by Ring's men! They're following the stampede!"

"Up handkerchiefs!" Colonel Stillman bellowed.

Kenny almost smiled. Colonel Stillman had his war, his command again. And he'd outfoxed Doc Ring so far.

Then the rocks seemed to shake, and there was more light now, and the flat land below became a seething torrent of plunging hoofs and clashing horns. A river of steaming, heedless flesh bolted by, drowning out all other sounds, lifting a pail of dust.

There was too much dust to see more than vague, masked riders, pressing into the flanks of the herd. The dike had split the stampede. It was passing on both sides. Into the flanks of it merged a small rush of other masked men, Colonel Stillman leading.

Kenny stood up, running down the slope toward a riderless horse whose dragging reins had caught under a rock. A gun sent a bullet *shooshing* shrilly past his head. It was Cinch Spalding, staggering on his feet, trying to get his gun up for a second shot. He fell down as Kenny looked. Kenny shook his head, swung on the horse, and rode into the dust. Cinch Spalding had his cut — of treachery and murder.

Red Wallace and his outlaws were mixed in the forefront

of the stampede. Doc Ring and his men were following them. Colonel Stillman, Baldy, and a few others were after Doc Ring. With the stampede, scattering out, and dawn rushing in now, the showdown was near.

A man could only guess at what happened first. Kenny heard gunfire while the cattle were scattering and slowing. He passed a body. It was Hi-Low Jack Bristol, who had been with Red Wallace. Then another body, also unmasked. Steve Creel. Doc Ring had struck them by surprise and hard.

A quarter of a mile off to the left a compact group of riders, faces masked, were riding easily. But in the dawning light Kenny would have known the erect posture and empty sleeve of the colonel at twice the distance.

He galloped on, knowing the colonel was cannily waiting for the fighting to ease off ahead. There'd be fewer for those few loyal men to handle. Kenny could have joined them, but he'd brought this about. Red Wallace and Bo Creel were ahead, and Doc Ring. There they were in the dust ahead, riders maneuvering at full gallop in two groups, guns slamming shots as the slowing stampede fanned away from them.

Even Jimp was there, his huge ebony figure hatless as he sat one of Doc Ring's fine horses. That was how Kenny spotted Doc Ring, since Jimp was keeping close to him. He saw Doc Ring wheel toward three men, reins dropped on saddle horn, and Doc's hands, each gripping a gun. All three men opened up on Doc Ring and Jimp. One man pitched off, and Doc swayed and dropped a gun. He fired again, got his man, and it was Bo Creel. But Doc was slipping from the saddle, too, as Jimp wrenched his horse close and scooped the slight, bowed little figure into the crook of one long, powerful arm.

The man riding at them was Red Wallace, still shooting. Jimp yanked his horse to a stop. Almost with slow dignity he slipped down with his burden and laid it on the ground. Lead

146

struck him and dropped him, kneeling, still trying to protect Doc Ring.

In the chill gray dawn Jimp knelt by Doc Ring, watching, while Red Wallace put lead in him again. Wallace was hatless. His red hair was plain. His broad, muscular face had a sneering grin of satisfaction — until Kenny hauled the handkerchief off his face and rode at him.

Then Red Wallace brought his lathered horse up, rearing. He was thumbing cartridges into his smoking gun as the horse came down. A gun blasted once, and, when Kenny looked, Jimp was holding Doc Ring in a sitting position. Doc Ring had fired that one shot and hit Red Wallace's horse. Doc's mouth was bloody, his thin face had a death's grip as Jimp held him there, and the horse fell. Red Wallace was leaping clear, trapped in the open. Bob Kenny came on.

Doc Ring had done it. A kind of frenzy seized Red Wallace. He pumped shots at Kenny and ran off to one side, reloading as he dropped to a knee. Kenny hit the ground, running, not a hundred yards away.

"You yellow, Red?" Kenny called, walking forward.

Red bawled at him: "Yellow, damn you? This time I'll get you!"

Kenny was grinning. This was the way it should have been, that roundup day before the drive started. Now Red had it, no help, no tricks.

"You won't see the Pecos, Red."

Red shot at him, shot again, and paused to steady himself. Then Kenny, pacing evenly, opened fire. It was the kind of thing to break a man's unsteady nerve. Red broke. He was jumping to one side when Kenny's shot knocked him, spinning, and the next shot caught him.

Kenny stopped there, knowing the sodden fall of a dying man. He waited a moment. The stampede was rumbling across the plains. A few riders, a very few, were carrying on the running fight. When Kenny looked back, Jimp had fallen across the slight, lead-riddled body of Doc Ring, and far back through the clearing dust, the small, compact body of riders was coming easily on, Colonel Stillman commanding.

Kenny smiled a little. There'd be work in gathering cattle and reaching the Pecos, but the grass would be long and green up north, where the 5 X would settle. Tonight there would be a campfire, as Carol had promised. Kenny stood a moment, rolling a cigarette, hardly thinking. His gaze was on the butte, miles off in the southwest, and he was smiling. They would see the Pecos together. They had sense enough now to know what they wanted, and they would have it — Colonel Stillman's daughter commanding. Kenny chuckled and started toward his horse.

LONG JOURNEY TO DEEP CAÑON

This was the only Western story T. T. Flynn wrote in 1950. In fact, he would write only three more Western stories for the magazine market. At the urging of his agent, Flynn turned henceforth to writing book-length Western fiction. In a sense this short novel, due to its length, may be regarded as his first effort at writing a much longer Western narrative than he had been accustomed to writing for magazines. His next long effort, indeed, was the short novel, "Two Faces West," that first appeared in the Toronto *Star* in 1952, was later expanded to the book-length TWO FACES WEST (Dell First Edition, 1956), and would eventually serve as the basis for a television series. Mike Tilden, editor of *Dime Western*, was known for changing authors' titles for their stories. He had a formula he used for every issue of the magazine. It employed certain key words in the various titles — such as "gun," "death," or "murder" — whether or not they were appropriate to the stories. He would also sometimes use the same title more than once for stories by different authors. "Bull's-Eye On Your Back!" by Cliff Farrell had appeared in *Star Western* (5/47). Tilden used that same title again for this story by T. T. Flynn when it appeared in *Dime Western* (7/50). For its appearance here the author's own title for it has been restored, with its intentional reference to a deeper psychological dimension meant to conjure an intimation of something beyond mere physical action.

I

Calhoun was in Mormon country, buying fine horses, when he hit Salt Lake City to pick up his mail. Among other letters a scrawled note said Grady Smith had been let out of prison, months early. Calhoun thought it over for all of five minutes and decided to ride through, cross-country, instead of taking the long way around by faster train.

Old Pete Wade and two young Mormon hands, hired along the way, had moved the horse herd to fenced, rented grass on the benches above the dry Angel Flats. Calhoun reached camp around midnight and was up at dawn. He told his decision to Wade while the two stood apart from the small camp fire and drank strong black coffee.

Old Pete had gone north with Calhoun four years back. They had wandered the Black Hills together while the blacker bitterness in Calhoun's heart seethed and simmered. Later they had moved over into Wyoming, where Calhoun had bought a small place on water, with enough grass around for the half-hearted ranching he was minded to try. More to keep busy than anything else. But the past moved into Wyoming with them.

Now with the coffee cups steaming in the crisp bite of dawn, old Pete spoke his first blunt conviction in four years. He was bowlegged, gnarled, with a fine pair of grizzled mustaches, a man mostly silent and observing. But this was a time for talking. Pete said it, growling through the steam of his coffee.

"Don't be a damn' fool, Dave! Nothin' but more trouble for you back in that Kingsville country. You sold your half of

151

the V Loop to Dal Carter, an' told him you figgered he'd been a skunk as a partner. You got offa the damn' range without a killin'. It's all over, an' gone, an' oughta be forgotten. You're doin' all right. Ain't had one of them black moods fer months. That there girl at Seabrook's ranch sure fancies you. . . ."

Pete caught the look on Calhoun's face and gulped at his coffee. He knew he had said too much. Calhoun stood big, broad-shouldered, smiling. It was a new kind of smile, hard and satisfied at the prospect of action.

"I'll take that big red roan and ride some of the fire out of him," Calhoun decided. "Move the rest of them toward home, Pete. Sell off as you go. Don't bargain too hard. We're out of the horse business. I'll see you at the ranch."

"If you ain't killed, which you will be, or worse," Pete growled.

Calhoun laughed. He was feeling good, in the way of a man who had been roped helpless and was now free to fight.

"There's a paper in the bank gives you the ranch and the bank account if anything happens to me," Calhoun said.

Wade stood motionless for a moment. Then he muttered, "Why, damn you, Dave, gettin' a idea like that!" Pete drained his tin cup and turned away, still muttering.

Calhoun grinned after him, enjoying old Pete's confusion. Then he drained his own cup and went about the business of leaving.

Eight days later Calhoun rode down through the Harco foothills into familiar country. He'd traveled light and fast, blankets tied behind the saddle. The roan was fined down and trail steady now. Calhoun was the same. A sort of windy excitement stirred in him today. And some of the bitterness was back, under the excitement, as he headed for Ferd Tyndall's small Half-Bit Ranch. He'd never had much use for Tyndall — but the outlying Half-Bit might have news of Grady Smith and how things were in the Kingsville country. Ferd Tyndall had his own dislike of Grady Smith and might talk, if given an opening.

It was early afternoon when the roan plodded a cattle track that angled to the crest of a brushy ridge. In the brush at the top Calhoun pulled up and looked down the long slope ahead to the Half-Bit buildings. Easing in the saddle, big and trail stiff, with a two-day's growth of beard stubble, Calhoun started a cigarette and watched three men, hunkered some yards in front of the log ranch house. They were a quarter of a mile away, but clear enough from the ridge.

They were talking earnestly. One man was using a short stick to draw map lines in the hard-packed yard dirt. The other two were making comments and pointing, in turn, at the drawn lines. They had the look of men planning closely together. The main corral back of the house was filled with horses. Calhoun's sweeping glance picked out five other men — three loitering at the corral, and two standing in front of the log bunkhouse. The Half-Bit wasn't big enough for all that. Calhoun wondered what it was all about.

The roan looked to the right, pricking ears. Calhoun's glance that way met a lifted carbine barrel, covering him. He said: "All right. Why the gun?"

Then he saw a second man, moving quietly toward him. They must have seen him coming and gone to cover in the brush, waiting to see what he'd do. The first man had a gray mustache and a face like weather-dried leather, dark and furrowed. He moved closer, into the open, holding his cocked carbine hip-high.

"You like the looks of things down there, stranger?" His voice was twangy, provocative.

A stir of temper made Calhoun perverse in his answer. "What if I don't like it?"

"You got a name?"

"I've got a name," Calhoun said shortly, and finished shaping the smoke.

The second man now moved closer, carbine carelessly ready in one big hand. Calhoun saw that rifle come up and took it for a silent threat. The flat sharp punch of the shot moved Calhoun's black hat awry on his head. He looked down the slope and saw the three men leap to their feet in front of the cabin. The men at corral and bunkhouse were staring toward the ridge like stiff toy figures.

Calhoun threw the rolled cigarette down onto the ground. Then he pulled the hat off his head and looked at the hole in the crown. Only then did his gaze go directly to the thick-set, powerful man who had fired that shot.

The fellow was grinning with malice and threat. He wore a working 'puncher's clothes, vest, hide chaps, black hat with the brim shaped up at the sides. His meaty face showed a bully's satisfaction in holding another man under his gun's threat.

Calhoun put the black hat back on his head. He spoke with almost insulting indifference. "Do you corral-hoppers hide out and shoot at everyone who comes by to see Ferd Tyndall?"

Glance narrowing, the smaller man studied him. His twangy voice lacked any regret. "Let's go down an' see Tyndall about it. Shuck off that gun belt an' drop your saddle gun on the ground. Mister, you weren't lookin' the place over like no visitor. I didn't hear no eager answer about who you are."

"The hell with you both!" Calhoun said, letting his temper out that much. He lifted the reins off the horn. "I don't want to see Tyndall that bad."

The twangy challenge was sharp as Calhoun moved to knee

the horse around. "Easy, stranger! Our friend don't always hit where he aims. But he's loose with a trigger. Drop them guns. Let's ride down an' tell Ferd about it."

The bigger man's grinning malice waited expectantly. The other one, the smaller man, had a coldly dangerous look. Calhoun weighed them both.

"If Tyndall's down there, we'll straighten this out. If he's not, I'll need my guns. I'll just gamble the two of you can't stop me before I get one of you." Temper jeered in Calhoun's dare. "Try it!"

Some of the grinning malice went off the bigger man's face. He stood indecisively. Calhoun took his measure right there, a bully who wanted it all his way before he took a chance.

The smaller man's dried-leather face creased into deeper lines of abrupt humor. "I'm Scotty," he said. "If you're bluffin', stranger, it's good enough." He spoke to the other man. "Burger, get my hoss. I'll ride down with him an' let Tyndall settle it."

Their horses were hidden farther along the ridge, in thicker brush. Scotty climbed a black horse Burger brought and swung in beside Calhoun. His manner had no particular animosity as they dropped down the slope toward Tyndall's spread.

"Been watchin' for sneakin' visitors," he said. "You seemed to fit. If Tyndall's your friend, it'll be all right."

Nine men were gathered in front of the log ranch house when they rode up. Tyndall was one of the biggest, a slouch-shouldered man with a flat jaw and thin mouth. Heavy black brows roofed his squinting stare at Calhoun.

"What you got there, Scotty?" Tyndall demanded. His unpleasant grin followed immediately. "Dave Calhoun! I'll be damned! What was he doin', Scotty?"

"Lookin' things over."

"Who fired that shot?"

"Walt Burger got hasty when his orders wasn't followed quick."

Calhoun climbed down and stretched, grunting. "Well, Ferd, what kind of dirty business have you got your hands in now?" he asked calmly.

Tyndall scowled. Then his grin crept back, thin and thoughtful. "Still acting big. Who you with now?"

"No one."

"I ain't heard you were back."

"Just back," Calhoun said, looking the other men over. "Riding in from Salt Lake."

Tyndall studied the trail-tired red roan and the blanket roll on the saddle. He ran another glance over Calhoun. "You look like it," he conceded. His thin grin spread. "Aim to team up with Dal Carter again?"

"Hadn't thought of it," Calhoun said idly.

Tyndall's snicker had some meaning beyond Calhoun's range of knowledge. But then all this had meaning. Tyndall spoke to the men who'd come from the corrals and bunkhouse.

"It's all right, boys. No trouble."

They straggled away.

Scotty said: "Dave Calhoun! I'll be damned!" His chuckle had a rusty sound. "That's one fer Walt Burger to think over," he said to no one in particular. "Walt shot him through the hat. Dave Calhoun!" Scotty wheeled his horse back toward the ridge, chuckling in his throat again.

The two men who'd been inspecting map lines in the dirt stayed with Tyndall. The thin one was Bud Storrie, full sixty miles off his little hardscrabble Box S ranch in the Benbow Hills to the north. The other one, with the black untrimmed mustache, was a stranger to Calhoun. That one's eyes were strangely pale. His nose had a bold slashing hook, which might be a sign of his nature.

Calhoun started another cigarette. "Haven't had word from these parts in a couple of years. How's everything? You meeting strangers with a gun these days?"

"If they ain't friendly."

Calhoun glanced at the spot where the map lines had been drawn. They had been scuffed out with a boot sole. Ferd Tyndall laughed. "Calhoun, you're mighty curious for a man just ridin' by."

"Too many men here for horse stealing," Calhoun guessed, still prodded by the bullet hole in his hat. "Bud Storrie never went in for cattle rustling, that I ever heard. But you're up to something slippery, Ferd. Only kind of dealing you ever knew. A bullet through my hat makes me curious."

"Don't be so damned free with your remarks!" Tyndall said sourly. "You ain't half owner of the V Loop any more. There'll be two hats lifted to me in Kingsville to every hat you'll draw." Tyndall was working himself into anger. Bud Storrie was covertly smiling. "*I* didn't get tried in court for shootin' *my* girl's old man in the back!" Ferd said viciously. "An' it ain't *my* old partner who's fixin' to marry the girl. You sneakin' back to shoot Dal Carter in the back, too, like you done old Sam Morton when he didn't want you hangin' around his Stella?"

Calhoun hit him in such fury that the shock from the flat jaw ran numbly up his arm. Tyndall catapulted back against the cabin logs. The back of his head slammed soddenly against a log. A jump then put Calhoun's back to the cabin wall. His right hand felt paralyzed. He had a moment of savage doubt he'd be able to cock and use his belt gun, if needed.

Bud Storrie stood with his mouth slightly open, as Tyndall tilted loosely and then fell heavily, out cold. The other man with the bold hooked nose hadn't moved.

Calhoun said: "Who wants to take it up?" He flexed his right hand. It felt like a knuckle bone might be broken. He thought bleakly in that moment: *Pete Wade was right. Trouble right straight through. Even with a horse thief like Tyndall. No one's forgotten. They never will.*

Then he saw the hook-nosed man smiling faintly. "Your trouble, Calhoun."

"You two walk around the corner of the cabin."

They obeyed. Calhoun backed toward the opposite corner, leading the roan. Screened from Storrie and the other man, he swung fast into the saddle and put the roan into a run.

His guess was wrong. No one tried a shot after him. A glance back showed the men at the corral, gaping uncertainly. The hook-nosed man had stepped back in front of the cabin. He was standing in an attitude of unconcern, watching Calhoun ride away. Calhoun could almost guess he was smiling faintly again. And then he wondered why, wondered who that man was, and what that gathering at the Half-Bit had meant?

As if in answer, all that Ferd Tyndall had said came rushing in. Stell' Morton was going to marry Dal Carter. Even Tyndall had speculated if that hadn't been what had brought Calhoun back. Others would speculate on the same thing.

Calhoun laughed bitterly. Stella Morton was long out of his life. So was Dal Carter, his former partner. Grady Smith had brought him back. But who was going to believe that now?

Calhoun watched his back trail, and, when he was convinced the Half-Bit men weren't following him, he put the roan steadily over the miles to town. The black, bitter mood was on him again, and he wasn't sure why.

II

The Pacific Corral was at the lower end of town, near the little dun-colored railroad station. Calhoun left his horse there, ordering grain, giving the hosteler a dollar to rub down the roan well.

The afternoon was running out fast when Calhoun left the feed corral with only scabbard and carbine tucked under an arm. There was time to buy clean clothes, bathe, and shave before night. Townspeople were drifting to the depot to watch the train come in. Leaning indolently against the end of the station, where he'd usually been at this time in past years, was the urbane, graying figure of Rory McCloud, wearing his sheriff's star.

Calhoun saw McCloud come up straight on his heels and stare across the wide-rutted dust of Railroad Street. Then McCloud wheeled away from the depot and cut across the street with stiff-legged strides.

McCloud called — "Howdy, Dave!" — before stepping up on the boardwalk and falling in with Calhoun.

"Howdy, Rory."

McCloud had the usual toothpick in the corner of his mouth. Tall, slack-shouldered, the years of lawing rested deceptively on him. He looked pleasantly harmless.

They rounded the corner into Grand Street. McCloud had to break the silence. "Just get in, Dave?"

"Just."

"Staying with us long?"

"Depends."

"On what?"

"On me," Calhoun said without turning his head. "You trying to tell me something?"

"Anyone ever tell you anything and make it stick?" asked Rory McCloud mildly.

"It's been tried."

"I ain't fool enough to make that mistake," said McCloud. He spat the toothpick away and fingered a fresh one from his vest pocket. "Dal Carter," he added vaguely, "will be surprised."

"Dal have anything to do with my movements these days?" Calhoun asked evenly. Rory was probing at something. Calhoun held in to see what it was.

Jackson, the mercantile man, and Kennedy, a cattle buyer, came walking toward the depot. Jackson, a florid, hearty man, lifted his hand in greeting at McCloud. Then Jackson recognized Calhoun. The hand froze a second. Jackson mumbled — "Hello, Dave!" — and lumbered hurriedly by, his red face a study in startled surprise.

They made the first step up on the boardwalk along the east side of Grand Street, heels thudding in rhythm.

"Grady Smith will be surprised, too," McCloud said idly.

"Grady's in prison, isn't he?"

"You ain't heard? He's out?"

Calhoun ignored the sheriff's dry question. "So Grady's back?"

McCloud's puckered look was estimating him. "Not yet," he replied. "But if Grady comes to Kingsville, I wouldn't want anything to happen to him."

Calhoun walked in silence.

Rory McCloud sighed softly. "You heard that, Dave. Think it over."

They reached the stale beer smell around the open doorway of the First Chance Bar. Calhoun's recollection was dry, too.

160

"Right here is where you killed Kirk Clelland. I was at the tie rail there. Heard you speak to him. Saw you beat him to the draw."

"I hated it, Dave. Always hate to kill a man," McCloud said regretfully.

"I saw you kill Tom Shattuck, too," Calhoun added. "You did the same thing with Shattuck you did with Clelland. If Tom Shattuck had been watching for it, he'd probably have dropped you."

Rory McCloud digested that for several strides. "Joshing me, Dave?"

"Not today."

"Now," said Rory McCloud, "I'm real interested. What did I do with those two?"

Calhoun said soberly: "Think it over, Rory. Think it over real hard. Chances are I'm the only one whoever noticed it. And I'm not telling you, Rory. Might need it myself."

They came abreast of Svenson's Gold Dust Bar.

"Drink?" Rory invited.

"Some other time," Calhoun said, not pausing or glancing that way as McCloud turned into Svenson's.

McCloud would have his drink, too. He'd stand, thinking hard about those two gun fights, and what he'd done. It would stay with him, puzzling, disturbing him. Calhoun smiled faintly at the thought.

Grand Street had its false fronts, red brick, clapboards, weather-roughened adobes. The street dust, the boardwalks and tie rails, the business and pleasure along both sides, sliced through Kingsville like the richer center of a drab cake and thinned out into the stage road, striking toward the northwest range and Caddo Peaks — toward the hardscrabble Box S.

Little had changed. Yet the way ran ahead of Calhoun's gaze like a strange street. He walked it like a stranger, who had

161

seen it in a picture and so knew it, but it lacked any warmth of association. Across the street a wiry man in leather chaps, dark leather vest, and gray hat came briskly off the steps of Deever's Mercantile. He flipped reins off the rail and climbed a burr-tailed sorrel with one swing of easy agility.

The sorrel was wheeling into the street when the rider sighted Calhoun. He looked a second time, then almost violently swerved the horse in a quick slant across the rutted dust.

Calhoun stopped at the edge of the plank walk. He spoke first as the rider wheeled in alongside. "Looking for trouble?"

"Bet I've found it," the wiry one said, easing in the saddle. He spat. He reached for a tobacco sack in his vest pocket. His eyes, under bleached brows, were bright and keen. About Calhoun's age he dusted thirty. Chaps, vest, run-down boots, and old gray hat had seen hard use. So had the rifle in the saddle scabbard and the gun at his belt. His jaw had square lines. His cheekbones were high, and nose blunt. He looked tough. He was tough in the way of strong rawhide. His name was Curry Waldron, and he spat again. "You damn' long-legged polecat!" he said disgustedly, with the deep fondness a tough one like Curry Waldron would go to any lengths to hide.

Calhoun's smile hovered behind his eyes. "You knew I'd be back some day."

"Who told me?" Curry Waldron demanded. He sneered. "Not you. Nary a word from you." His disgusted look once more ran over Calhoun. He spat again.

Calhoun chuckled then. "I didn't mean to meet you on the street this way. Where you bunking?"

"Deaf Tom Keller's old shack in Blue Cañon. Got a few head in there under Keller's brand. Bought it from him last year before he moved on." Curry Waldron licked a cigarette, flared a match across the scarred leather of his chaps, and spoke cautiously through blown smoke. "Dal Carter's in town."

162

Calhoun nodded, not interested in that. "Seen any sign of Grady Smith? He's out."

Curry Waldron straightened to attention in the saddle. The news seemed to please him. "Might have known Grady was loose when I seen you." He spat again, thoughtfully now. "I'll look for him. You want Grady shot?"

"I want to talk with Grady *before* he is shot," Calhoun said with emphasis.

Curry thought that over. His look narrowed shrewdly. "If Grady's found dead, an' you're suddenly back, too, guess who'll be blamed?"

"Grady will be back, and Grady will be killed, so he can't talk to me . . . or anyone else," said Calhoun with flat conviction. He paused while two women walked past with their store packages. He heard their talk die suddenly, then take up furtively, heads closer together as they went on.

Curry grinned mirthlessly. "Cap Toller's wife an' Miz Sadie Bunch. Might as well yell it out now. They'll trot till bed time, tellin' how you're back."

Calhoun shrugged, his thoughts hard on something else. "Grady," he said, "won't believe he's in danger until the bullet hits him. Grady thinks he's safe and on a long-time payroll. He don't mean to talk to me. That's as far as Grady's thinking."

"When did you start reading Grady's mind?" Curry wanted to know.

"I've been to the prison twice to talk with Grady. I offered money for the truth of who shot Stella Morton's father. Grady sneered at it. Said he had all the money he needed."

"First time in his life he ever had any," said Curry flatly. "The snake was lyin'."

"He was telling the truth, Curry. The warden told me money came every month, to be banked for Grady."

Curry's lips formed a silent whistle. "Who'd send that one money?"

"It always came in bank notes. No name. The warden wouldn't tell me how much. He did say the letters were mostly postmarked Tipton City."

"Thirty miles from here," Curry said.

They eyed each other, as men do across common understanding. "If you cut Grady's sign, let me know," Calhoun said.

"Would Dal Carter like it?" Curry wondered casually.

"We can see."

Again they eyed each other. Curry said: "Be a pleasure to see." He put the burr-tailed sorrel up the street at a lope.

Calhoun continued on to the hotel, regretting the public encounter with Curry. He had considered Curry as good as an ace in a stud game, wickedly useful if not turned up. Now Curry might be less than useful. He might be in some danger himself if he made an overt move in this business, after talking in public with Dave Calhoun. But then Curry would expect that to happen.

Calhoun crossed the street and continued to Clackham's Grand Hotel at the next corner. His right hand had swelled a little. The knuckles hurt. It brought his thoughts back to the bunch at Tyndall's ranch. He wished now he'd mentioned all that to Curry Waldron.

Clackham was standing behind the little corner desk at the back of the hotel lobby — waiting for the train to bring him trade, Calhoun guessed. Orry Clackham was a small man, neat, precise. He wore black cloth sleeve guards, combed thinning sandy hair precisely from a side part. His eyes were bird-like, cautious. He was a covetous little man who barked thin-lipped commands at his help, strutted on his worn hall carpets, and scuttled from any real trouble.

Clackham whirled the register around and plucked a pen from the small shot-filled bowl at the end of the counter. "Yes, sir . . . room?" he greeted warmly. Then Clackham blinked, leaned forward against the counter a little, peering.

"Hello, Orry," Calhoun said, and a devil that was loose with his black mood since Tyndall's made him reach out and grip Clackham's other hand. "Good to see you, Orry."

"Uh, yes, yes," Orry Clackham stammered. "Uh, you're back, Calhoun?"

"No," said Calhoun gravely. "I'm somewhere else. Going to hang onto that pen, Orry?" He took the pen from Clackham's fingers, dipping the point in the crusted inkwell.

Clackham was not glad to see him. The wheels in Clackham's precise mind were plainly turning on the possibilities which might arise with Dave Calhoun in the hotel.

Calhoun signed his name boldly. Then the slightly swollen hand held the pen motionless for an instant above the page. A name near the top had leaped out at him. **Miss Stella Morton, Cross T Ranch.** Stell' Morton had registered yesterday. She was under the same roof. . . .

Clackham evidently hadn't noticed Calhoun's slight freeze. He turned and plucked a key from the rack. "I'll put you in two-ten, at the back," he said without any enthusiasm and laid the key on the counter.

Calhoun took it and slid the scabbard and carbine beside the register. "I'll go up later. Got some cleaning up to do after a long ride."

As he went out, Calhoun realized he hadn't really worried so much how he looked until he had seen Stella Morton's name. He thought that over bleakly and almost turned back to the hotel.

He'd been tried in court on the charge of killing Stella's father. All the past between them had ended before the trial.

Ferd Tyndall had said Stella was going to marry Dal Carter. But a man had to look decent. He'd intended to buy clothes when he reached Kingsville. And hunt up a barber the first thing.

Calhoun carried his purchases to Deak Preston's barber shop, on beyond the hotel and across the street. The very fat, genial barber was not Deak Preston. He said Deak Preston was dead, and his name was Lang. He wielded a skillful razor and shears. When he was through, Calhoun carried his packages into the back room where tub and hot water waited.

He soaped himself, let the hot water ease into the long days of riding, and put his thoughts on Grady Smith. It was on Grady's sworn testimony that he'd been tried for the death of Stella's father. Grady wasn't a man to go through with a lie like that without backing. Grady had been convicted that same week of rustling. The jury had let Calhoun go free, most of them not caring to hang a man on Grady Smith's testimony alone. But the damage had been done.

Now Grady had been free almost two weeks and hadn't appeared around Kingsville. Calhoun wondered blackly if Grady Smith might have decided never to come back. He'd often put himself in Grady's mind, and did so again, sitting in the hot soapy water. The answer he got reassured him. Grady would come back. He'd be safer around Kingsville range than anywhere Dave Calhoun might hunt him down. Grady would expect help from the man who'd sent money every month to the prison. He'd return, and his trail would lead to the man who'd backed him in wrecking Dave Calhoun. *Unless Grady was killed before Calhoun puzzled out the trail.* It was, in a way, a race to beat Grady's certain death, for which Calhoun would be blamed now that he was also back.

Calhoun dried himself deliberately and dressed in new underwear and dark broadcloth pants he let stay outside his boots. He had bought a plain gray shirt and black tie to wear with the broadcloth coat in town. His hat, with the bullet hole through the crown, he'd kept.

When he stepped out, the fat barber approved. "You ain't the same man, mister."

Calhoun looked in the mirror at his weather-dark, rather long-jawed face, impersonal now. "Clothes help," he said, paid, and walked out.

Lamps had been lighted in the barber shop and were glowing in stores and saloons. Calhoun walked with a gray thoughtful hardness in his eyes. He lost the hard look when he glanced through the window of a small café and saw the girl serving at the counter. He stopped.

She must have sensed the intensity of his look. Her head turned. She waved, almost as if she'd expected him to be there at any moment. Calhoun was already wheeling back a step to enter, realizing at the same time he was ravenously hungry. It also hit him that Gail Baker had waved the first friendly greeting he'd had, save from Curry Waldron. Gail was a friendly woman.

He walked to an empty stool at the back of the counter. The place was moderately filled. Gail was flushed and busy as she brought him a glass of water, knife, fork, spoon.

"I heard you were back, and wondered if you'd stop in."

"Wouldn't have looked for you, working in town," Calhoun told her.

"Working?" said Gail proudly. "I own this place."

"What about the ranch?"

"Uncle Bill's running it . . . what's left." Gail laughed softly. She had always been gay and competent, with a rich strong repose of strength beneath. She said now: "This is the most profitable pasture on the Anvil Ranch."

167

Calhoun could guess what was behind that comment. The small ranch hadn't been doing well. Gail was doing this to help out. He looked for sign of hurt in her brown eyes. Gail might have read his mind. She laughed again.

"Busy time, Dave. Are you going to eat?"

"All I can hold. Fix it and I'll like it."

Gail hurried to the kitchen. She had been Dal Carter's girl, and now of course she was not, with Dal and Stell' Morton going to marry. Calhoun frowned and started a cigarette. Everything that had seemed right and good was wrong now.

He saw, by the number of customers who came in, the little café evidently was profitable in a moderate way. Gail brought him a thick steak, perfectly browned potatoes, baked corn, stewed tomatoes, and a great wedge of dried peach pie. And rich strong coffee like he remembered she could make. Calhoun ate slowly, ignoring the tide of talk along the counter and at the three tables. When he was greeted, he replied pleasantly. And all the time he was aware everyone else was acutely conscious Dave Calhoun occupied the back stool.

He lingered, drinking more coffee, smoking, meeting Gail's glance now and then as she hurried back and forth. *Mavericks, both of them*, he thought. *Two left-overs, while the rest of it went on.*

The place began to empty. Gail came outside the counter and sat beside him, ignoring dirty dishes for the moment.

"Back for good, Dave?"

"No."

Gail hesitated. "You wouldn't want a job?"

"Cooking?" he asked wryly.

"That," said Gail cheerfully, "would finish wrecking the Anvil."

"That bad at the ranch?"

"It could be worse, I suppose. Uncle Bill's not a fire-eater." Gail's face had shadowed. She asked abruptly: "Why not, Dave?"

"I'll be busy."

"I thought so," Gail said under her breath. She picked a bit of bread crust off the counter and rolled it absently between her fingers. "You're back because of Stella and Dal."

Calhoun looked at her in astonishment. "You think that, too? Why . . . I wouldn't care. . . ." He stopped at the relief he caught, swift and secretive, on Gail's rounded cheeks. "You were worried about Dal," he guessed in a low tone.

"Of course not!" Gail denied. Her flush gave a lie to it.

Calhoun shook his head wonderingly. "I'm out of that," he said. "Got other business on my mind. I'm sorry, Gail."

There seemed nothing more to say. He stood up to pay and leave. Gail stood also, quickly. "Stay a little longer, Dave. I . . . I'm worried about something."

He nodded and sat down. Gail walked around behind the counter and brought him a fresh cup of coffee. Then she busied herself clearing off the counter.

Smoking, waiting idly, Calhoun noticed Gail glance often toward the front of the counter. Two customers paid and walked out. It left one man. He sat on the front stool, elbow on the counter, his back to Calhoun, his gaze through the front window on sidewalk and street. He wore the bib overalls of a nester. His old black hat had a defeated-looking sag to the brim. The same kind of sag was in his broad shoulders as he sat without moving. He'd come in since Calhoun had entered and evidently ordered one cup of coffee. The cup was there, ignored, at his elbow.

When Gail went to the man and spoke, he shook his head, not looking at her. Gail lingered a step away from him, behind the counter, and she looked worried.

Calhoun waited, puzzled. Gail also seemed to be waiting. Now and then she looked intently out the window. Always it was when someone was passing, on foot or horseback.

Then came the sharp trot of several riders, coming into town. The man stood up, big and quick-moving for all his clumsy look. He placed a nickel on the counter and lumbered out hurriedly. He carried a shotgun that must have been upright between his knees, hidden by his legs and body from where Calhoun sat.

Gail said: *"Dave!"* Calhoun was already on his feet. "He's Mister Soderholm, who lives out beyond the ranch, on North Fork," Gail added rapidly. "He's not himself tonight. Go after him, Dave! Don't let him get into trouble!"

"Who rode past just then?"

Red which might have been shame came on Gail's face. "Dal Carter and three of his men."

Calhoun's look was disgusted. "I'm not nursing Dal Carter these days."

"It isn't him!" said Gail fiercely, and she might have believed it. "It's the Soderholms. His wife and children. He's a good man. But something's cracked in him. I could see it in his eyes. But I wasn't sure until Dal rode by, and he hurried out."

Calhoun shrugged, wondering if Gail knew what she was asking. He was already on his way to the door. Soderholm had walked left, after the riders. He'd been striding fast.

170

III

Calhoun had lost his man. The widely spaced street lamps spread pools of wan yellow light in the black night shadows. Lighted windows made stretches of the boardwalks clear enough. At the corner, where Mountain Street crossed Grand, the hotel diagonally opposite, Calhoun paused for a moment, peering along Mountain Street.

The shadows were thicker either way on the side street. There was no stir of movement to suggest Soderholm's lumbering figure. Calhoun muttered displeasure at being caught in a business like this. *Anyone but Dal Carter!* As he crossed Mountain Street, he surveyed the hotel porch and horses at the hotel hitch rails. No group of four horses suggested Dal Carter and his men had tied there.

Then, as he passed under the street light at the corner, he had a clearer view of the block ahead to Valley Street. He made out, midway in the block, a high-sided freight wagon and, just beyond it, several riders had reined up, still in the saddle, discussing something. The night stir of people was moving on the walks. Looking ahead at the figures passing from wan light to darker shadow, it was hard to separate them.

Soderholm, unmistakably, moved out of a dark doorway ahead. He was plodding now, one deliberate step after another, as if he'd set his big, clumsy-looking body into motion, and was letting it carry on. Calhoun stepped out fast, brushing roughly by two men, not caring what they thought about it. Anger was gray and building in him at what he was caught with. He considered turning back, telling Gail Baker it was none of his business, or hers. He should have told her when she asked his help.

He thought of shouting roughly at Soderholm's back. But there was a dull, inflexible purpose about that back which warned that Soderholm wouldn't stop, or probably even hear. He had the look of a man moving automatically now, beyond the line of thinking or reasoning.

Calhoun broke into a half run, his fury growing because he was not sure why he was doing it. Perhaps because he and Gail were mavericks, and, because of the past, her trouble belonged with his.

Soderholm passed the leaders of the freight team. In a few steps he'd be able to look clearly along the high side of the wagon at the riders still bunched, talking. The shotgun came out from under his right arm, into the grip of big fists. There was no longer any doubt in Calhoun's mind about what would happen.

He wouldn't have cared. Scores of times in the past four years he'd tasted the thought of having Dal Carter under his own gun muzzle. But this, in a way, was different because Gail Baker didn't want it.

Calhoun came up fast, running on his toes lightly. He saw Soderholm stop, swing up the double-barreled gun. Calhoun drew the heavy Colt .45 from under his coat. He clubbed the long heavy barrel to Soderholm's sagging black hat. The tearing blast of one shotgun barrel flicked muzzle light and concussion against the night-shrouded street as Soderholm staggered.

The four men fell out of their saddles. Calhoun thought furiously: *A second too late . . . !* Probably buckshot had been fired. At that short distance it could tear a man into shreds. Not only Dal Carter, but the men around him.

Dal would have been the one closest, too. That silver-mounted saddle and bridle on the flashy cream horse, wheeling

172

in fright, would be Dal's. He'd always been a man for fancy trappings.

Soderholm was collapsing like a blasted tree, slowly, reluctantly. The shotgun bounced off the edge of the plank walk. The second cocked barrel went off with a roar into the dirt under the empty stretch of tie rail. The walk shook under Calhoun's feet as Soderholm's big body struck heavily.

Everyone in sight along the walk had found a doorway. Calhoun stood alone with the Colt in his hand. He saw with an odd sense of relief that the reins of the cream horse were being held firmly. The rider was keeping the horse between himself and the walk. The shot must have been high.

"It's all right, Dal!" Calhoun called curtly. "No more trouble."

"Who'n hell's talking?" the angry demand came back.

"Dave Calhoun."

"So this is what you were riding into town to try! I might have known it!"

"A man named Soderholm drew down on you with his shotgun," Calhoun said. "He's flat on the walk here. You're safe enough now." Calhoun let sourness blanket his anger. "You can come out from cover."

Then Calhoun stood very still as a thought knifed at him. *What had Dal said? So this was what you were riding into town to try? Dal had said . . . you were riding into town. How did Dal, just getting into town himself, know Calhoun had been riding to Kingsville? How, unless Dal had been to Tyndall's ranch, or talked with someone from Tyndall's?*

Dal hauled the cream horse's head cautiously to the tie rail, flipped reins around the rail, and ducked under. He'd drawn his side gun. He stooped, picked up the shotgun, and cursed from shaken nerves as he stepped on the walk with it.

The doorways were giving out people now. Feet were beginning to pound on the planks toward the spot. Dal Carter's three riders stepped up fast behind him. Soderholm was stirring, groaning at Calhoun's feet.

"Did you bring him here?" Dal demanded thickly.

He'd been a tall young man with ropy muscles and underlying explosiveness. He'd had a way of speaking with an echo of challenge, as if thrusting himself at opposition, whether it was there or not. He'd had short curly hair and tightness at the mouth corners. In four years Dal had put on weight. He was different, somehow. He even moved differently, with a new kind of arrogance. His manners held only challenging dislike as he stood, scowling.

"You know better than that," Calhoun retorted, ignoring the townsmen, beginning to flank around them. "If I ever go for you, Dal, it wouldn't be through another man."

"How'd you happen to be here?"

"I was asked to watch him."

"Who asked you?"

"Guess, damn you!" Calhoun sneered. "How's everything at Tyndall's?"

Dal exploded furiously. "What do I know about that horse thief?" Soderholm was dazedly trying to sit up. "This is what I know about!" Dal gritted. "Try to buckshot me, will he?" He kicked Soderholm square in the face. The man fell back. Dal's boot heel gouged down on Soderholm's nose and mouth, twisting. "I'll show him!" Dal said viciously.

Calhoun knew bleakly he was a fool, even while he whipped up his gun barrel. It caught Dal a smashing blow on the line of the jaw, dropping him so that he pitched against the bystanders.

The walk shook as the spectators stampeded away again. They expected Dal's three men to take it up. So did Calhoun. None of the three had worked on the V Loop while he was

174

half owner. He waited a moment, then said impatiently: "All right, all right. What about it?" His gun barrel tapped his leg.

The nearest one put hands out a little in front, empty. "The boss'll give orders," he said sullenly.

"Well, damn it, turn your backs then until he can give orders!"

They turned their backs.

Soderholm staggered up. His broad stolid face was a red smear, blood dripping from crushed lips and nose. Teeth had been broken, too. He spat one out dazedly.

"Get out of town quick, while you're alive," Calhoun told him coldly. "Get out of the country fast. That's the best advice I can give you, unless the sheriff hauls you back."

Soderholm spat out a mouthful of blood and mumbled in a bitter daze: "I was gettin' out, anyway! What else can a man do when his woman an' kids are hungry?"

He gave Dal Carter's lax figure a look of pure, dazed hate. His bloody mouth worked silently. He turned away, smearing the back of his hand across his mouth.

Calhoun spoke to the backs of the three men. "If Soderholm is murdered, taking his family off this range, the town will know who did it. Tell Carter to think hard, unless he owns the sheriff. And tell Dal to think hard twice before he stomps a helpless man in public."

Calhoun walked away, holstering the gun under his coat. He chanced the risk of a bullet at his back, but this was Rory McCloud's town. McCloud had never looked with favor on bullets in a man's back.

Pete Wade was right, Calhoun thought again blackly. *Nothing but trouble.* He wondered if he'd been a fool to mention Tyndall to Dal. He'd wanted to see what Dal would say before witnesses.

Calhoun cut across the street toward the hotel, thinking

about Carter. Dal had always been cold-blooded, if you penetrated his veneer of easy affability. But that kick, and grinding boot heel in Soderholm's helpless face had revealed a new, coldly arrogant viciousness in Carter. Dal had changed in four years, and for the worse. Yet, Stella Morton was going to marry him. She'd never seemed that kind of girl. Nor had she seemed the kind to be fooled by the man Dal Carter was now.

The hotel lobby had emptied to the verandah. A man, who looked like a drummer, asked an almost cheerful question as Calhoun tramped up the steps.

"What's the trouble over there, mister?"

"A gun went off," said Calhoun briefly without stopping. Orry Clackham was hovering nervously in the doorway. "Where's my carbine?" Calhoun demanded.

"The trouble over?" Clackham asked with obvious apprehension as he went to his lobby desk.

"Ask Dal Carter, if he comes in."

Clackham was pale as he stooped behind the counter and came up with the scabbard and carbine. He turned to the key rack, then gestured helplessly. "You kep' the key."

Clackham's fear that gun play might break out in his hotel was so obvious it struck some chord of humor in Calhoun. "Orry, I'll be in my room, trying to rest. Had a long day. Don't let anyone come up and disturb me." Calhoun made the request gravely. He winked. "Not even Dal Carter."

Clackham licked his lips, then nodded silently, as fear built in his bird-like, cautious eyes.

Calhoun smiled as he started up the carpeted stairs with their brass tread guards. Orry Clackham's fear for his property was the needed touch to put everything in perspective. Dal Carter wasn't going to invade the hotel, seeking Calhoun. It wouldn't be Dal's way.

Still smiling wryly, Calhoun walked back toward his room.

This hall upstairs was very quiet. The worn rose-patterned strip of carpet muted his steps. He looked almost against his will at room **207**. Clackham's precise writing had put **207** after Stell' Morton's name in the register. Dingy white paint covered the transom glass above the brown-painted door. Light glowed behind the transom and made a shining thread under the door.

This was the greatest folly of all. Calhoun did it from the satanic urge still stirring through his veins. He stopped and rapped on the door. He was smiling when brisk steps came to the other side, the knob turned, the door opened.

"Why Stell'," he said, "prettier than ever."

She had the tawny, burnished hair of the Mortons. It was down around her shoulders now in a curly, gleaming cascade. Not a tall girl, Stella's erect shoulders and restless grace gave an illusion of added height. She had fair skin and long lashes over stirring, green-blue eyes. There was a soft, provocative spirit in the width of her full-lipped mouth. And temper, too. The Morton temper, bred in all of them. But in Stella the temper had added spice to tangy richness.

Now there was no temper at first, as Calhoun had expected. Stella's hand caught the edge of the door frame, her other hand holding the doorknob. She was wearing a crimson dressing gown.

"You . . . Dave!"

"Hadn't you heard I'm back?" Calhoun questioned, smiling.

Stella shook her head. Uncertainty leaped into her eyes. "Those gunshots! Were you in that?"

"Must you," said Calhoun, "always believe I'm connected with shooting?"

Stella caught her breath. She said thinly: "Damn you, Dave." That was the Morton temper taking over.

"This will cause eyebrows to lift," suggested Calhoun. "And I've a thing or two to say to you." His grin was faint. "Might be the last chance . . . but if you're afraid to ask me in . . . ?"

Stella stepped back, wordlessly. He walked in. Stella closed the door and turned quickly away from it, restlessly, in small slippers whose heels padded against the carpet with her nervous steps.

"What is it?" she demanded in the same thin voice. Then she moved to the window, under lip caught between her teeth, and swung around, gazing full at him through the lamplight.

This was the girl he'd held in his arms, all fire and love. Calhoun said: "I built a house for you, and Dal bought it along with my half of the ranch." He chuckled. "If you live there with Dal, will the ghosts walk, Stell'?"

She said again, huskily: "Damn you! Is that what you wanted to say? If that's all, get out!"

Calhoun shook his head, sobering a little, still smiling faintly. "Not what I had on my mind, Stell'. I'm back for reasons of my own. Nothing to do with you . . . or Dal, as some people seem to think."

"Who thinks?"

Calhoun's gesture dismissed names. "You'll probably think so when you hear what happened across the street. Those shots were from a man named Soderholm, trying to get Dal Carter with a shotgun. I got to Soderholm in time." Stella had caught her breath. "He didn't hurt Dal," Calhoun assured her. His face and voice hardened. "But I did, with a gun barrel to the jaw. Dal will be all right. But I want you to know it had nothing to do with you."

Stella asked accusingly: "Why did you do it?"

"Ask Dal. You two seem to understand each other," Calhoun said disgustedly. It was in his look, his voice. It brought red, flaming, to Stella's cheeks.

"Dal," said Stella, "I can understand. But you . . . ?" She pushed her hand out, damning him.

"Once more . . . after four years . . . I didn't shoot your father."

"Then why did you run away after the trial?"

"Why did you run away from me when I needed one person who believed in me?" Calhoun asked with a bitterness he'd never wanted to show again. He stepped toward her, his voice lowering roughly. "A man you wouldn't dirty your quirt on accused me, and you believed it."

"It was my father who was killed!"

"And who was I?"

Steps came off the stairs and along the hall. Stella brushed past Calhoun and ran lightly on her toes to the door. Quickly, silently she turned the key. She was stepping back when knuckles rapped the door. The knob was tried.

"Stell'?"

That was Frank Morton, Stella's brother.

"What is it, Frank?" Stella replied calmly. She was forcing the calm.

"I want to talk."

"Not tonight. I'm getting ready for bed."

"You'll want to hear this!"

"I don't want to hear anything tonight. I'm sleepy."

Frank was exasperated. "Dave Calhoun is back! He's already hurt Dal!"

"Has he? How badly?"

"Enough! Don't you want to hear about it?"

"No."

Frank Morton, always notorious for his temper, spoke guardedly through the door. "Calhoun should have known better than to come back. We'll talk about it in the morning." Frank must have heard that Calhoun had gone up to his room on this floor. He must have felt sure that Calhoun could hear what was said in the quiet hallway. His voice had an ugly note.

After a moment Frank's steps went back to the stairs and down. Stella slowly opened her clenched hands. She was pale again. Her eyes had stayed almost fearfully on the scabbard and carbine Calhoun held.

"Frank has brooded about you, I'm afraid," Stella said abruptly. Her lips were stiff.

Calhoun said coldly: "Frank will start it, not me. But don't expect me to stand and let him kill me."

"Why are you back, Dave?"

"My business."

"There's trouble wherever you are," said Stella huskily.

Calhoun glowered at her. "Do you know who asked me to keep Dal from being shotgunned?"

"I don't care."

"You will. Gail Baker begged me to do it." Calhoun asked slowly: "Did you warn Gail you were going to take Dal from her? Or don't you warn your friends?"

Stella could move like an angry cat when aroused. She reached him in two quick steps and slapped him furiously.

Calhoun rubbed the smarting cheek and grinned. "Thanks, anyway, for keeping your brother out," he said as he stepped to the door.

"I was trying to protect Frank, not you!"

When he'd turned the key and his hand was turning the knob carefully, while he listened for other steps in the hallway, Stella asked suddenly: "If you didn't shoot my father, Dave . . . who did? And why?"

Calhoun glanced back at her. His look darkened. He was unconscious of the hardness dropping on his face. "Some day I'll know," he promised evenly. "I'll tell you then . . . and Frank, if he's alive."

The hallway was empty. Quietly he walked back to his room door at the head of the back stairs and got in, he felt sure, without anyone knowing he'd been in Stella's room.

It had been a fool thing to do. Frank Morton — Dal Carter . . . either one could have turned that harmless visit into a bloody gun fight, grudges, hates being what they were now.

He was asleep quickly. His last thought was of the cascade of gleaming, tawny hair about Stella's angry face.

IV

Early morning sun was warming the high false fronts along the west side of Grand Street when Calhoun walked into the small Home Café for breakfast. Gail Baker, fresh and briskly busy at her half-filled counter, gave him a grateful smile and nod as he walked back to the same rear stool.

On her hurried way to the kitchen, Gail said under her breath, "Thanks, Dave."

A little later, when she brought the platter of ham and eggs he had ordered, Calhoun said: "Any message for your Uncle Bill?"

"Are you going to take the job?" Gail asked with quick hope and a quick smile.

"I might."

Her look had relief and pleasure. Calhoun leaned forward. His question was audible to Gail alone. "Did anyone ever say where Dal got the money to buy my half of the V Loop?"

Gail was a good actress. Only her brown eyes were startled, speculative with a light shade of apprehension. She shook her head slightly, denying it. "Why, Dave?"

He cut into the ham, smiling. "Merely curious," he muttered. "Dal told me he borrowed it, but wouldn't say where."

"Does it matter now?" Gail was still caught by apprehension.

Calhoun halted the first bite of ham at his mouth. "How could it?" he agreed.

Gail gave him a doubtful look. It stayed on her mind, he saw, as she passed back and forth. He finished eating, rolled a smoke, and, when the adjoining stools were empty, his slight gesture brought Gail around the end of the counter to stand beside him.

Again Calhoun spoke under his breath. "One favor back."

Gail nodded instantly.

Calhoun said: "You hear all the town talk in here. Has Grady Smith been seen around?"

Gail's lips parted slightly under the impact of what that meant, coming from Dave Calhoun. She shook her head.

"If you hear anything about Grady, send word to your Uncle Bill at once. Or tell Curry Waldron, if he's in town." Calhoun made the request mildly.

Gail's sober look considered him before she nodded. Her hand, warm and firm, went out and touched the back of his hand. "I never believed his story, Dave." Gail hesitated. A slight flush heightened her color. "I don't think Stella did either . . . in her heart."

Calhoun looked at her impassively. "Does that matter now?"

He stood up, wondering about the ways of women. He was still wondering, as he went down the street and bought a range outfit, including a bedroll, to be picked up by the Anvil wagon when it came to town. He was coming off the steps of Deever's Mercantile Store when his name was called from a two-horse buggy that had pulled up.

The gnomish figure, hunched on the seat, looked hardly the size of a boy. But no boy ever had that bony face with high-arched nose. Or the red-flecked eyes with their steady glare. The man had a slight arch in his back that threw his narrow shoulders into a bad stoop. He was bone mostly, with dry parchment-looking skin tightly drawn over those bones. His lips were thin, bloodless as the man himself seemed. And yet, for all that, there was no aura of hate, malice, or evil about the hunched figure.

He was Bror Neilson, and he had been rolled and broken by a horse when a boy. What grew into the man was this, and more. Behind that red-flecked steady glare, Bror Neilson could think as fast as anyone. Faster than most. He'd pulled together the sizable Buzzard Wing Ranch, as Neilson had called his wing-shaped brand. He used a buggy, mostly. But perched lightly on his specially-built saddle, with stirrups adjusted for one shorter leg, he could ride with any man.

"Howdy, Mister Neilson," Calhoun greeted politely, going to the buggy wheel.

Neilson had a high voice with the sound in it of paper crackling. "Heard you were in town, Calhoun. Want to ride for the Buzzard Wing?"

"No," Calhoun said calmly.

"Going to work for anyone else?"

"Perhaps."

"Who?"

"No short answer meant, Neilson, but that's my business."

Bror Neilson's cold glare rested on him. "Ride out, if you change your mind," he said. His team of big blacks surged to a shake of the reins, leaving Calhoun standing there in a drift of dust.

Calhoun crossed the street, pondering this meeting. He saw Rory McCloud, the sheriff, step out of the doorway of Sill's Saddle Shop and swing to fall in with him as he stepped up on the walk.

"Neilson hire you?" McCloud inquired, taking a toothpick from the corner of his mouth.

"No. Did he talk to you about it?"

"Nope. I guessed that it was on his mind when I seen him waitin' for you."

"What are you going to do about Soderholm's try at Dal Carter?" Calhoun inquired.

"Nothin'," said Rory McCloud matter-of-factly. "What's Carter goin' to do about you dropping him?"

"Ask Dal."

"His jawbone is cracked. He can't talk much." Rory McCloud sighed. "I can figure lots of things . . . but I ain't figured yet how come you jumped in an' saved Carter's skin, an' then dropped him cold before you walked away."

"Think on it, Rory," Calhoun invited soberly.

"I keep busy thinkin' what I did wrong in them gun fights with Kirk Clelland an' Tom Shattuck," said McCloud gloomily. "You wouldn't want to tell me now?"

"No."

Calhoun had the bleak, wary feeling the sheriff was talking all around what was on his mind. But McCloud was that way. He was a man to watch and wait, and to make no hasty moves. Which, perhaps, explained why he'd been sheriff so long. He offended few people unless forced to act.

McCloud seemed to make up his mind about something. He said — "I'll see you later." — and wheeled off the walk to cross the street.

Bror Neilson's buggy had stopped at the depot. Five armed Buzzard Wing riders were about the buggy now, almost like a bodyguard. But when Calhoun turned along Railroad Street toward the feed corral, the buggy cut over toward him without the riders following.

Calhoun halted as the buggy sided him. Bror Neilson's high crackling voice said: "I forgot one thing." He was peering coldly. "Last night, did you ask Carter how everything was at Tyndall's?"

"I did."

"Why?"

There was something about Bror Neilson that held Calhoun for a moment. Something, he restlessly felt, which should have meaning to him. But it eluded him. He said almost absently: "Not wanting to give you another short answer, Mister Neilson. . . ."

"But it's none of my damned business!" Bror Neilson's high voice finished without rancor. Neilson hunched, glaring. "A fool four years ago . . . a fool now!"

"So?" said Calhoun, suddenly alert. "Why?"

Neilson mimicked him, mockingly. "Not giving a short answer, young man . . . but none of your business . . . unless you're riding for the Buzzard Wing."

The blacks sprang forward again at an almost invisible signal through the reins. The buggy wheeled so fast it rocked dangerously. This time the five riders lined out from the station and fell in behind, as the buggy swerved fast into Grand Street and vanished.

Calhoun smiled sourly. He'd invited that, and Neilson had come off best. For Calhoun had been left with a gnawing black desire to know all that was in the gnomish man's mind. *A fool four years ago* . . . when he'd sat in court, accused of killing old Sam Morton, on Grady Smith's testimony? *A fool then, a fool now?* — and Bror Neilson spoke like a man certain of his knowledge.

The Anvil was a small ranch in the Caddo foothills. Uncle Bill Baker owned it. He'd raised Gail. She'd have the ranch some day.

Calhoun had cut directly across the range. He rode easily down the last short stretch of grassy slope to the small, neat clapboard house. A squatter, sturdier log bunkhouse was out back, near the corrals and sheds. The whole place had a neat, pleasant look. The flowered curtains at the windows were Gail's touch. So were the flower beds at the side and front of the house. Calhoun hardly noticed that the flower beds had not

186

been spaded and planted this year. He was scanning, speculatively, an old rickety four-horse wagon, standing behind the house, loaded with a few pieces of battered furniture, lumpy mattresses, a stove, plow handles showing over the side boards.

A thin, expressionless boy about nine in patched overalls was standing at the nearest corral bars, listlessly eyeing four gaunted horses inside. A smaller girl in a faded cotton dress stepped out the back door. She saw Calhoun, riding into the yard, and darted back into the house.

Calhoun rode to the corral. "Where's Bill Baker, son?"

The boy pointed north. "He jis' rode off."

"What's your name?"

"Mark Soderholm."

Calhoun had guessed it already, but when he said — "Where's your father?" — and the boy said sullenly — "I dunno." — Calhoun guessed again, with almost explosive irritation. "He didn't come with the rest of you?"

The sullen, frightened look on the boy's face was enough. Calhoun rode the way the boy pointed, pressing the red roan into a high run. In less than a mile he raised a trotting rider in the distance ahead. A shot from his Colt turned the rider back to meet him.

Bill Baker, a wiry, aging man with a close-cropped gray mustache had brown eyes like Gail's. Usually free with a wry humor, Baker was sober today behind his surprised and welcome greeting.

"Going after Soderholm?" Calhoun inquired.

"That squarehead fool!" Baker exploded. "His fam'ly drove in a little while ago, scared. Soderholm come home late last night with his face a mess."

Calhoun told about it, leaving out Gail's part, and adding casually that Gail had hired him for part-time help, if her uncle was agreeable.

"Hell, yes," Bill Baker agreed instantly. "Part time, full time, any time, Dave! Wisht I had forty like you. I'm mad an' gettin' madder. Light an' roll one while I figger you in."

Calhoun said: "I don't know anything, Bill. I've saved the questions for you to answer."

Presently, sitting cross-legged on the grass across from Calhoun, scowling with his thoughts, Bill Baker said: "It ain't a long story . . . but it's dirty. Frank Morton took over the Cross T after his father was killed. Dal Carter had all the V Loop after he bought you out. Somethin' happened to them two. They began to crowd an' gobble. They got bigger an' got greedier. The lawyer you had at your trial, young Hilar Sudbury, had been lawin' for them with more tricks than old Judge Rideout ever guessed. But bein' legal ain't stopped 'em when they had a move ready. Latest trick they've done is buy, steal, an' lease water rights up the Cahona Valley. Cross T done that. But you'll find V Loop waterin' there, usin' the free grass to the west."

"Which cuts off Bror Neilson that way," Calhoun interjected instantly. Now he began to understand the gnomish little man's offer of a job. He asked: "What about Soderholm?"

"He's one of them homesteaders over on North Fork," said Baker glumly. "I don't like 'em too much myself. But all the land they can fool with lays in that stretch of bottoms. They can't spread off the bottoms to any real cow land. Last two years there was drought, an' it was bad on them, like on everyone else. Worse maybe. They come in with a plow, a prayer, an' a sack of meal. And always kids to feed. Things don't go right . . . they're in trouble, fast."

"Soderholm wasn't in town shooting at a drought."

"V Loop took over Mobey's land on the benches this side of North Fork. That seven mile stretch of bottoms is all plowed an' fenced in," said Bill Baker. "Soderholm took up farthest this way."

Calhoun thought a moment. "That puts Soderholm at Mobey's Crossing," he estimated. "No good plow land this side."

"Smack at the crossin'," Baker agreed. "North Fork is high cutbanks an' quicksand, either way from the bottoms. An' quicksand an' fences through the bottoms now. There never was no right-of-way road at Mobey's Crossing. A mulehead like Soderholm just squatted an' plowed an' fenced. It didn't matter until Dal Carter wanted that crossing, to connect with the benchland on the other side."

"He could have bought or bargained."

"Ain't Carter's way any more. He just had the mulehead's fences cut, an' he run in a few hundred steers night before last. What they didn't eat, they walked down. Made three bad years in a row for Soderholm an' busted him, with nothin' ahead for winter. Joe Farley, the tough V Loop ramrod Carter put on after you left, told Soderholm to hire a lawyer. Soderholm didn't have grub money for his family, let alone lawyer money an' a year or two to law about it."

Calhoun asked thoughtfully: "How about the other homesteaders?"

"Soderholm is the best of them. The rest ain't in any better shape for a fight. They're squattin' the bottoms there like chickens with a fox under the roost, each hopin' he won't be grabbed."

Calhoun snorted disgustedly, then shrugged. "Poor devils. Can't blame them, I guess. Bill, has Soderholm proved up his homestead?"

"I think so. This summer, seems to me. I ain't sure."

Calhoun stood up. A bitter, bleak humor was in his half smile. "I'll get Soderholm. Go to work for you a little later,

Bill. If your wagon goes to town, there's some stuff at Deever's for me."

Bill Baker regarded him narrowly. "One man can bite so big he chokes."

Calhoun laughed. "I've seen a beaver-cut tree brought down by small bites."

"You interested in bringing Dal Carter down?" Bill Baker demanded tartly.

Calhoun shook his head. "Just curious," he said. "Dal backed off when I needed a partner siding with me in that Grady Smith business." Calhoun's bitterness sawed in his tone. "In fact, Dal had a loss of memory about some things that would have helped me. He offered a skinflint price for my share of the ranch. I knew by then he'd steal it from me if I went to prison, which looked likely at the time. That or hanging. I took the cash and let Dal go until later."

Bill Baker's cagey nod understood many things. He rose himself. "Sure you don't want me along?"

Calhoun's shake of the head denied it. "Might not be back for a day or so," he estimated as he approached his saddle. "Soderholm will be in tonight. Tell his wife so."

Frank Morton was inclined to be sulky with his sister while Kingsville blurred behind them in the distance. It was midday under a brilliant blazing sun. Frank rode with his gray hat pulled forward, shading his handsome, aggressive face. He was a tawny, golden-tanned, broad-shouldered young man, with the marks of his reckless temper molded into assertive impatience.

"Fine thing, leaving Dal alone in the hotel," Frank said finally.

They rode alone, Stella in a divided skirt, her tawny hair up under her own gray hat, soft leather gloves on her hands.

Some distance back a buckboard trailed them, carrying purchases and a small leather trunk with Stella's town clothes.

She said sharply: "Dal's jaw is his own business. I can't help him there."

"Fine talk about the man you're going to marry!" Frank charged irritably.

"I heard what Dal did to that man's face. It was cruel, unnecessary."

"What was buckshot at Dal's back?" Frank reminded angrily.

"More trouble with our neighbors. I'm getting tired of it, Frank. Don't forget I'm half owner of the Cross T."

"And doing all right, thanks to Dal and me."

"I'm not so sure," said Stella under her breath. "You had all the answers after father died. You and Dal. I didn't care much about anything for a time. Now . . . ," Stella caught her lip under white teeth, frowning.

Frank's sulkiness turned ugly, as it often had the last year or so. "Mind your own business, Stell'." He used a brother's insight to jeer. "Don't let Dave Calhoun get under your skin again! We've been waiting for him to come back."

Stella's hand went furiously to the braided leather quirt at her saddle horn. Frank saw the gesture and placated sulkily. "Cut it out, Stell'. You know how I feel about you."

After a moment Stella nodded, forgiving him. "What about Dave Calhoun?" she persisted.

"You know what he did to us," Frank said with ominous calm. "I've been waiting."

Stella reminded tightly: "Dave could always shoot faster, straighter than you. Remember?"

"Leave that to me. I'm the man of the family."

"I've left things to you," Stella said absently. "And to Dal." She turned the subject. "I spoke to Hilar Sudbury about that man, Soderholm. Hilar said Soderholm was in a rage about Dal's cattle getting into his crops, and it was a legal matter now. Hilar said it wouldn't amount to much."

A sly, amused satisfaction entered Frank's look. "Hilar was right. A homesteader always makes trouble."

Stella decided abruptly. "I want to hear Soderholm's side of it."

"You keep out of Dal's business, Stell'!"

"When I marry Dal, his business will be mine. A funeral isn't my idea of a wedding. I'm going to see that homesteader. Want to ride with me?"

"I do not!"

Stella quirted her horse off the road, taking the straight line for North Fork. Frank watched her go with angry indifference. Stella was in no danger from the homesteaders. She'd not hear anything she'd not learn later, anyway. His simmering thoughts were back on Dave Calhoun.

In Kingsville Rory McCloud patiently tramped the worn stair carpet to the second floor of Clackham's hotel. Rory's knock at a front corner room was answered by one of the V Loop riders. The man's hand was close to his side holster until he saw who it was.

McCloud said: "This a fort or a sick room?" He walked in and looked at Dal Carter, in a rocking chair by one of the front windows. Dal had plaster tape all along the right side of his jaw. A quart whiskey bottle and a glass of water rested on the carpet by his chair. "It looks bad," he said with bland sympathy. "You want a paper served on Calhoun?"

Dal's look was baleful. "I'll tell you if I do." He had to speak with mushy thickness because his jaw was taped almost motionless.

"How about that nester?"

192

"Get out," Dal said thickly. "I'll tell you when I need you."

"You been doin' it," Rory McCloud said humbly. "You and young Morton." Rory fingered in his vest pocket for a toothpick, found only a broken one, and looked at it regretfully. "That Soderholm kind of got excited, I guess. He ain't bad. No use bringing him in to jail. He'll move out like Dave Calhoun told him to."

"Don't bother me about him."

"Shouldn't have, bad as you feel," decided McCloud mildly. He put the toothpick stub in the corner of his mouth. "Must be old home week," he remarked absently. "Dave Calhoun comes back. Now Ike Morris, my deputy, comes in on the train from Tipton City, an' says he seen Grady Smith, buyin' a saddle hoss. Grady come to Tipton on the train. Told Ike he aimed to ride out and find a job."

Dal sneered. "You better lock up that thief."

"Can't, until he breaks a law," McCloud said patiently. "Hope you heal quick, Dal."

McCloud went back down the stairs with a certain frustration in his look. But when, less than an hour later, Ike Morris, the ruddy-jowled, hearty deputy, came into McCloud's cluttered office in the courthouse, McCloud turned from the old rolltop desk expectantly.

Ike's hearty face was grinning ruefully. "You hit another guess right, Rory. A V Loop 'puncher just got Carter's cream horse out of Reddick's Stable. You sure it was only a guess Carter would pull out?"

"Uhn-huh," Rory said. "But don't go talkin' about my guesses." Rory turned back to his desk. "A man can get too good at guessing," he muttered.

V

The day blazed, hot and silent, as Calhoun rode across the benchland toward North Fork. This was good grass. He could understand Dal Carter's scheming to get it. The few V Loop cattle he sighted were probably some of the bunch shoved onto Soderholm's land, then moved across the ford.

The benchland ended abruptly in a deeply dropping slope. A sluggish channel hugged the bottom of the descent. The fertile bottoms were on the other side, a quarter to a half a mile wide, six or seven miles long, built up high enough to miss flood water. The bottoms lay in a great curve. Only the upper portion was visible from the ford. Above and below the bottoms, the channel ran between high, impassable banks.

A cow could wade across at any point along the bottoms and would probably mire in quicksand. Only here, at this upper end, did the shallow current run over firm bottom. Soderholm's log cabin and pole horse shed stood about a hundred yards from the river. Calhoun let the roan drink and rode, splashing, for the other side.

He pulled up suddenly as the dull boom of a rifle shot warned him. The moan of a heavy bullet passed close. Calhoun pushed a palm out, empty, and rode slowly on. As he neared the cabin, Soderholm's heavy figure emerged from the doorway, finger on rifle trigger.

He'd changed to clean bib overalls and had shaved. The whole front of his stolid face was still raw and swollen. Something had happened to the man. Shoulders had straightened out of their defeated sag. The bleached, blue eyes held a desperate ferocity.

"Know me?" Calhoun inquired laconically.

Soderholm's swollen mouth mumbled, "Yep . . . now." His big hand gripped an old Sharps buffalo gun, long-ranged, deadly.

"Sounded like a Sharps when it passed," Calhoun remarked. He looked out at the broken fences and trampled corn and row crops. "Your wife got to the Anvil."

Soderholm nodded.

"A dead man here won't help her raise the kids."

Soderholm swept one arm at his small homestead, his trampled crops. "That don't either," he said thickly. "I've had enough."

Calhoun dismounted. "I'll buy your crops like they are. I'll rent your place for a year. Four hundred cash in eagles, when you write it, sign it, and promise to move your family on for a year."

"Gold? Four hundred?" said Soderholm vacantly. The ferocity in his look began to blaze. "You lie! Bound to be a lie! The crop's ruined!"

Calhoun went into the soft leather money belt under his shirt. In his hat crown he dribbled gold double eagles. They caught the sun in yellow sheen. Sweat started on Soderholm's puffy face.

He mumbled, "Grub for two years."

Calhoun passed him the hat.

"Write it out. Two copies. Date it three days ago. It's not charity, Soderholm."

The homesteader's big callused fingers hesitantly forked down through the gold coins. The hand became unsteady. Soderholm wheeled and lumbered blindly into the cabin with the hat and Sharps rifle.

Calhoun walked slowly around the bare, but clean, yard. He was studying the lay of the homestead, the ford, the higher land beyond the bottoms.

Soderholm came out. He had the look of a man born again. His bleached eyes were excited. His raw mouth smiled apologetically. "Best I could find to write on," he said, tendering two old envelopes.

With a chewed pencil stub he'd written on the back of each envelope:

I, Mark Soderholm, sell my crops and rent my homestead land on North Fork for one year from this date, to Dave Calhoun, for cash in hand, now paid to me.

His hat shoved back on his head, Calhoun read the text carefully, checked the date, handed one copy to Soderholm.

"Give this one to Bill Baker at the Anvil," he directed.

Soderholm hesitated. "Mister . . . I'm curious."

Calhoun smiled bleakly at him. "You're on my land now, Soderholm. Ride off to your family." A thought struck Calhoun. "Another fifty for that Sharps and all the loads you've got for it."

Soderholm thrust the heavy rifle at him. "About twenty shells. No money for it. I've got enough."

Soderholm had kept one sag-backed, old plow horse in the pole shed. Calhoun watched him vanish over the higher ground beyond the ford. Then Calhoun explored his property, whistling softly between his teeth.

Soderholm had charcoal-lettered **KEEP OFF** on soap-box boards and nailed them to fence posts, facing the ford, and on the opposite side of his property. The cabin was barren inside, save for three empty boxes, upended. On one box were piled the Sharps cartridges. On another box were some corn dodgers,

196

wrapped in newspaper, and a dressed rabbit. Wood coals smoldered in the fireplace.

Calhoun made sure the Sharps was loaded. He left it in the cabin and rode leisurely out of the bottoms and to the east. He had been prepared to wait a day, even two. From a low knoll he sighted a drift of dust, then a bunch of cattle trailing lackadasically toward the bottoms. About a hundred head, three riders. Calhoun kept behind the knoll and returned to the bottoms. This was luck.

The other homesteaders were keeping away from this upper end of the bottoms. A great waiting stillness hung over the scene as Calhoun loped back to the cabin. He led the roan horse in a tight squeeze through the front doorway and tied his handkerchief over its nervous, inquiring eyes. Then, again whistling softly between teeth, Calhoun put the Sharps' cartridges in his coat pockets, carried the box into the lean-to kitchen room behind the cabin, sat down comfortably, and rolled a smoke.

The cabin faced the river. He could look out through the one-glassed back window and see over most of the homestead. The cattle finally came on the skyline and poured down to the homestead bottoms, where broken fences were now no bar. The 'punchers pulled up and let the herd spread out into the trampled corn, mashing and eating.

The 'punchers watched the cabin for a few minutes. Then one rode to the nearest **KEEP OFF** sign. He bent down and wrenched it from the post. He went on to the next sign and ripped it away, too. Then he saw one of his companions head for the cabin, and joined him.

Calhoun closed the door into the front part of the cabin where his horse stood quietly. He leaned the Sharps rifle in a corner and placed himself beside the back doorway.

The plank door was open. A man would have to thrust

head and shoulders in, or enter, to see him standing against the wall boards. Calhoun had no exact plan. He'd have to take it as it came. It was logical the deserted cabin would be investigated.

The two 'punchers pulled from a trot to a walk as they entered the yard. Their talk was audible. "Looks like that damn' sodbuster sure pulled out."

"Don't it? Clean as a whistle. Knowed what to expect after last night in town, I guess."

"We better see if he took everything. Farley'll want a report on that."

They stepped down

"Sure gone," said one as he reached the doorway. He tramped in. The other man followed at his heels.

"All but me!" said Calhoun mildly.

Their startled jumps were almost ludicrous. So were instinctive slaps toward their side guns, then a quick lift of hands as they backed away from the cocked Colt in Calhoun's fist.

The one with the thick-set torso, shortish bowed legs in hide chaps, and a knotty, mottled face, had been with Dal Carter last night in Kingsville. Surprise narrowed to a watchful glitter in his dark eyes. "Hired out to a sodbuster, huh, Calhoun?"

The other one was younger, lanky, with high, wide cheekbones, heavy, blotched freckles, and a narrow, sly mouth. Calhoun spoke to him.

"Fun tearing down those keep off signs, wasn't it?"

His name had added a shock of surprise to the younger one's gaze. That passed now in an uncertain grin, a look at the older 'puncher.

"Who's the other one out there?" Calhoun questioned. He was mild, patient, and could see them weighing his manner.

The older one said: "He's Carter's ramrod, Joe Farley."

198

"Big man for a little job like this," Calhoun murmured. "Your names?"

They were Bates and Hagan.

Calhoun ordered: "Backs to me. Drop your belts and guns, walk over to the wall, and hug it."

Hagan, the older one, sneered. "Calhoun, I wouldn't like to be you!"

"I like it," said Calhoun dryly. "Quick, now."

Their heavy belts, with cartridge-filled loops and guns in the holsters, thudded to the rough-sawed floor planks. They marched to the wall and faced it in stiff, surly silence.

Calhoun tossed the belts over beside the door. The easy trot of Farley's horse was coming into the yard. Calhoun said almost idly: "Don't call my hand, boys. It's not worth it. Let him come in."

Farley, not at all suspicious, stepped down from his horse and walked in, calling: "You two going to bed down in here?"

"Hold it!" Calhoun said sharply from the right side of the door, against the wall.

Farley, a lean, quick-stepping man, had sighted him with a sudden side look and clawed at his gun. Fast, too, while he plunged on in from the door, making a tricky target. This one was a natural gunman, gambling to match surprise with surprise.

Calhoun jumped too, following the man. He saw by the desperate look that Farley hadn't expected it. Now it was too late for either to stop. Farley's long-barreled revolver was clearing the holster when Calhoun's smashing shot drove it out of his hand, spinning it to the floor.

Farley's moving legs crossed under the shock. He almost fell, then recovered balance, blood dripping from his lacerated fingers. The other two had ducked and turned hopefully as the shot crashed. They now froze there as Farley turned a wild and mounting rage at them.

"Damn it, why didn't you warn me?"

"You didn't do any better than we did," Hagan retorted defensively. "He's Dave Calhoun!"

The name brought Farley's rage to a calculating focus on Calhoun. "Last night in town. Now here," he said, and lifted his bleeding hand. "What are you trying, mister?"

Calhoun spoke impatiently for he'd been close to killing a man, and didn't like it. "I'll stand outside the door while you three step out and turn to the right. Don't make a try for your horses."

They did it silently.

When they were at the corner of the cabin, Calhoun ordered with the same dark impatience: "Now walk back the way you came. Sit on the slope, outside the fences. I'll bring your horses when I'm through."

They headed across the field, stepping awkwardly over trampled cornstalks, arguing angrily. Farley was binding a handkerchief over his injured hand.

Calhoun took their carbines from saddle scabbards and collected their gun belts. He carried the lot to a well dug a few steps behind the cabin and dumped them over the log curbing. Then he walked around front and led the roan horse out. From the saddle he watched the trudging men reach the rising ground down which they'd driven the small herd. They stood and watched Calhoun begin to bunch the cattle, then drift them slowly to the lower end of the homestead, below the ford. This, too, Calhoun did not really fancy. But the black, hard mood was on him, fanned by the Mortons' Cross T brand on many of the steers. Frank Morton and his sister were preying on Soderholm's helplessness as cold-bloodedly as Dal Carter. The lot of them were working together, as Bill Baker had said.

When he had the bunched cattle moving right, Calhoun

drew his six-shooter, yelled, and drove them into a run with roaring shots. The leaders ran out into the shallow current with tremendous splashing. Calhoun turned back to the cabin. He saw the three V Loop men, watching helplessly.

The lead steers got almost halfway across before they bogged down. There was frantic scrambling and splashing. Some of the cattle had stopped and were turning uncertainly back. A third, at least, were in the quicksand.

Calhoun got the Sharps out of the kitchen, gathered the reins of the three horses, and led them out into the middle of the homestead. He left the horses there, ground-tied, and rode to Farley and his men. They were watching the bogged cattle in futile anger.

"I tried to put 'em across for you," Calhoun told them blandly. "Looks like they ran into quicksand."

"You knew damn' well they'd hit quicksand!" Farley accused furiously. "By God, you'll pay for this!"

"My rent receipt is only dated three days ago," Calhoun told him with bland truth. "I haven't tried to put any cattle across before. Yours have downed my fences, trampled the crops I bought, and raised hell generally. It'll cost you an order on the V Loop for two hundred dollars to come on my land with your horses and start roping your beef out of the sand. Read this."

Calhoun handed down Soderholm's envelope. Farley turned dark with rage as he scanned the writing. He slapped the envelope back in Calhoun's hand.

"I ain't giving any order on the V Loop!"

Calhoun rode back to his land without comment.

Stella Morton heard the thin far echoes of Calhoun's gun, driving the cattle into a run. She reined up, listening, heard no more shots, and rode on leisurely. She was at the drop of

201

the grassland before she sighted the river, and the struggling mass of bawling cattle. Wide-eyed, startled, it took her a moment more to note the three riderless horses in the trampled cornfield, and a man lounging near them on a fourth horse, evidently interested in the cattle.

Then Stella saw the men on foot at the bottom of the slope. She recognized Farley, and quirted her horse in a reckless rush down the long slope to them.

Joe Farley, rage fanned by the pain in his hand, forestalled her questions. "Dave Calhoun ran 'em in the quicksand! He wants a V Loop order for two hundred dollars to let us get our horses in the field there and yank them critters out before it's too late!"

Stella's lip curled. "Dave Calhoun put the three of you afoot?"

"He hid in the cabin an' surprised us. Shot me in the hand," said Farley, showing the blood-soaked handkerchief around his fist. "Gimme your horse, Miz Morton! Lemme get help here to settle this!"

Stella said angrily: "It's a twenty mile round trip. I'll talk to Dave Calhoun for Dal Carter."

Calhoun watched her quirt toward him and greeted her politely. "Stop and rest a while, Stell'."

"So you lied about last night in town," Stella accused hotly. She lashed her quirt tip at the floundering cattle. "You're really back to get at Dal."

Calhoun handed her Soderholm's envelope. "Not as good a house as I built for you, Stell'. But it'll do, if I'm left in peace. You can see what's been done to me already. Fences down. Crops I bought ruined. And now this bunch of cattle run in today." A bland, cold demand was in Calhoun's question. "You and Dal trying to run me out of the country? Half of these cattle today are Cross Ts. Yours."

"*You*, a homesteader?" Stella said a little wildly, righteous anger suddenly left unsupported. Her look hated him for the chill amusement shading his impassive politeness.

Calhoun took back the envelope. "Two hundred dollars from the V Loop or the Cross T, like I told Farley, or the whole lot can go down in the sand tonight." He patted the heavy Sharps, resting across his saddle. "It's a good strong cabin to fort up in," he added thoughtfully.

Stella was white with anger, made worse because everything was wrong. Because Dave Calhoun had tricked himself into a righteous stand.

"I'll pay," Stella yielded angrily.

"Cash, or an order on the Cross T," Calhoun requested impassively. "I can law about an order, if it's not paid."

Stella said in a breathless scorn: "You fool, you fool! Dal and Frank won't take this peacefully." She tore off a glove, fumbling in a saddlebag for her leather handbag. It held checkbook and pencil.

Calhoun scanned the check she scrawled. He jutted his chin at the three horses. "There they are. Tell your bullies I threw their guns down the well. They can duck under water for them, later on."

It was a hot windless afternoon in the bottoms. Calhoun stayed near the cabin, watching Farley and his men wading, roping, and hauling the bellowing, struggling steers out of the sand grip. With the Sharps rifle at hand, Calhoun watched the grassland rims for strangers approaching.

He built a small fire in the open, cooked the dressed rabbit Soderholm had left, and ate most of it and all the corn dodgers. Stella was helping the men. She rode to the cabin as Calhoun was finishing the rabbit.

"Can I have a drink from your well?" Stella requested coldly.

She was hot, mud-daubed, hating him.

"Cartridge grease floating on it, but I can splash most of that off," Calhoun said agreeably.

He drew up the wooden well bucket for her. When Stella rode back to the work, Calhoun drank slowly, then climbed on the roan horse. He rode across the ford to the higher ground and watched the sand-bogged cattle while he smoked half a cigarette.

The racket on the Soderholm place had drawn homesteaders from lower down the river. Two buckboards, a wagon, men, women, even children, were at the wagon ruts on the other side of the bottoms, watching. The story of all this would be carried to town. It would spread swiftly. There would be sly laughter at Dal Carter and Frank Morton.

Calhoun turned the roan away from the river and rode toward the piling slopes under the Caddo peaks. Strangely he was angry himself, dissatisfied. Bror Neilson's half-contemptuous words kept coming back to him. *"A fool four years ago . . . a fool now!"* How big a fool, Calhoun wondered darkly.

He reached Curry Waldron's place in Blue Cañon three hours after dark. Curry was not in the old one-room cabin. The single small corral was empty. Calhoun put his horse in the corral and went to sleep in Curry's bunk.

By noon the next day he was chafing, wanting to leave, wanting worse to talk with Curry. Half an hour later Curry rode in on a tired horse. He was not surprised to find Calhoun.

Curry dropped saddle and bridle by the cabin door and slapped the hard-ridden sorrel up the cañon. "I been scouting ever since I seen you in town," Curry said. Under his bleached brows, Curry's keen eyes held a suppressed satisfaction, excitement.

"So you're homesteading?" Calhoun remarked as they went in to the pot of coffee Calhoun had hot on the sheet-iron stove.

Curry's tough grin followed. "Why didn't you say you were back for an open fight with Dal Carter and Frank Morton?"

"Soderholm needed help," Calhoun said. He sat in an old splint-bottomed chair with his coffee. Curry sat on the bunk as Calhoun went on. "That homestead could keep folks from wondering why I'm back."

"Find Grady Smith dead, or Dal Carter dead, an' they'll think of you fast enough," Curry differed. He swigged at the black coffee. "Carter has plenty of enemies. Here you are, to take the blame if anything happens."

Calhoun nodded dourly.

"I stopped by Bill Baker's place," said Curry, watching him. "Bill was just back from Kingsville. Gail sent word by him that Grady Smith bought a horse in Tipton City. Said he was riding out to find a job."

Calhoun set his cup on the floor and stepped to the open door, rolling a smoke in silence. Staring out, he inquired: "You remember everything that happened four years ago?"

"Who don't?" Curry asked bluntly. "You owned half of the V Loop. You were younger an' full of oats. Sometimes you went on a mild tear for the hell of it. There was folks didn't approve of you. Sam Morton finally told you to keep away from his Stella. You got mad. Sam Morton got madder, an' clouted you off your horse."

Calhoun rubbed his jaw in recollection. "The old man hit like a bronc's kick."

"Couple of Morton's men up the road saw it, an' talked, of course," said Curry. "You rode on to Phelps's Store, on Crabtree Flats, an' bought a bottle of pain killer."

"I rode up in the mountains, drank that quart of whiskey, and thought it over alone," said Calhoun with bitter wryness. "After I sobered up late the next day, I headed for home, knowing Morton was right. I was ready to steady down for life."

"Sam Morton went on to town, then rode to Castleman's ranch, to look at some horses," Curry said quietly. "He short-cutted for home, alone. Never got there. You had a story about where you'd been. But folks did wonder, after Morton was found dead at the edge of some brush near Bone Creek. Shot in the back. Then a few days later Grady Smith was caught cold with three rustled steers. Grady asked the sheriff to get you. Dal Carter was in town, so Rory McCloud brought him to Grady instead."

"My partner," said Calhoun slowly.

VI

Curry got up and poured himself more coffee. "Both the preachers said Carter did right. Grady told Carter he'd heard a shot about where Sam Morton was found dead. Grady hid in the brush, not knowing what was up. He told Dal Carter it was Dave Calhoun who slipped away from where that shot had been fired. Later, when Grady heard it was Sam Morton who'd been killed, Grady was afraid to talk. But Grady needed help now. Dal Carter washed his hands of murder. He told that to Rory McCloud on his way out. So you got tried for murder. Dal Carter bought your half of the V Loop. Grady's story stuck in some craws, so you weren't convicted, but Grady was . . . for steer stealin'. You lit out an' vanished."

"Waiting for Grady to get out," Calhoun said gently from the doorway. "Grady lied about me. He was paid to lie. Paid to keep his mouth shut while he served his time." Calhoun swore in a burst of black anger. "Grady's kind will need steady paying. He's back to get it. Sure as hell he'll be killed for it before I can get the truth out of him."

"Grady Smith ain't a fool," Curry decided. "You notice he got off the train at Tipton City. He's movin' cautious."

"He'll have to see the man who's been paying him."

"Grady waited in a cell four years, thinkin' it over," Curry reminded. "No tellin' what Grady thought up."

Calhoun gave a helpless gesture and told what had passed between him and Bror Neilson.

"A fool four years ago, an' a fool now?" Curry repeated. "An' he wanted you to work for him? An' then he wanted to be sure you asked Dal Carter about Tyndall's ranch?"

"That's right."

Curry's tough grin came back. "Dal Carter slipped there, lettin' out he'd been in contact with Tyndall, where you saw that bunch gathered. Trouble is shaping in the Cahona. Bror Neilson and the smaller outfits over his way have been cut off from the free grass west of the Cahona."

"Bill Baker spoke of that."

Curry urged: "Think it over. Tough strangers at Tyndall's. Dal Carter in contact with 'em. V Loop an' Cross T must plan to use guns in any argument about their Cahona grab. But the killing will be done by strangers. Dal and Frank Morton will be looking the other way."

"Neilson must suspect something about what went on at Tyndall's," Calhoun mused.

"Anyway, it's plain why he wanted to hire you, Dave. Neilson could trust you in trouble with Carter and Frank Morton."

Calhoun scowled thoughtfully at his cigarette end. McCloud must have guessed all that in Kingsville. A restless uncertainty gnawed at Calhoun. The gnomish Bror Neilson, with his parchment skin, high-arched nose, red-flecked glare, had made him restlessly uncertain in Kingsville, made him feel that Neilson had some hidden meaning to him. Now in Blue Cañon, frustration in Calhoun nagged at what that meaning could be. Bror Neilson had suddenly become important.

"Neilson must know something about Sam Morton's death," Calhoun muttered.

Curry said: "A fool four years ago! And now, huh . . . ? Dave, he could have been baiting you on."

"I'm baited," said Calhoun in abrupt resolve.

Frank Morton's anger ruined breakfast for himself and

Stella. "You were foolish to pay Calhoun. You or Farley could have ridden for help."

"And lose part of those steers in the quicksand?"

"Damn the steers!"

Stella pushed back her plate. She had come in late last night, disheveled, weary, resentful. Frank had been asleep. She had told him this morning.

"Dave Calhoun was right," Stella decided so bitterly Frank regarded her in narrowing calculation. "I saw what had been done to Soderholm's place. No wonder Soderholm tried to shoot Dal. You'd have done the same thing in his place. So would I!" Stella stood up. She had put on man-jeans this morning, a plain blue work shirt, and had caught her tawny hair back with a red ribbon. Her eyes were smoldering.

Frank kicked back his chair. "Nice talk again about the man you're going to marry. Dal and I aren't sullied-up homesteaders. Soderholm wanted trouble. He got it." Frank's tawny aggressive look turned ugly. "Calhoun is looking for trouble. Damned if he hasn't set it off, too. Joe Farley isn't a man who'll take an injured hand. Or Dal a smash on the jaw like Calhoun gave him." A dark satisfaction yeasted Frank's thought. "I've got my own tally with Calhoun. This is about what we all want."

It would have gone on like that, but they both looked at the open window beyond the breakfast table. A rider was coming to the house at a full run.

Frank said — "Now who's that?" — and started outside to see.

The rider was a Cross T 'puncher, Slim Perkins, who flung himself off a lather-flecked dun and spoke to Frank in suppressed excitement.

"Buzzard Wing men took over Deep Cañon Springs and Clark's Tank about daybreak this mornin'. I was riding to

Clark's to see Johnny Wood. Three Buzzard men turned me back."

Frank's oath exploded in the warming sunshine. He did not bother to look toward the bunkhouse and corrals. Only Hewlitt, the ramrod, and three men had used the bunkhouse last night. They had ridden off an hour ago.

"Get a fresh horse and ride to the V Loop," Frank snapped.

Perkins nodded, climbed his horse, and ran it to the corrals. Stella came out from the back door where she'd listened. The house behind her was long, low, built solidly of stone by their father when they were both very young. Something of Sam Morton had gone into that solid house. A shadow of the same thing was in Stella now. She was not angry. She was concerned, steady.

When Frank turned back toward her, she said to him: "So trying to take the Cahona range has finally set Bror Neilson at you?"

Frank had sobered a little, too, at the news, but his reckless aggressiveness now took hold again. "We counted on a show-down with Neilson."

"*We?*" asked Stella. Her lip curled slightly. "The Cahona was your venture, Frank. Cross T made all the moves."

"It was Dal's idea. He's with me, of course."

"It's always Dal's idea, isn't it?"

"I don't know what you mean by that, Stell'."

Hands in her jeans' pockets, under lip caught beneath her even teeth, Stella estimated her brother levelly. They were six years apart in age. Stella was the younger. Frank was a head taller. They'd always fought, made up. Frank had been something of a hero to Stella, big, handsome, reckless. Her green-blue eyes were not hero-worshipping now.

"How much right has Bror Neilson to take over Clark's Tank and the Deep Cañon water?" Stella asked evenly.

"None! He can go to court about it, but damned if he'll grab it this way. He's trying to break us."

"Can he?"

"If he gets enough cattle on that free grass west of the Cahona, which is what he's up to. Dal and I have counted on that grass. We need it."

"How badly?" Stella prodded. "You've kept all this quiet, Frank."

"Well, you're hearing it now," said Frank harshly. "We've got to have that grass! Before you get worked up about Neilson, remember I'm your brother, and Dal's your man."

Stella said: "First trouble with Dave Calhoun . . . now Bror Neilson." She turned and walked into the house.

Curry Waldron led the way up Blue Cañon and across the northeast shoulder of Caddo mountain. They traversed a narrow defile whose left side was sheer rock a thousand feet up. A treacherous shale slope dropped them into the pines where the dry needles lay, deep and yielding.

"I've never stole a horse, exactly," said Curry, "but a horse thief showed me this way to some of the flat land fast."

They came out on a bald granite ridge and looked far down on brush- and tree-dotted foothills that undulated into the flatter rangeland north and east. Out there Bror Neilson ran his Buzzard Wing brand, neighbored by smaller outfits.

"Cattle bunched an' moving," said Curry, pointing. "Look! Two . . . three bunches. And off there another 'un."

They dropped off the granite on an almost invisible thread of trail. An hour later they rode down a sparsely grassed coulée, droughted and grazed close, and headed toward the nearest moving cattle. Curry knew the men.

The Sullivans, father and two sons, were shoving along less than two hundred head. Sullivan, a big hearty man with a brown beard, said: "Hell, we're all movin' stuff on the open range west of Clark's Tank. Buzzard Wing took the lead. Neilson's at Deep Cañon, or Clark's, now."

They turned ahead of the Sullivans toward Deep Cañon. Curry was wry about it. "That's how foxy Bror Neilson is. Gets his neighbors behind him when he tackles V Loop an' Cross T. You still want a piece of it?"

"All I want is a talk with Neilson," said Calhoun restlessly.

"If he knows anything you want, he'll trade you into his fight," Curry warned. He speculated: "If Neilson's got Deep Cañon and Clark's Tank, he's split the Cahona range. Must've run off what Cross T men he found."

The Cahona was a long, well grassed, shallow valley with a V of black lava roughs ten miles wide at the upper end, separating it from the Buzzard Wing line fences. A dike of high rock ridges — probably an eroded fault line — formed the west boundary of the Cahona that had no water in running streams. West of the Cahona were miles of good grass on open range. But no water, except at Deep Cañon and Clark's Tank, that also served the whole middle stretch of the Cahona.

Cross T, by taking up all the middle Cahona water, had gotten not only Cahona grass but all the free range to the west, as far as a cow could graze from a water hole, which was far. Bror Neilson now had the main water and that gave him the grass. But what Neilson was doing hinged on more than grass. Despite two drought years and short grass this year, cattle were in no extreme danger. Calhoun speculated aloud about it to Curry, riding close at his right.

"Neilson's got a plan an' a reason for it," Curry was stating when the flat blurt of a rifle shot came from rocks and brush, topping a low ridge not a hundred yards to the left.

Calhoun felt the bullet graze his forearm. He heard the meaty *thunnnnk* as it struck Curry Waldron.

Thinly, vacantly Curry gasped: "Now who done that?"

The spur-raked rush of Calhoun's roan toward the low ridge was savage, because Calhoun was instantly, wildly savage. He'd left the cumbersome Sharps in Blue Cañon. He ignored the lighter carbine at his knee and cocked the Colt gun as he reined the roan hard in a weaving rush at the ridge. It was reckless, foolish, but the only way to get in at the hidden killer. Calhoun bent low against the roan's neck. He heard another meaty *thunnnnk*. He barely had time to kick feet from stirrups as the roan went down.

Calhoun struck hard, sliding, rolling. The floundering, dying horse was almost on him when he scrambled groggily to hands, knees, then up in a hatless, dodging run toward the hidden gunman. Calhoun had instinctively lowered the Colt hammer as the roan stumbled. The gun was still in his hand. The whinging scream of a third bullet missed him. He marked the bald, front rocks that hid the man and fired twice at the spot as he ran.

There were no more shots. Calhoun went up the steep slope, smashing through low brush like a wild man. Curry had been his closest friend here.

Great breaths whistled from him as he lunged at the rocks from one side. But as he expected, the man was gone. Calhoun heard the hard gallop of a retreating horse off the back slope of the ridge. He ran that way and found gouged tracks in the brush. This was a spot of thickets and uneven terrain. The rider was already out of sight.

Calhoun went at the tracks like an Indian, stooping low over them while he gasped for breath. He stopped over a bare washed spot, printing one track forever in his mind. That right hind hoof print, toed in slightly. The shoe calks had twisted slightly to the right in the earth, because of the toe-in, mashing the print a little on that side. It was repeated in tracks farther on.

Calhoun turned back, running again. His horse was dead. The carbine stock was splintered. Curry Waldron was lying quite peacefully on the ground, knees drawn up. The bullet had gone in Curry's left side, at the heart, and emerged opposite in a hole bigger than Calhoun's fist. It was a miracle Curry had been able to utter words. His last words.

Curry's black horse, looped reins on the saddle horn, had already wandered off some distance. Calhoun used up ten minutes walking the nervous horse down.

The Sullivans were far behind. Perhaps an hour of the afternoon was left. Calhoun took Curry as Curry was, across his knees, on Curry's horse, and rode for Deep Cañon.

VII

The cañon was deep only on the south side. There the rock face was abrupt and high. The rest of the cañon was really a side arm of the Cahona, cleaving in an irregular curve through the western boundary ridges, debouching in a fan-shaped mouth on the dry, lower range west of the ridges. The springs were in the Cahona half of the cañon, three small springs in the space of a hundred yards, finding their common pool and pushing a sluggish rill west through the cañon — that was a full eighth of a mile wide and well grassed.

Calhoun got there after dark, passing cattle and guards in the Cahona. He found cattle being pushed through the cañon tonight. Campfires blazed at the springs. Three chuck wagons were already there. Saddled horses stood ready on picket ropes. Armed men, lounging at the fires, gathered quickly and put Curry's body on a blanket.

Questions. Answers. Calhoun saw a familiar buggy beyond the chuck wagons and was told Bror Neilson was there. He found the gnomish little man cross-legged on a blanket by a small fire, his hat pushed back on his head, a chunk of cold meat in one hand, a biscuit in the other. Bror Neilson was talking through the bawl of passing cattle to Stella Morton.

Stella stood quickly at sight of Calhoun's lowering face. Bror Neilson got up more slowly, gnawing at the meat. He listened to Calhoun's heavy, chopped account of Curry's death.

Stella had looked angry. Now she seemed to freeze. "No Cross T man would have killed Curry Waldron," she said.

215

"The man tried to kill me and hit Curry instead," Calhoun told her simply.

Stella swallowed. "Or you, Dave."

Bror Neilson was standing now, one leg a little shorter, narrow shoulders stooped. In the fire flicker his high-arched nose and the narrow bloodless lips in the parchment face gave him an unreal look. His infrequent smile came thinly. "How about V Loop men?" he asked Stella in the high, crackling voice.

"No!" Stella denied, coloring.

Bror Neilson studied her, still smiling thinly. He gnawed another bite of cold meat and seemed to gulp it without chewing. He gestured with the chunk of meat at the other fires, the men, the cattle streaming west.

"Young lady, tell your brother he's not old Sam Morton. He'll do better when he knows it."

"And what shall I tell Dal Carter?" Stella asked coldly.

That struck a rusty-sounding chuckle from the gnomish little man. "More of whatever you've been telling Carter, my dear. Now, I'll have a man ride with you to Rimrock Camp."

"I'd like to have Dave ride with me."

Bror Neilson seemed to enjoy that. "We'll take care of Waldron's body," he told Calhoun.

Dourly, after a moment's indecision, Calhoun nodded his agreement and went for Curry's horse. Stella, tonight, wore a divided skirt and a soft gray wool jacket. She had brought a saddle gun, he noticed, as they rode off together. She could use it too, better than most men.

He wondered, almost resentfully, why Stella had asked this of him. Their way was east out of the cañon, south through the Cahona. Silence held them both as they turned south. Stella broke it, with the sound of dejection in her voice.

"I had to wait a long time for Neilson. No one seemed to

know exactly where he was. I might have known you'd be in this, too."

"Did Frank send you?"

"He doesn't know I came," said Stella wearily. "I wanted to hear Neilson's side. He told me he's going to break us. Cross T and V Loop both, and he likes the idea."

"Just for the fun of it?"

"He seemed to enjoy the prospect. He said the whole middle part of the Cahona was patented land. It was true. But Frank bought Deep Cañon and the piece that holds Clark's Tank from heirs who held cloudy titles. Frank, he says, hasn't recorded any deeds because all Frank got were quitclaims. He says Frank tried to run a big bluff, and no one but Bror knew better. He says Frank can go to court, which might take several years. Meanwhile, Bror has seized the water and gets the grass."

"Will it break Cross T?"

"Bror says it will. And break Dal, too. He says they've borrowed all they can. They've held cattle and bought cattle, counting on all that grass and free range to come through. The market's down now. Their cattle are poor, after two drought years. They can't buy feed for this winter. They don't dare sell at a big loss, but they'll have to. Bror's throwing every head he and his neighbors can gather onto that range. They're going to eat off all this year's grass by overstocking heavily, then pull back on their own rested range for the winter. By then Frank and Dal will be smashed."

"Should I say I'm sorry?"

"No."

"Frank and Dal will fight, and not in court," said Calhoun matter-of-factly.

"I'm afraid so. Men will be killed," Stella responded resentfully. "You'll be in it, killing for Bror Neilson. Was this what you came back for?"

"If you want to think so," Calhoun said indifferently.

Stella turned her head, studying him. Coyotes spoke along the far ridges. The stars were bright blobs, pouring a silver glow in which Stella's face looked pale, worried. She said: "Grady Smith was in Deep Cañon half an hour before you got there. I saw him ride in."

Calhoun checked his horse abruptly.

Stella wheeled to face him. "So it's Grady you're back for, Dave. I wondered."

A barren, cold urgency chilled Calhoun's demand. "Which way did Grady ride in from?"

"The way you came." An edge of taunt sharpened Stella's tone. "If Grady's so friendly with Bror Neilson, aren't you in strange company there?"

"Stranger company right here, Stella. Dal Carter won't like this. Let's get on."

"I know the way. You can turn back!" Stella flared at him.

"I might shoot a lady's father, but I wouldn't let her ride home alone," Calhoun said.

Stella's horse bolted under the strike of her quirt. Calhoun had to ride hard to hold her in sight in the starlight.

They were at least four miles from the Rimrock Camp when shadowed riders burst out of the scattered brush clumps to the right and left. They headed Stella and closed on Calhoun.

Stella pulled up. Calhoun heard her call: "Cross T?"

Calhoun wheeled his blowing horse back, not liking this. The move was a mistake, he knew instantly. At the same moment his horse was shot from under him with rifle fire. Calhoun hit the ground in a staggering run, Curry's carbine in his hand this time. Then he saw how useless it was, stepped to the floundering horse, and ended it's misery with a bullet. He was standing quietly as Stella galloped back.

"Dave! Are you hurt?"

"Not yet," Calhoun replied when she reached him. The other riders were ringing the spot. "Nice planning, Stell'," Calhoun told her. "I rode right into it, didn't I?"

"I didn't expect this!" Stella said sharply. "Dal, he was bringing me to camp, from Deep Cañon!"

It was Dal Carter who pulled up beside Stella on a dark sorrel horse tonight. Starlight touched the fancy silver on Dal's bridle and saddle, and the white plaster tape on Dal's jaw. Looking around, Calhoun recognized the flat jaw of Ferd Tyndall. The starlight was bright enough to show him the thick-set Walt Burger, who had put the bullet hole in Calhoun's hat at Tyndall's ranch. The same grinning malice was on Burger's meaty face tonight. Joe Farley, the V Loop ramrod, was there, too, with white plaster strips on his lacerated hand. And Bates and Hagan, the 'punchers who had been with Farley at Soderholm's place.

"Don't jump, men," Calhoun warned. The sarcasm was idle and cold. "I'm only going to smoke."

"Dal," said Stella. "Give Dave a horse. Let him go." Her voice sounded tight.

Dal's reply had a mushy thickness from a mouth still stiff. "Sure Stell'. Frank's worried about you. Bates can ride with you to camp."

"You come, Dal. I want to talk with you. But first give Dave a horse and let him go."

Dal was tolerantly agreeable. "Hagan, give Calhoun your horse."

Dal kneed his sorrel over to Tyndall. "Ferd, do like we planned. I'll meet you. . . ." Dal's voice lowered on the rest of it. Then he reined away toward Calhoun. "Leave your guns here, Dave, if you're going back to that thief, Neilson."

"Why not?" Calhoun agreed indifferently. He wondered if Stella believed all this. He dropped the carbine and gun belt.

219

Hagan had dismounted.

Dal said: "All right, Stell'. Let's ride to Frank. He's worried."

Stella hesitated. "Good bye, Dave. Thank you."

"Thanks," Calhoun said absently, "for everything." As he stepped up on Hagan's horse, he heard Stella and Dal leave. He'd marked Ferd Tyndall's covert grin at the nearest men. It was all plain enough, except to Stella. Something black and stubbornly fatalistic held Calhoun from appealing to her. He carried the thing on with ironic calm, wondering if it were possible to break through the ringing riders.

A wrist-flipped rope dropped over Calhoun's shoulders and ended that idea. He looked around. The other end of the rope was dallied to Walt Burger's saddle horn. Burger was grinning.

"Carter says drag him up in the ridges, but don't kill him . . . quite," Ferd Tyndall said. "The lady wouldn't like it." Ferd spat. "You got anything to say, Calhoun?"

"Come close, Ferd, and listen."

Ferd Tyndall rode in close, his humor expectant. Calhoun silently spat in the flat-jawed face. Tyndall struck him viciously in the face.

"Drag him, Burger!" Ferd Tyndall mouthed in thick fury.

Groggily Calhoun held to the thought that this was Dal Carter's doing. Burger's rope was doing the dragging. Ferd Tyndall had issued the order to Burger. But the decision had come from the same cold-blooded viciousness that had taken Soderholm's livelihood and pulped Soderholm's helpless face with a grinding boot heel.

The first hard fall off the horse had slammed the breath out of Calhoun. After that, for a time, it wasn't so bad. They rode slowly, and there wasn't much grass. Then Burger found low brush and rode through it. Branches whipped, stabbed, broke. Bear grass spines cut like knives through Calhoun's clothes. Small cacti, no bigger than his fist, needled into him.

It was a slow thing, of stabs, rips, bumps, clothes ripping and tearing. Agonizing strikes against rocks. Calhoun clumsily shielded face and head when he could. Aches, pain, the slippery feel of blood merged into one dull, burning focus. *Dal Carter was doing this.*

"Lemme look at him!" Ferd Tyndall ordered. He stepped down, struck a flaring match, bent close.

Calhoun spat weakly at the grinning face.

"Damn it, drag him faster!" Ferd ordered angrily.

The stars began to spin dizzily. More brush crackled, broke as the horses surged through at the slowest of trots. Calhoun's snaking, bouncing body caromed off heavier growth. His head struck a rock. The stars vanished. Pain went away.

Calhoun heard coyotes clamoring again and found himself looking at the sky. The west ridges of the Cahona loomed close, dark against the glassy gray-green of dawn. Calhoun stirred, groaned.

He was on his feet, staggering north, when the first golden strike of the rising sun reached through the morning chill. Arms, legs worked. No bones seemed broken. Over that framework of a man, he was lacerations, cuts, crusted blood, ribbons of clothes, puffy swellings, dizzy weakness, and pain outside, inside, through muscles, nerves, and pounded flesh.

He was a man bruised, battered, torn, weak, ghastly thirsty. But he was still a man who could move one step after another toward Deep Cañon with focused purpose. The buckboard and the eight men riding with it were almost to him before Calhoun was aware of them. It was then two hours after sunrise, and he was growing weaker. With dull, detached interest he recognized the gnome-like figure, perched lightly in the saddle of the lead horse, one stirrup shorter than the other.

Bror Neilson's high crackling voice greeted him. "Didn't look for you to be walking, Calhoun."

"Fell off my horse," Calhoun mumbled through puffy lips.

Five days later Calhoun crawled out of an old pup tent in Deep Cañon where he'd spent most of the time, inert on a borrowed bedroll. Rory McCloud, the sheriff, had dismounted outside and called his name, then moved forward.

Rory stood slack-shouldered, gray and quiet, toothpick forgotten in the corner of his mouth as he sized up Calhoun.

"It must've been a hell of a high hoss, runnin' fast when you fell off," Rory decided mildly.

Calhoun nodded.

Rory let it stand. "I stopped about Curry Waldron, Dave."

Curry had been buried in a sheltered, grass-grown bench a little up the north slope of the cañon. It would have suited Curry. He had no family.

Calhoun wore overall pants, borrowed underwear, a blue cotton shirt. He'd borrowed the gun belt and gun beside the bedroll in the tent. He was more of a man than he'd been five days ago. He was still covered with court plaster and crude bandages. His face was patched and swollen. Aches, pains stirred sharply when he moved. But bone, muscle, and the man inside were a wondrous mechanism that could take dark, fierce purpose and heal and strengthen.

The very fierceness of Calhoun's purpose had made him wait stoically until his body could be used. Now, through lips still swollen, he told McCloud: "Curry was murdered. It was meant for me. I haven't talked about it. But I'll warn you now, Rory. When I find a horse track with the right hind hoof toed-in a little, and the calks messing dirt on the right side of the print, the rider's mine. He left that sign when he got away."

"Two murders don't right one murder, Dave. You got any idea who did it?"

"I've got my trail sign. It's good enough."

Rory took the toothpick from his mouth and sighed. "Grady Smith's around. I told you once, Dave. I'll tell you again. I'd hate to see Grady found dead."

"Then Grady better not be on the horse I track down." Calhoun made a harsh gesture. "The whole damned country around here is full of men set to shoot each other. But you come to me about one sneaking killer. Use your law, Rory, on the rest of them. Don't bother me." Calhoun's dark disgust taunted Rory. "Are you afraid to meddle with the big trouble?"

"Nope," said Rory mildly. "But I can't arrest 'em all for getting ready to kill each other." He studied the toothpick. "Frank Morton's got quitclaim deeds to the Springs here an' the land around Clark's Tank. Bror Neilson bought himself a couple of quitclaim deeds from the same heirs, on the quiet. Makes everything even on that. Bror and his neighbors are using the water now. It's a case for Cross T to take into court. Until the shootin' starts, all I can do is watch. I've got Ike Morris peelin' an eye on Cross T and V Loop. I'm sorta watching this end."

"And nothing you can do about it when the fighting does start," Calhoun said with heavy cynicism. "You can't lock up the whole range."

Rory nodded sadly. "I've been watching this build for several years. Couldn't stop it. Now, good family men are set to be killed, if something don't head it off." Rory's tone was mournful. "That's all, Dave. I've told you about Grady. Hope you don't ever have to worry with the sheriff's job. Keeps a man awake, sometimes."

Rory rode off. Calhoun walked to the nearest chuck wagon and drank from the wooden water barrel lashed to the side.

He then started a dogged plod to the other end of the short cañon, to limber a body that still protested each move.

He hadn't seen Grady Smith, or spoken of Grady to anyone. He'd hardly spoken to Bror Neilson. The hunched, limping little man was riding out most of the time. Neilson was like a general, commanding forces on the battle line. His troops were stubborn, determined neighbors of Buzzard Wing, their 'punchers, and other small cowmen who had felt, or knew they would feel, the pressure of Cross T and V Loop.

Calhoun had no great interest in all that. He'd lain in a stupor of weakness and pain at first, with Grady Smith and Dal Carter focused steadily in his thoughts. They were in his mind now as he walked slowly, scanning all horse tracks he passed. The toe-in print might show here in Deep Cañon. He looked, somberly, carefully.

He wondered again how Bror Neilson had happened to ride out, searching for him. Bror had seemed to know what he'd find. Calhoun halted abruptly. Bror's high-arched nose had linked by some obscure twist of thought with another bold, arched nose at Tyndall's ranch. That axe-blade of a nose at Tyndall's had made no move to stop Calhoun's retreat that day. The same man had been silent, in the background, when Burger's rope had started to drag Calhoun. And hours later Bror Neilson had known about it, evidently.

Calhoun reached the fanned-out mouth of the cañon. Ahead the land swelled and dipped into distance. The dry grass was high and plentiful. But as far as a man could see cattle were already on it so thickly the grass wouldn't last long.

VIII

High above the cañon mouth a guard was posted on the rocks. Two armed men waited at a crude stone breastwork where Calhoun stopped. One was a Sullivan.

"Any trouble?" Calhoun inquired.

"Too quiet," the man said soberly. He was big, like his father, but young. The laughing exuberance of the other day was gone. He guessed: "Cross T is schemin' somethin'." His thumb jerked at a rifle, leaning against the dark rock. "We're ready as we can be."

Ready to die, like Curry Waldron, Calhoun thought bleakly. Rory McCloud was right, in a way. These men with Bror Neilson were sons, husbands, fathers who had no business dying. But they'd been pushed too far. They'd not be stopped now. Some of them would die.

The other man was older with a short untrimmed sandy beard. He drawled dryly: "You about ready to climb back on that hoss you fell offa, Calhoun?"

"Soon," Calhoun said somberly.

It put Grady Smith in his mind again as he walked stiffly back to the Springs. How did Grady happen to be with Bror Neilson's men? And why had Bror said — *"A fool four years ago!"* — as if Neilson might know something about Sam Morton's death?

Calhoun had put off demanding answers from Bror until his strength returned. He was ready now, he decided. When Bror rode in, they'd have a showdown.

Then, as he came to the pup tent again, Calhoun forgot all

that. A powerful blood bay horse was nipping the short grass in front of the tent. Stella Morton was sitting cross-legged at the tent mouth, waiting.

Stella saw him and stood up quickly. She had on the same divided riding skirt but a jacket of matching brown woolen cloth with big red cloth-covered buttons. Her gray hat had been tossed on the ground.

Stella had looked utterly dejected as she had sat waiting there. Now, as she saw Calhoun up close, hurt, pain grew, dark and miserable, in her eyes. "Dave! Dave!"

"I fell off my horse," Calhoun said with a wry twist of puffy lips. He wondered why he should be trying to reassure Stella. "You couldn't guess that would happen," he added.

They were in sight of men, guarding the Springs, men who must be vastly curious. Stella was searching Calhoun's battered face as if each cut and bruise were being printed in her mind, just like the toed-in track had become fastened in Calhoun's memory.

"One of our Cross T men told me this morning," Stella said. "He wasn't there when they dragged you, Dave, but he didn't like what he heard about it. Frank had nothing to do with it. He hadn't been told, either. All he said this morning was that he didn't care what had happened."

"I suppose not, Stell'."

Stella's throat moved as she swallowed. "Dal told me I'd heard his orders about you. He said Tyndall had a grudge against you. It was Tyndall's doing, if it happened at all. Dal said he hadn't heard about it until I told him."

Calhoun's nod did not argue. "Dal wasn't there, either," he agreed.

"Dal was there when he mashed Soderholm's face." Stella's voice was small and steady. "In a fair fight that would have been Dal's business. But not the way he did it to Soderholm."

Stella held out her hands. "I've taken Dal's ring off. I gave it back to him this morning. It doesn't matter, I know . . . but I had to see you, and then say it." Stella picked up her hat and walked to her horse, gathering the dragging reins.

Calhoun stepped to her side. "Thanks, Stell'. But why Dal at all, when Gail Baker wanted him?"

Stella ran her hand slowly over the blood bay's muzzle, not looking at Calhoun. "Dal had quit Gail. She knew she was through. If he'd quit her once, he'd quit her again, when it suited him. Gail is sensible. We talked it over."

Calhoun shook his head, wondering again at women. "Then you took Dal, knowing that!"

Stella's fair pale face showed quick color as she moved around and turned the stirrup. "It was an engagement that went on and on because nothing ever seemed to happen to end it. I didn't marry him, Dave." The bay shifted as Stella reached for the saddle horn. She said in a small voice: "I talked with Bror Neilson, two years ago. He's an understanding man."

Calhoun barely heard that. His glance, by dark habit now, had run absently over the ground, then had shifted suddenly under the bay to the right hind hoof. His swollen left hand dropped on Stella's arm.

"Wait!" he commanded. "Who's been riding this horse?" His glance raked up to the bold Cross T brand on the bay's flank. "Who?" Calhoun demanded again roughly.

Stella's dejection stiffened. The Morton temper answered him. "What does it matter? What's wrong with you, Dave?"

"Has Frank been riding this horse?" Calhoun asked coldly.

"What if he has?"

"The man who rode this horse five days ago killed Curry Waldron in trying to kill me. Was it Frank?"

All the blood drained from Stella's face. "Not Frank, Dave. Not Frank. He hates you because he thinks you shot our father.

227

But he'd try it in the open." Stella beat one fist into the other palm, crying her own fierceness under her breath at what she saw on Calhoun's maltreated face. "I know Frank! He's my brother! He's been a swaggering idiot. He's been wrong. Now he's paying for it. He's losing everything father left us both. I can't even blame Bror Neilson and the men helping him. I've tried to stop Frank from fighting Bror, and I can't. He may be killed before it's over. But he didn't hide and try to kill you."

"Then who rode his horse?" Calhoun asked with such bitter persistence that Stella's temper wiped away. Fright haunted her look.

"I don't know," Stella denied from stiff lips.

Darkly Calhoun guessed: "Dal's been riding him!"

Stella closed her eyes, shutting out his face. "Hasn't there been enough killing? And enough to come?"

Calhoun waited a moment, then said quietly: "Not quite enough, Stell'. Frank's fight with Bror isn't my business. I'm back to find who really killed your father, and why I was blamed. I'll talk to Dal about it." Calhoun took the bay's reins from her. "McCloud will want to see this horse's track. You can send word to Frank that you'll be all right."

He waited for the Morton temper to challenge. But after a moment Stella gave a helpless gesture, stepped back, and watched Calhoun beckon the nearest armed man, who had been covertly watching them.

The first few miles of riding were the worst. Then the bone and muscle accepted it, or numbed a little. Calhoun had the best horse he'd been able to borrow from those kept ready in the cañon. He had a Winchester in an old saddle boot, a .45, and enough shells for both. Cold meat and biscuits were stuffed in a pair of old saddlebags. A battered canteen filled with water hung from the horn. Everything was borrowed, and, when he rode out on the dry range from Deep Cañon, he had no belief he'd return. He was heading for a chuck wagon camp some twelve miles out. From that camp a handful of riders were patrolling the line of the Wild Horse Breaks, off which cattle could wander into miles of bone-dry badlands — or be driven.

One of the men at the Springs had thought Grady Smith was at the line camp, or Clark's Tank. A man in from Clark's Tank at noon had said Bror Neilson had left there with half a dozen men, to ride the edge of the breaks south and talk with all the men over that way. Neilson had been certain the first move against them was coming swiftly. It had been held back too long now.

Cattle dotted the rich dry grass, almost like sheep the way they were taking it down. *It's like a big roundup,* Calhoun thought — and, in a way, it was. The wind-stroked afternoon held a brassy heat under a cloudless sky. The breaks were still miles away when the brush-hummocked rise and dip of the range poured out a thin line of riders.

Calhoun pulled up warily. One rider turned back. The others came on, dipping out of sight again, then into view, nearer. One small, hunched figure could only be Bror Neilson.

And it was. The man looked more bone and dry skin than ever, Calhoun thought when they met. Neilson's red-flecked glare sized him up. "Going somewhere, Calhoun?"

"Sort of."

Neilson said impatiently: "Turn back. There'll be trouble tonight. I don't know exactly what it is, but it's planned. We'll need you."

"Who was the man who rode away?" Calhoun inquired.

Bror Neilson rubbed the back of a skinny hand over his arched nose. His glare studied Calhoun. "Grady Smith," he said abruptly.

"I thought so, Bror. I want a word with you alone."

The gnome-like little man swung his horse from the others, snapping: "Have it then, fast! I've more to do than talk with you today."

When they were out of earshot, Calhoun said deliberately: "Couldn't your man, with the nose like yours, find out what's going to happen?"

Bror looked startled. Then his humor was a faint line of satisfaction. "My cousin," he stated. "Drifted in from Texas. Played along with the tough ones until he was hired for some trouble that was expected. Tyndall hired him, and kept quiet about what the trouble was. You gave it away when you paired Carter with Tyndall. It was time, then, to make my move fast. I did. I met my cousin a while ago. They're ready for something. He can't find out what it is, but he's going back to try."

Calhoun said with a cold lack of emotion: "Dal Carter killed Curry Waldron. What about four years ago? Why was I a fool?"

"Still a fool, if you have to ask it now." Bror shifted in the saddle, shrugging hunched shoulders. "Carter borrowed money from me, on the quiet, to buy you out. Then, later, he borrowed from Frank Morton, paid me back, and teamed with Morton to crowd me." Bror's high-pitched scorn sawed on the breeze. "A humpbacked little scarecrow like old Bror Neilson wasn't much of a bite for bright young schemers like Carter and Morton."

Calhoun, sifting his own dark thoughts, said slowly: "So Dal borrowed from you? That doesn't tell me much."

"He started sounding me out on a loan two months before Sam was killed." Bror's bloodless smile watched the dark drive of that knowledge set flinty on Calhoun's face.

Slowly, reflectively Calhoun said: "Dal knew then I wouldn't sell. I'd built a house. I was going to be married. I planned to be on the V Loop for life. Only something like Stella's father

. . . shot in the back, supposedly by me . . . would break all that up. It makes me wonder who Grady Smith saw riding from Sam Morton. And how much Grady got to make it me."

"Wondering never proved anything."

"It helps," said Calhoun with flinty patience. "Stella says she talked with you about some part of all that."

Bror snorted at the memory. "You left a girl who'd cared for you. You never stopped to think her life might have been overturned, too. A real man wouldn't leave someone like her to be claimed by another man. He'd have come back for her. Which was what a girl might well hope." Bror spat to one side. "But you didn't come."

"Why is Grady siding with you, Bror?"

"Figure it out," Bror invited acidly.

"You're set on smashing Frank Morton?"

"Frank's father was my friend. The son's a fool, inflated with windy pride. Why not?"

"If he changed . . . ?"

"Fools never change," Bror sneered, and ended the talk by wheeling his horse into a run toward the Springs. His men followed.

Calhoun rode north, away from where he'd sighted the distant retreat of Grady Smith. Bror's words mocked along the threads of memory. *Fools never change.* Bror could have meant Dave Calhoun. Grady Smith was the one man who could help. It was like a wolf hunt now. First Grady, then Dal Carter. If Grady were watching, he might be reassured by Calhoun's progress north toward Clark's Tank.

Calhoun rode at least two miles with the hot dryness of the south wind fingering his back. Then, in a brush-screened dip, he turned west for another mile and doubled back south.

Grady might have kept going. He might not even have

recognized Calhoun in the first place. But there had been no sign of Grady's riding on toward the Springs after Bror and his men. That should put Grady somewhere ahead.

Calhoun kept to the low spots, taking his time to dismount, belly-down at the rises, and scan the land ahead. His battered body protested. He ignored it.

In one more shallow coulée Calhoun walked up the slope and bellied in a patch of rabbit weed, rustling and pungent around him in the wind whip. Only cattle were in sight ahead. He injuned back down the slope a little, laid the carbine in the grass, and stood up to roll a smoke. Ahead, east a little, was about where Grady had disappeared. South was the V Loop and Cross T thread out of Rimrock Camp. Grady had probably turned his trail back west to the wagon camp.

Calhoun sealed the smoke and stooped for his carbine. A slamming blow knocked him rolling on the gun, and off it in numbed helplessness. A spiteful gun report echoed off the opposite rise of the coulée. In that helpless moment Calhoun ate the bitter dregs of all his folly. *Fools never change!* He'd been so intent on hunting Grady, he'd not conceded that Grady might be hunting him.

He lay face down, gasping. Only the abrupt, turning stoop had saved him from a center shot through the upper middle. His side had been hit. A second bullet ripped through the high dry grass, inches from his shoulder. Prone in the long grass, he was a difficult target now. But Grady had him.

Calhoun hugged the earth as another bullet just missed. The worst of the sick numbness was passing. His hand touched the carbine's stock. He could move both arms. And legs. And body now.

A soaring murderous rage sent him rolling with a great gasp, bringing up the carbine, levering it. He came to his knees in a drunken lunge that showed him a standing figure on the

232

other crest of the coulée. Pain knifed Calhoun's left side as he fired and levered the gun again. Then Calhoun blinked. Grady Smith, a medium-size, chunky man, had fired awkwardly, one-handed, at Calhoun's horse, and bolted back, dodging.

Calhoun's second shot evidently missed. Grady vanished behind the screen of the coulée rim. Calhoun swore. His borrowed dun horse had bolted, reins dragging, a bleeding welt crossed the animal's hip, where Grady's bullet had ploughed.

Calhoun took his own measure. Grady's bullet had ripped into the heavy leather cartridge belt above the left hip. Two shells and loops had been torn away. The slug had glanced up against a lower rib, evidently cracking it, and glanced on by. There was blood. Pain knifed the rib region when he moved. Calhoun wadded a handkerchief against the bleeding gash and started after the horse.

It took him half an hour to walk down the snorting, terrified animal that kept backing up, lunging away. But in the saddle Calhoun was a man again. The bleeding had slacked off. He had a slightly lame horse, a condition that would only worsen. The tracks of Grady's horse, when he worked them out, headed toward the wagon camp.

IX

The late afternoon sun brightened the weathered canvas of the solitary old chuck wagon. It was a dry camp, by a sparse thicket, less than a quarter of a mile from the gullied badlands. Half a dozen horses grazed on picket ropes. A single saddle horse stood by the wagon. Two men stood there. One looked like Rory McCloud. Watchfully on his rapidly laming horse, Calhoun rode in.

The second man was older than Rory. A flour sack apron marked him as cook. Then, as Calhoun passed scattered bedrolls, he saw a third man on the ground beyond McCloud. A dead man.

A savage sense of failure seized Calhoun. Grady Smith, dead, would be forever silent about who had murdered Sam Morton. Then, as Calhoun reached the rear of the wagon, he saw the dead man's black mustache and axe-blade of a nose.

"Who killed him?" Calhoun asked McCloud. He dismounted stiffly, glance roving narrowly around.

"I seen some buzzards, found him, an' brought him in, so he wouldn't get pecked over," Rory said. "Two holes in his chest, sometime this afternoon."

"He must have been seen talking to Bror Neilson," Calhoun said. He told briefly what he knew of the man.

Rory's deceptively mild eyes were weighing the bloody furrow on the dun's hip, the blood-stiff cloth at Calhoun's side. "I'd almost think you killed him, Dave," said Rory mildly. "Only he never got his gun out to shoot back. Also, Jimmy Briggs here says Grady Smith fogged in with a bullet-smashed shoulder a little while ago. Said you tried to kill him. Got Jimmy to tie his saddle on a fresh hoss an' took off, with God's fear in him. I was waitin' for you to come after him, Dave."

"Which way did Grady go?"

"South," said Rory mildly. Then Rory's jaw dropped. The flicker of his hand toward his holster gun froze. Calhoun's gun was already covering him. Pained chagrin gleamed in Rory's look. "What'd I do that tipped you off, Dave?" Rory drew a breath and suggested hopefully: "Just guessed it, huh?"

"Cookie, change my saddle to the best horse and keep out of this," Calhoun directed.

"Friend," the wrinkled, almost toothless Jimmy Briggs said calmly, "I ain't never got in it, an' don't mean to."

Calhoun backed around where he could watch the saddle being shifted. "Rory, when you decide to snatch your gun, you dip your chin a little. A man, watching for it, has got you."

Rory's disgust was mournful. "Ain't that a hell of a thing to hang over a sheriff's head? Now I'll never be sure." He yanked at the gun belt buckle, allowed the heavy belt to slide to the ground, and stepped away from it. "Ride after Grady an' get killed! He's headed for the one man who'll team with him against you." Rory's disgust mounted. "I waited a long time for all that to work out. Now you come into it."

Curious, Calhoun asked: "For what to work out?"

"Four years ago Grady Smith looked like a gun was at his head when he seen Dal Carter at his cell door instead of you. But after they talked alone, Grady perked up. Through the front window I seen Dal Carter's grin when he stopped outside to light a cigarette. That didn't prove Grady lied when he swore you must've killed Sam Morton. But I been waitin' for a liar an' a killer to fall out."

Calhoun reminded him coldly, balefully: "You're still waiting. The horse with the toed-in print is a Cross T blood bay.

Stella rode him to the Springs today. Five days ago Dal Carter was on him. Waiting for two snakes to fall out got Curry killed. I warned you, Rory, what I'd do when I found the man."

The wrinkled, impassive Jimmy Briggs brought a short-coupled blue roan with a look of run and bottom on muscular withers, sloping haunches. Calhoun stepped back and into the saddle.

"It's still the law's business," Rory insisted.

"Use you law on the big trouble tonight," Calhoun advised in the same baleful tone.

He lifted his hand, not really unfriendly, and let McCloud have a chance at his back as he rode off. As he had expected, the sheriff looked on him as a dead man already and did nothing.

Grady Smith, with a fresh horse and good start, would get where he was going. The one thing Grady would not believe, or Dal Carter, either, if Grady joined him, was that Calhoun would come there, too.

Dark caught Calhoun miles to the west and still north of Rimrock Camp. He had ridden cautiously, keeping to cover as much as possible. If Cross T guards were riding out, he missed them. But Cross T hardly needed guards. Bror Neilson was holding water, not seeking a fight.

Calhoun started a swing that brought him in from the south, before moonrise, to Rimrock Camp. The steady wind whipped the night's coolness about his body and checked some of the feverish pain in his left side. He saw the campfires from a distance and pulled up in the dark, studying them, then rode in more cautiously.

At Rimrock Camp, the south end of the Cahona narrowed. The belt of rocky ridges ended in a low rimrock. There was a quarter circle spur of descending rocky slope at the west end of the rimrock. In the shelter of that spur, against the vertical rock, a small seep spring furnished meager water to this end of the Cahona. A hut of flat slab rock, mud-chinked, with a soddy roof, and an old pole corral had long been there. Rimrock Camp was the last toe hold from which Frank Morton could look north at the miles of grass he'd lost to Bror Neilson.

There were three campfires, one larger than the others. The dancing red light and occasional swirling rise of brighter sparks showed the stone hut, at least three wagons, and many horses in close. It was a big camp. Calhoun estimated Cross T and V Loop must have pulled all their men to Rimrock Camp, plus Tyndall's bunch, and other hardcases they might have hired. No mounted figures outside the camp area moved between Calhoun and the sparking fire. He dismounted finally, close-fisted the reins under the bit, and walked the roan slowly forward.

Near thirty animals were picketed and rein-tied in a loose semicircle near wagons and fires. Calhoun merged in among them with the roan. He could hear talk, laughter, and finally make out unshaven faces at the fires. He picked out the meaty face of Walt Burger, who had dragged him. He saw Joe Farley, the V Loop ramrod, Bud Storrie, Scotty, then Hagan and Bates, the V Loop 'punchers who had come to Soderholm's place with Farley. Grady Smith was not among them. Or Dal Carter, Ferd Tyndall, or Frank Morton. Lanterns glowed inside the open door of the stone hut. Men were in there, talking. Planning the raid on Neilson tonight, Calhoun guessed.

He thought of the dead man Rory McCloud had found. Many more would die tonight — including Dave Calhoun, if he were caught here. He dropped the roan's reins and moved slowly left until the dark bulk of a chuck wagon screened him from the fires. Carbine carelessly in his left hand, he walked toward the wagon.

Then it happened. A big 'puncher ambled around the end of the wagon, peered in the dark, saw Calhoun's figure, and swerved to meet him, speaking peevishly: "My God, are they gonna talk all night before they start?"

"Guess so," Calhoun mumbled. There was no stopping, no turning back now. One yell of alarm, a shot would bring the whole armed camp boiling at an intruder. The 'puncher's eyes would adjust to the dark here in a second or so. Calhoun asked as they met: "Where's Carter?"

"In the cabin. Say, you . . . ?"

Calhoun's unsweeping Colt barrel smashed in against the 'puncher's throat. What would have been a warning yell gobbled and choked. Calhoun hit him again, furiously, desperately. This time behind the ear. He grabbed the caving figure and let it down on the grass.

He took the man's six-gun and rammed it inside his pants. Pain ran white-hot through his side again from the effort as he went on to the wagon. Firelight reached under the wagon to his legs. Laughter rose on the other side of the wagon, and suddenly a voice called: "Tell Morton his sister's come back!"

The 'puncher would be found any minute now. If his head was thick, the man might stand up himself, bawling alarm. Calhoun stepped on the front wheel hub and swung over into the wagon bed. The canvas sheet, rolled to the second wooden bow, slatted above him in the wind as he knelt against a sack of dried beans. In black shadow under the canvas he watched Stella ride the lather-flecked blood bay into the big circle of firelight. Stella looked pale as her eyes took in the armed men and saddled, waiting horses.

Frank Morton, big and broad shouldered, hurried out of the hut ahead of Dal Carter. Ferd Tyndall followed them. Stella rode over toward the wagons, away from most of the men. Frank's temper was edgy as he reached her. "What

238

happened, Stell'? Where were you?"

"Deep Cañon again," Stella replied. From the saddle she gestured toward the men. "So Bror Neilson was right. You're coming at him with guns tonight. And he's ready for you. He said to tell you."

X

Frank waved that aside. "We suspected it. Dal caught one of the men, talking with Neilson himself." Frank sneered. Calhoun could hear the grate in Frank's voice. "We're going to fire the whole range west of Deep Cañon! While Neilson's worrying about that, we'll take the Springs and Clark's Tank. Don't think those small cowmen will be standing at the water when they see fire."

"Frank! You can't do that!" Stella threw the words at her brother. "Dry as the grass is, and the way the wind is blowing, you may kill all those cattle." Stella sounded sick, angry. "Did *you* think of that?"

"It was Dal's idea," Frank admitted.

"It would be Dal's idea. Where is Ike Morris, the deputy?"

Dal Carter stood just beyond Frank, dark-faced and sullen as he watched Stella. "Couple of the men are watching that fat deputy!" Dal said. He could talk clearer now. "Have they found Calhoun's body?" he asked.

It was a second before Stella's thin voice demanded: "Dal, did you kill Dave today?"

"Of course, he didn't!' Frank said impatiently. "Calhoun tried to kill Grady Smith. Put a bullet through Smith's shoulder. But Grady knocked Calhoun over with a shot before he rode away. Probably killed him."

Still in the thin voice, Stella said: "Is Grady Smith here?"

"There in the V Loop bed wagon," Frank said in mounting impatience. "Go on in the hut, Stell'. Keep out of the rest of this tonight. You've meddled enough."

240

Stella whirled her horse. Dal Carter jumped, catching the bit. "Frank! Keep her away from Deep Cañon!"

Frank had already reached the stirrup. With a brother's angry assurance he reached to pluck her from the saddle. "You won't stop this, Stell'! Might as well quit trying."

Calhoun, kneeling in cold and dismal anger, thumbed back the hammer of his gun. Carter would never be any nearer than he was now. But a shot would open the bloody gun fight, with Stella in the midst of it. Frank Morton would probably have to be killed. Sweat sheened on Calhoun's face. There was a better way than this, now that he knew where Smith was.

He forgot Stella in the saddle, where she could see better than the men on the ground. For an instant Stella's look froze full at him. Then, as Calhoun moved back into the shadows a little, he saw Stella go suddenly docile and let Frank lift her to the ground.

He was not sure, until he heard Stella's clear voice say: "Dal! You killed Curry Waldron. You were riding the horse I took out today when you tried to kill Dave from cover and hit Curry instead. Dave recognized the track and knows it's you. Dave isn't dead. He's hunting you."

Frank Morton's surprise was quick and questioning. "Is that right, Dal? Did you try to drygulch Calhoun?"

"Why should I admit anything about a wolf who drygulched your father?" Dal retorted in surly anger. "Let's get going?"

Frank nodded, turning to follow Stella to the hut. His blunt warning — "You'd better get Calhoun on sight, Dal, or he'll get you!" — came back over his shoulder.

Men had drifted over, watching, listening. Dal Carter lifted his voice. "We're ready to ride! V Loop men with me! Tyndall knows what to do! Cross T men go with Morton!"

Dal uncinched Stella's saddle, threw it on the ground, and left the horse standing there. He was cutting past the nearest fire when he halted up with a yell. "Here's the sheriff!"

Rory McCloud had ridden hard, too. His horse was foaming, blowing as he rode through the firelight to Dal Carter. Calhoun missed their meeting. He was dropping over the outer side of the chuck wagon, pain stabbing his side again as he landed. The blob of the 'puncher's body still lay on the grass, not yet noticed by men moving to the horses. Any instant now the man would be found.

Calhoun had twenty feet of open space to cross before he reached the V Loop bed wagon. He missed what McCloud said but heard Dal's rough loud order: "Don't try for your gun, McCloud! You're covered! We can't use any mealy-mouthed law tonight. Climb down an' sit with your deputy."

Calhoun, moving steadily, reached the hind wheel of the bed wagon. He heard a shout behind the chuck wagon. "Somethin's wrong here!"

Calhoun climbed the front wheel of the bed wagon and dropped in. "Grady?"

"Yeah!" a sprawled figure in the bottom mumbled thickly.

Calhoun's gun muzzle prodded. "It's Dave Calhoun!" He heard Grady Smith suck in fear like a moan. "I won't kill you, Grady. Dal Carter will do that for me, you damn' fool."

"Don't know what you mean," Grady mumbled.

"I know who sent the money, and why!" Calhoun said, stretching it a little. The excitement was growing where the 'puncher had been found. Short moments now and the search would be on and the shooting would start.

"You've only got one friend in the world," said Calhoun calmly. "He's the man who wants to know who really killed his father. Get up and tell him, Grady."

Grady was shaking. "Carter'd get me."

"I'm closer," Calhoun reminded softly, balefully. "There's Morton coming out of the cabin. Last chance, Grady."

Grady Smith's fear again was like a moan. He rolled, coming up to his knees awkwardly. The firelight struck his face, unshaven, haggard with pain and fear. His hail was thick, urgent. "Morton! Quick!"

Frank's hard-set reckless face was scowling as he turned over to the wagon. Grady's shoulders hid Calhoun for the moment. Hands clutching the side board of the wagon, Grady got it out in a thick rush of fear.

"I lied at the trial, Morton. It was Dal Carter I seen leavin' where your father was shot. Carter paid me to change it."

"What's that? Dal did what . . . ?"

"He kep' sendin' me money to keep quiet."

Calhoun said: "Frank. Stand still."

When Frank Morton saw who backed the gun muzzle, threatening over the wagon side, his sneering bitterness blurted: "So that's why he's lying about Dal? A gun at his back."

Calhoun said calmly as the seconds ran out on him: "Your father would have believed Bror Neilson, Frank. Bror told me. He'll tell you. Two months before your father was killed, Dal was asking Bror about borrowing money he finally did borrow from Bror to buy me out. Two months *before,* Frank. Would *you* have thought then anyone could buy me out with the new house just built? Ask Bror."

Frank stood like a man clubbed.

"Dal's mine, anyway, for killing Curry Waldron," Calhoun warned. "But you've heard the truth, damn you. Now run with the man who did kill your father and has made a fool out of you ever since, but keep out of the rest of this for Stella's sake. I don't want to be the one who kills you."

Frank might not have heard him. "If Dal would skunk-hide and try to kill you, it must be in him," Frank said thickly. "Get that man in the cabin, safe!" Frank's great-lunged shout reached through the night. *"Cross T! Cross T men here! Quick!"*

243

Grady Smith, panting, scrambled out of the wagon and stumbled toward the hut. Stella, in the doorway, stopped him, listened, ran toward them as Calhoun dropped off the front of the wagon and levered his carbine.

"Frank! Is it true?" Stella called. "Did Dal shoot father?"

"Evidently! Get back in there!" Again Frank's great shout lifted. *"Cross T! All here!"* Frank's fury met the first of his men who came running. "We're not riding tonight! We're through with V Loop! Don't let anyone but the sheriff get at Grady Smith in the cabin!"

Stella faltered: "Dave. You took the blame. And I . . . !"

"Never mind," said Calhoun impatiently.

Dal Carter was coming, calling: "What's wrong, Frank?"

All the Morton temper roared from Frank. "Grady told the truth. You're through, Dal!" Frank yanked his gun as he started forward.

Calhoun was jumping to stop him when the loud burst of a rifle drove Frank, staggering, against the wagon. Calhoun, whipping the carbine up, found the quick-triggered gunman who had shot Frank. He was the thick-chested Tyndall man, Walt Burger, one of the two who had been holding Rory McCloud under their guns. Burger saw his danger. He tried to dodge. Calhoun's bullet struck the meaty face under an ear and tore flesh and bone into a spattering red blotch. Burger was dead as he collapsed.

Rory McCloud was still sitting on his horse. McCloud's chin was ducking a little as Calhoun whirled.

Stella was kneeling beside her brother, trying to lift him. She was crying silently. Calhoun called to the nearest Cross T men. "Get 'em in the cabin!"

Dal Carter had dodged back behind the chuckwagon. His shouted orders had an explosive viciousness. Calhoun crouched in front of Stella, trying to sort out the confusion.

One running man kicked the smallest fire into a welter of flying embers, swirling sparks. Men were running to join their outfits, puzzled, uncertain about what was happening. Rory McCloud's hand gun bellowed twice.

When Calhoun looked, the graying, slack-shouldered sheriff was dropping off his horse, gun cocked again. The other man who had been guarding Rory was staggering, bent over, holding his middle. Dal Carter's bawling orders were telling V Loop men to get Dave Calhoun and Grady Smith.

Men had heaved Frank up and rushed him toward the stone hut. Stella was following. A young 'puncher, gun in hand, was shielding her. He made Calhoun think of young Sullivan, standing guard at Deep Cañon. Those two youths would not be killing each other tonight. Good men — husbands, fathers, sons — would not die tonight. A wind-whipped line of fire would not race through the thickly grazing cattle. Right or wrong, hates, feuds, injustices of the whole range were going up in gunfire here at Rimrock Camp. There could be peace after tonight. But, while it lasted, the dying would be quick, and furious.

All that could pass in a molten flash through a man's mind while he dived under a wagon bed, pain searing at his twisting side. Dal Carter was the man who drove the dying on, who would keep it bloody with his hardcases . . . and his fear. Dal had spread his greed astride the range with murder. *He would murder now to keep from hanging.* That, too, was a flash of thought that whipped Calhoun into a wriggling rush under the wagon, and up to a crouch in the darker shadows by the hind wheel.

A dark, running figure, out in the night, drove a gout of muzzle flame at Calhoun. The bullet loudly smacked the wagon bed above his head. Two figures over there had been circling out to the rocky spur, where they could command the front of the stone hut from dark concealment. Calhoun used his carbine, aiming carefully. He dropped the first running figure.

The second man opened up as Calhoun levered the carbine. The bullet, smashing the stock, drove the gun out of Calhoun's hands. Splintering wood or disintegrating bullet ripped his hands and wrists. Both hands were numb from the shock. The left hand was almost useless.

Calhoun's baleful rage exploded. Near helpless, the galling fury of it sent him lunging forward, flailing hands to liven them. In ears ringing from the shots he could hear Dal's bawl of command behind the chuck wagon. He plunged toward it.

A bullet racked his back. He ignored the man off there in the dark. A flying step up on the wagon tongue and a scrambling dive over the seat put him into the cluttered bed of the chuck wagon, under the slatting sheet. Life tingled in his right hand as he stumbled back to the stout chuck box which filled the rear end of the wagon. There was a two-foot opening between the top of the chuck box and the canvas overhead.

Dal Carter was shouting: "Spread out! Get up to the rocks! Keep out of the firelight!"

Calhoun's right hand could cock the Colt gun he drew. When he tried his left hand, it had blood-slippery control of the 'puncher's gun he had thrust inside the front of his pants. Calhoun shoved both guns, and head and shoulders, across the top of the chuck box. Belly-flat on the box he looked out on all the protected area behind the chuck wagon. The frightened horses were milling, dragging reins and picket ropes. V Loop and Tyndall's men were gathering back there. Dal Carter was twenty feet away, his right side to the chuck wagon as the gun in his hand gestured toward the rocky spur west of the camp area.

"Dal Carter!" Calhoun called. When Dal swung, staring uncertainly, Calhoun called: "Up here, Dal . . . from Curry

246

Waldron!" He had another flash of thought in the second he bellied there, waiting. Back near Salt Lake City where old Pete Wade said: *"Nothin' but trouble back at Kingsville!"* It brought a mirthless grin to Calhoun's swollen face. Trouble — death. Dal Carter saw Calhoun's swollen, grinning face in the fire glare above the chuck box. He took in the blood-smeared fists, gripping cocked guns, waiting for a showdown that was long overdue.

Dal's fearful knowledge would have satisfied even Curry Waldron. Dal's jump was fast, his gun faster than any of his startled men. His bullet struck the top edge of the chuck box as Calhoun's guns roared back and did not stop their flaming, crashing crescendo.

Dal died, hopeless rage twisting his handsome face as he fell. Ferd Tyndall, a dozen steps over, tried to run. The bullet that dropped Ferd struck his back. Lead tore into cans and bottles in the chuck box under Calhoun. But the scattering V Loop men were not standing and making a fight of it.

Calhoun saw one man step out of the milling horses, waving his arms, yelling, pointing into the night. Those who heard him ran for their horses. Calhoun stopped firing. The bright rim of the moon was showing. And out there, beyond the saddled horses, in the first thin moonlight, was a dark moving mass that could only be bunched riders, moving cautiously in. They could only be Bror Neilson's men who had come to meet a fight and were not certain now what they had found.

Calhoun watched the fight break up as quickly as it started. Men without leaders did nothing but run for their horses. Slowly, in pain, Calhoun stepped back in the dark wagon and dropped on the same sack of beans he'd knelt against earlier. Almost absently he wanted to thumb fresh shells into his gun. Then, realizing what he was doing, he dropped the 'puncher's gun. He heard the pound of departing horses. A few scattered shots sent them on their way. Then the massed trample of the Deep Cañon horses entered the camp area. Calhoun climbed wearily, painfully, out of the wagon.

Both his hands were smeared with his own blood. He was looking at them when he was sighted. Grinning, puzzled men who had been kindly to him the last few days climbed down, calling questions.

Calhoun gave them brief answers as he started toward Bror Neilson, who had dismounted and was meeting Rory McCloud by the main fire. Rory had come from the front of the hut, where he had been with the Cross T men. He looked calm and deceptively mild again beside the hunched, gnomish figure of Bror Neilson.

Bror's glaring look held a great satisfaction. It was in his high, crackling voice, too, as he addressed Calhoun. "So you did kill Dal Carter? Good work. Saves the law a lot of worry."

Rory said mildly: "When I make a man a deputy, I look for him to shoot straight, like Calhoun done." When Calhoun shot him a frowning question, Rory said solemnly: "I forgot to tell you, Dave. I made you a deputy just before the shootin' started." Rory rubbed his chin thoughtfully and dipped it in reminder. "I'd rather have you helpin' the law than watchin' what I do."

Calhoun smiled faintly. "Is Frank Morton dead?" he wondered.

"Last word outta the cabin there, he's got a good chance. Holed bad in the meat, but he don't seem tore up inside," answered Rory.

Calhoun hesitated, then said: "Frank turned on Carter, Bror. Solved all your worries. He'll be more like his father from now on."

"Then we'll get together like neighbors," said Bror Neilson. "He may be one fool who's learned his lesson." Bror's glare

248

rested on Calhoun. "Is there another one around who's learned *his?*"

"Meaning?"

Bror Neilson spat. "V Loop will be for sale, won't it? You buying?"

"Can't swing it, even if I sell my place up north."

"I've got money to lend."

"I'll ask Stella," Calhoun said. As he turned toward the stone hut, walking lighter, he heard Bror Neilson's high, crackling voice, addressing Rory McCloud.

"Some fools do change! You've lost a deputy, McCloud! We'll have a new neighbor family. Look at him running to her."

Calhoun barely heard this last. The hut door had opened. Stella had stepped out, with lantern light behind her, the firelight and the brightening moonlight on her clearly. Calhoun had started a painful, slogging run toward her. That was the way he felt, and he had to tell her.

The End

T. T. Flynn was born Thomas Theodore Flynn, Jr., in Indianapolis, Indiana. He was the author of over a hundred Western short novels for such leading pulp magazines as Street and Smith's *Western Story Magazine*, Popular Publications' *Dime Western*, and Dell's *Zane Grey's Western Magazine*. His short novel "Hell's Half Acre" appeared in the issue that launched Star Western in 1933. He moved to New Mexico with his wife Helen and spent much of his time living in a trailer while on the road exploring the vast terrain of the American West. His descriptions of the land are always detailed, but he used them not only for local colour but also to reflect the heightening of emotional distress among the characters within a story. Following the Second World War, Flynn turned his attention to the book-length Western novel and in this form also produced work that has proven imperishable. Five of these novels first appeared as original paperbacks, most notably *The Man From Laramie*, which was featured as a serial in *The Saturday Evening Post* and subsequently made into a memorable motion picture directed by Anthony Mann and starring James Stewart. *Two Faces West*, which deals with the problems of identity and reality, served as the basis for a television series. Flynn was highly innovative and inventive and in later novels, such as *Riding Nigh*, concentrated on deeper psychological issues as the source for conflict, rather than more elemental motives like greed. He was so meticulous about his research that he once spent days to determine the exact year that blue- (as opposed to red-) checked tablecloths were introduced. All anachronism was anathema to him. Flynn is at his best in stories that combine mystery—not surprisingly, he also wrote detective fiction—suspense, and action in an artful balance. The world where his characters live is often a comedy of errors in which the first step in any direction frequently can, and does, lead to ever deepening complications.